CASSIE EDWARDS
THE *SAVAGE* SERIES

Winner of the *Romantic Times* Lifetime Achievement Award for Best Indian Series!

"Cassie Edwards writes action-packed, sexy reads! Romance fans will be more than satisfied!"
—*Romantic Times*

HIS HEART SOARED

"Did your wife make this broth?" Janice found herself asking. She felt a slight blush rush to her cheeks, and hoped that he didn't see it.

"No, I have no wife," White Shield said, his heart skipping a beat. She must be interested in him or she would not have asked such a question.

He started to ask her if she had a husband, and if his name was Seth, but she spoke again too quickly.

"My name is Janice," she said, extending toward White Shield a hand that was no longer trembling. Why should it? Before, her hands shook from fear.

Now there was no fear.

There was only a need to know more about this man.

White Shield reached out and accepted her hand in his, his heart soaring at the touch of her skin.

When he circled his fingers around hers, he believed he could feel her pulsebeat quicken. Certainly, his own heart was no longer beating at its usual pace.

Savage Devotion

Cassie Edwards

LEISURE BOOKS   NEW YORK CITY

A LEISURE BOOK®

July 2000

Published by

Dorchester Publishing Co., Inc.
276 Fifth Avenue
New York, NY 10001

Cover art by John Ennis
www.ennisart.com

ISBN 0-8439-4735-7

The name "Leisure Books" and the stylized "L" with design are
trademarks of Dorchester Publishing Co., Inc.

Printed in the United States of America.

I wish to dedicate Savage Devotion *to a sweet friend of mine . . . Mary Bahrns of Mattoon.*

Savage Devotion

She was such a thing of beauty,
As I saw her standing there,
I knew that to win her love,
Would be something quite rare.
Her eyes so blue, and hair like the sun,
Oh, how my heart was starting to run.
But would she have me, a warrior so bold,
I felt shivers that were quite cold.
My love for her was strong and true,
Would her heart be mine, too?
She looked at me with eyes so bright,
As I stood there in the pale moonlight.
And as she turned I saw in her eyes,
That she loved me too, and I felt so wise.
For to have this woman's love,
Was to be soaring like an eagle above.
I will cherish her until my dying day,
Because as a warrior . . . that is my way.

—Debbie Rogers
Poet and friend

Chapter One

Far or forget to me is near;
Shadows and sunlight are the same;
The vanquished Gods to me appear;
And one to one are shame and fame.
        —RALPH WALDO EMERSON

1893—The State of Washington

It was the bright-leafed season of September, when nights were cool, and shadows long.

A slow fire burned in the center of a large longhouse-style council house built of cedar posts and planks. Shadows from the fire leaped and danced along the walls and peaked ceiling of the house, and upon the Bear band of

11

Skokomish Indians. There were no women attending the council. Only the men had gathered to speak among themselves of things of importance to their people.

Dressed in a buckskin outfit devoid of decoration and ankle-high moccasins, and with bands of twisted and woven shredded bark at his wrists and ankles, White Shield, the sub-chief of this band of Skokomish, sat proudly. Beside him was Night Fighter, his chieftain grandfather. The people of the council sat in a half circle facing them.

White Shield's square jaw was relaxed, his steel-gray eyes were at peace, and his dark brown hair hung straight and thick down his back as he gazed proudly at his grandfather. The *tyee*, chief, wore an elk-hide cape thrown loosely around his lean, old shoulders for warmth and a buckskin outfit beneath it.

White Shield listened as his grandfather spoke in a deep, authoritative voice about what was now being called the "Business Panic of 1893." Especially affected was the city of Tacoma, where the markets had collapsed and business was paralyzed.

The council had met to discuss the effects of the business panic on the Skokomish people. In previous meetings they had already decided among themselves that it was beneficial, not harmful, to them. Because of the crash, the lumber companies had closed down. All

Tacoma banks but one had closed their doors to the public.

But the Skokomish knew better than to get too confident. It was best to frequently discuss the ways they could maintain their independence of whites.

As Night Fighter continued talking, White Shield watched him. His grandfather was resting his weary body against a backrest of woven shredded bark stretched across a framework of wood. His cape had now dropped down to rest around his waist. His clinging buckskin shirt revealed how deep-chested he was, and how thin his shoulders had become now that he had seen seventy-five winters. His face was leathery and serene, and he had the look of infinity in his ancient eyes.

Through the years White Shield had watched and learned from his grandfather, studying the ways of leadership. Since he was a child, White Shield had been told that along with his great lineage went great responsibility.

White Shield knew that when his grandfather passed on to the other side, which he feared would be *winapie*, soon, his people expected White Shield to become chief, and White Shield felt certain that his grandfather had prepared him well for the proud task. He was confident that he knew everything required to be his people's leader.

But it saddened White Shield when he was

forced to face the reality of that day that lay before him, when his grandfather's body would be wrapped in a cedar bark mat for burial. It would be the hardest thing of all things that had happened in White Shield's life. He did not even like thinking about saying that final good-bye to his grandfather.

He had already said good-bye to loved ones too many times, his grandmother most recently. She had been buried high on a hill that looked down over the full width of the Skokomish island, where the wind blew from across the Sound, so sweet with the smell of cedar in the forests.

White Shield went often to visit her grave. He had felt her presence there as the wind brushed across his cheeks in a soft caress. It had been his grandmother who had told him that each wind was the breath of some being who had once lived, who was now a part of the unseen world, where she, herself, also resided.

The sadness in White Shield's grandfather's eyes, and the emptiness in White Shield's heart, bespoke how they both missed the woman they had both loved. They were both struggling to accept that void in their lives but knew they must get past their loss. There were always responsibilities to be seen to in order to keep their people's lives as free as possible of the white man's interference.

Again White Shield listened to his grandfather as he addressed the council. The *tyee* looked like an aged philosopher, a man of much insight, White Shield thought. He admired the elder's intelligence and bravery, which were tempered with patience that only time could bring.

White Shield hoped that he could live up to the expectations of his grandfather when the time came for him to take over the leadership of their people.

His thoughts were stopped when his grandfather suddenly turned to him, reaching out a bony hand to rest it on White Shield's shoulder.

"Grandson, tell our people *your* view of things," Night Fighter said. His thin lips quivered into an affectionate smile, the deep pride that he felt for his grandson evident every time he looked at him. White Shield was fine-boned. He was a tall man with a handsomely planed face and well-muscled body. He always reminded Night Fighter of himself when *he* was youthful and muscled.

White Shield recognized the proud look in his grandfather's eyes. White Shield's heart was warm with love for this old man whose life had been devoted not only to his people, but also to his grandson. As White Shield spoke, he looked around the circle of men, his eyes sometimes lingering on one special warrior or another. His deep voice, his way of speaking succinctly, drew everyone's attention. Each man seemed to lean forward in anticipation of what White Shield had to say.

This sort of attention sometimes embarrassed him, yet he knew that his grandfather ate it up as though it were fine honey being sucked slowly from the tip of his finger after dipping it into a honeycomb fresh from a bee's nest.

"*Sikhs*, friends, companions, warriors, elders," White Shield began, then looked over at his grandfather and slowly smiled. "*Grand*father."

After his grandfather gave him a proud smile and nod, White Shield looked again at those who sat listening. "Like you, I believe the 'Business Panic,' as it is called by the whites, is good for our people. I hope that many of those white people who have lost so much will leave, and the land occupied by them will return to the ownership of the Skokomish."

"But if that happens, would you move from our island, where we have made our homes for so many sunrises and sunsets?" a voice rang out, drawing attention to the elderly man whose eyes had lost their sight long ago. "I have grown fond of our island. I feel a quiet joy when I walk through the forest and trust each step that I have memorized. Living somewhere else would be too difficult for this old man whose eyes are now only empty sockets in his head."

Always feeling deeply for this old man, who was Night Fighter's best friend, White Shield rose to his feet and went and knelt down before him. He placed his hands on Six Feathers' feeble shoulders. "No matter what happens, no matter how much land we might again claim as ours, Six Feathers, *this* is our home," he said softly. "I, too, have grown too fond of it to leave. I smell the same wondrous fragrance of the flowers as you. I hear the same calls of the birds, and I, too, enjoy sitting on the riverbank and running the sand slowly through my fingers. It is our home, Six Feathers. No matter if we were forced to live here, it is a paradise on earth. If the whites knew how lovely it is, they would realize the foolishness of having given it up to the Skokomish."

The elderly man smiled. "And let us not forget that the people of Tacoma chose the name of their city based upon the Indian word *Tahoma,* our name for the great nearby mountain," he said. "Because of this Indian name, the people of Tacoma are always reminded of their connection with the red man."

"But *we* are reminded each time *we* look at the mountain that this name no longer reflects our heritage, but instead the *white man's,*" Night Fighter grumbled. "It is now called by a white man's name . . . Rainier!"

"But in everyone's hearts it will always be *Tahoma,*" White Shield said softly. He hugged Six Feathers, then went and sat down beside his grandfather again.

"Those whites who have remained on land stolen from us Skokomish are so poor now from the money crash, they are relying on clams for their meals instead of the red meat called 'beef' they were accustomed to eating,"

White Shield then said, chuckling softly. "As you all know, we Skokomish are profiting from this, for those whites who were once so rich and snobbish still cannot bring themselves to do such a lowly, menial thing as digging on the riverbank for the clams. What small amount of money they have is being paid to our Skokomish children, who take delight in digging the clams for the white man's money."

"Do you believe the children who are digging clams for whites on Tacoma's side of the Sound are safe without adult supervision among the whites?" another voice asked.

"As long as the children go in groups, *ah-hah*, they are safe," White Shield said softly.

"It is strange how things changed so quickly for the people in Tacoma," another man said. "It seems only yesterday that young whites left the logging camps of Maine and Utah to set up a new life in the untouched forests around Tacoma."

Another elder exhaled in annoyance. "*Ah-ha*, yes," he grumbled. "Our world of towering green groves became shaped into false-fronted temples of whiskey, where ambitious schemes flourished."

"It pleases my heart that things *have* changed," Night Fighter said, drawing all eyes to him again. "For us Skokomish, it was bad that Tacoma was selected as the western terminus of the Northern Pacific Railway. The railroad made the city the heart of the timber empire of the Pacific Northwest."

"*Ahnkuttie*, not long ago, foreign sails crowded Tacoma's harbor," another warrior said, his voice bitter. "Great ships were moored at the longest dock in the world to load logs from forests that once belonged solely to the Skokomish. Cargoes of grain from far away arrived daily by rail to be poured into the holds of ships from around the world."

A low laugh drew everyone's eyes back to White Shield. "The white men of Tacoma named their city 'The City of Destiny' when it became such a boomtown," he said sarcastically.

"And, Grandson, the white men succeeded only until greed caused their downfall," Night Fighter said tightly.

"Now it is our turn to win out over the greedy whites of Tacoma," White Shield said. He smiled. "Our Supreme Being, our people's Transformer, has again set things in order for us Skokomish."

"While things were going well for the white men of Tacoma, you, my grandson, purposely became a part of the white man's world," Night Fighter said, patting his grandson's knee. "But it was done only for our people. You encouraged selective logging in the forests around Tacoma." He laughed throatily. "The white men and women even called you a 'Forester,' a man who works without pay to save as many trees in the beautiful forest as you can."

"I was fortunate, we were all fortunate, that most of the lumber barons grew to trust my judgment about which trees should be spared so that the forest would not be totally stripped," White Shield said. "Of course I said that was important so that new tress could sprout and be there in the future for other lumbering companies. But deep in my heart I was only thinking of the welfare of our children and grandchildren."

"But, Grandson, there were those who did not want you anywhere near the lumber companies," Night Fighter said, in his eyes a great weariness. "They did not like the idea of a redskin dictating to whites what they could and could not do."

"It was, and still is, the lumberjacks who truly hate your grandson," White Shield said, placing a gentle hand on his grandfather's shoulder. "The fewer trees that were cut, the fewer jobs there were to be had in the white community."

White Shield did not say it aloud, but he knew that it was those men who had threatened—who might even now be plotting—to kill him.

Chapter Two

I am going to my own hearthstone,
Bosom'd in yon green hills alone—
A secret nook in a pleasant land,
Whose groves the frolic fairie's planned.
                    —*RALPH WALDO EMERSON*

The steamer *Hope* was bound down-Sound for Tacoma. Clinging to the ship's rail, Janice Edwards stared skyward with a thundering heart when she saw dark storm clouds suddenly overhead. Only moments ago she had been enjoying the sight of the cedar, fir, and madrona trees that grew lush and green along the high, forested shoreline of Puget Sound.

She had been admiring occasional small

islands to her right, all misty blue and bronze-green, their timber as yet untouched by any lumber baron's ax.

Looking in another direction, she had admired majestic Mount Rainier, lifting its snow-clad summit many thousand feet into the sky.

And only moments ago the September sky couldn't have been a more luminous blue.

But now, in just a matter of minutes, smoke-gray clouds and streaks of fog had erased the sky's glistening blue.

Janice's long red hair whipped around her face and fluttered wildly down her back as the wind picked up.

With land so near now, when she looked into the waters of Puget Sound she was able to see massive tangles of bull kelp that had been ripped from the rocks, now bobbing and swirling in water that had suddenly become turbulent.

"Janice!"

Janice could just barely hear her older brother Seth calling her name through the howling of the wind.

She returned his cry, but she was too scared to release her hold on the ship's railing, afraid that if she did she might be swept over the rail and into the angry sea.

Her lips tasted of sea salt.

The wild spray of ocean water stung her eyes.

But she ignored both, for she could now only concentrate on one thing.

Seth!

Had he heard her?

Oh, Lord, would Seth come to her and help her back to their private cabin down below?

She soon knew the answer.

He had not heard her or he would not be frantically shouting her name over and over again through the thunderous sound of the waves that were now crashing dangerously against the ship's hull.

Humbled by the whims of the ocean and its power, Janice was transfixed by the towering waves that were rumbling onto sculpted boulders and reefs. To her horror, she saw that the ship was being forced toward the rocks, the wind and the waves now more in command than the ship's helmsman.

The ship was so close now to the boulders along the shore, Janice could see the gooseneck barnacles that clung to the rocks.

Time and again towering waves rumbled onto the boulders, disintegrating into pools of frothy, hissing foam.

"Lord, Janice, where are you?" Seth shouted as he tried to see through the sprays of water that leaped up over the ship's rail like some demon set loose from the depths of the sea.

He desperately held on to Janice's adopted child, ten-year-old Alexis Jade, whom he carried

Cassie Edwards

in his arms while continuing to search for his sister.

Now and then he bumped against another body as someone else stumbled through the blinding, stinging sprays of water.

He could hear screams and shouts splitting the air, which only moments ago had been sweet with sunshine and the perfume of flowers that grew along the shores of this usually beautiful place.

He had grown to love the serenity of the area, but now the brewing storm seemed to mock everything that was precious to him.

His sister.

His niece.

His wife, who awaited his return to Tacoma!

If the wind and water had their way, he would never see any of them again, for he believed that the ship would soon be dashed against the rocks.

Janice felt panic rising. She had left her brother standing with Lexi just a short while ago. Seth had been pointing out Mount Rainier to the dear child, whose curiosity kept Janice and her brother busy with explanations about everything.

A sob caught in Janice's throat when she recalled a day not long ago when she had jokingly told her adopted Chinese daughter that curiosity killed a cat.

Were her daughter's curiosity, and her

brother's eagerness to please, going to be the cause of her never seeing Lexi again, or Seth? Janice despaired. If the storm had its way, no one on this ship would survive.

Determined to find her way back to her brother and daughter, Janice started to let go of the rail, but then clung even more desperately to it again when all at once the low-hanging gray clouds tore open, spilling water from them as though monstrous buckets had been turned upside down in the heavens. It was such a heavy, thick rain, Janice could no longer even see the raging waves.

But, oh, Lord, she did still hear them.

They were deafening.

They were like large claps of thunder as they beat against the sides of the ship.

And when she momentarily did get the chance to see through the falling rain and sprays of seawater, what she saw made her heart sink, for she knew that she might be only moments away from dying. When the ship collided with the boulders, there would surely be no way to survive.

Suddenly images of the past flew through Janice's mind, as though she were looking back in time through a looking glass. She was remembering her older brother Seth telling her as a child that when she was of marrying age, men would fall over each other to have her.

As a child of twelve, all of the boys *had* raved

about her, saying that she was beautiful with her flowing red hair, luminous green eyes, and oval face.

Now, at twenty-one, she had grown up into a petite woman with perfectly shaped lips and lovely dimples. She was soft-spoken and fragile.

But even though she was very wealthy, she had a kind, caring heart, and was always looking for someone to help.

She had found the perfect way to express that compassion one day three years ago when she had found a seven-year-old Chinese girl walking alone, orphaned and half-starved, on an empty street of San Francisco.

Janice had taken the child in, and after unsuccessfully searching for her parents, she had legally adopted the waif. She had given this beautiful Chinese girl the name Alexis Jade, but she called her Lexi.

Had it been only a few days ago that Janice, her brother Seth, and Lexi, had boarded the steamer *Hope* and sailed away from San Francisco toward Tacoma, where Seth had lived the past year as he had labored over seeing his dream of an opera house take shape?

The plans were now complete. Soon his dream of owning a magnificent opera house would come to fruition.

His wife, Rebecca, even now awaited his return in his fabulous home in Tacoma.

As for Janice, she was traveling to Tacoma to

care for her ailing grandmother, Hannah, who only a year ago had moved there after Seth had had a log cabin built for her in the forest. Although Hannah had become quite wealthy after her husband had struck it rich during the gold rush, when he had died, she had decided to return to a simpler life.

Before he struck it rich, her husband had been a trapper. And when Hannah and Clarence first got married, they had lived a rugged life in a log cabin just outside of Tacoma.

It was the gold fields that had lured him away from his trapper's life.

Hannah had always hungered to return to the more serene existence they had first known together, but her husband had gotten caught up in what his sudden wealth could buy for them . . . fancy houses, horses, gambling.

After Janice's grandfather was shot at a gambling table, her grandmother had finally gotten her wish to return to the Northwest. Having always hated the conventions of society, happiest when she was strolling in the forest, far beyond the sounds of horse's hooves upon the cobblestones of the streets, Hannah had settled down in the forest outside Tacoma. There, she would be close to Seth, who lived in a mansion in the city; he would be there for her, should she need him.

Neither Seth nor Janice had thought anything could happen to their precious grandmother, but as fate would have it, just as she had become content in her simple life in the forest, she had been downed by a stroke.

Upon hearing the news, Janice had made plans to go to her grandmother as quickly as possible. She had decided to make her grandmother's last days the best she could have.

And now this?

Janice doubted that she would ever get the chance to see her grandmother again, much less give her the best of care.

Her mind quickly darted to someone else. Janice's and Seth's father, Hannah's son, had been dead now for several years. He and his wife Susanna had died while on a steamer cruising to England. Their vast wealth had been left to their son Seth and daughter Janice, equally divided between them.

Janice had hoped that while she was living with her grandmother she could begin a new life away from her riches in San Francisco, and possibly find a man who would know nothing about her wealth, who would marry her for herself only.

Although beautiful and sweet, Janice had found that men mainly courted her for the money they would gain from marrying her.

Janice had made a deal with her brother that when they reached Tacoma, they wouldn't openly behave as brother and sister, so that no one would know she was as rich as Seth. If a man desired her, she wanted it to be for herself alone, not for her money.

She and Seth had agreed that they would meet only in private. Janice had to have it that way or she would never know whose love for her was genuine.

Although Janice was used to living in a mansion on Nob Hill, one of the most affluent districts of San Francisco, she had looked forward to living a simpler life in her grandmother's log cabin.

And she had planned to keep Lexi home with her to tutor her instead of sending her to a public school. Janice had already seen the prejudice against her Chinese daughter when Janice had sent her to school in San Francisco.

She was determined to protect her daughter from further abuse.

Janice raised her eyes heavenward and began praying as the storm took on the fury of a tornado.

She screamed, and her body lurched sideways when the steamer was tossed against the rocks and torn in half.

Janice screamed over and over again. Just as she felt herself falling toward the swirling, thrashing water, she caught sight of Seth holding Lexi in his arms. Together they plummeted toward the angry arms of the sea.

Just as Janice hit the water, she saw her brother and Lexi being swept away in the rage

of the waves. Her heart broke into a million pieces.

Sucked over and over again into the depths of the sea, Janice fought to stay alive.

And although she was petite and fragile, she found the strength and the will to swim to shore.

As she crawled onto the rocky embankment and stretched out, choking and gagging as she desperately panted for air, she relived those last moments when she had seen her brother and daughter swept away from her. Overwhelmed by despair, she fell into a deep, dark tunnel of unconsciousness.

Chapter Three

Dreams in their vivid coloring of life,
As in that fleeting, shadowy, misty strife,
Of semblance of reality, which brings,
To the delirious eye, more lovely things,
Of paradise and love—and all our own!
—EDGAR ALLAN POE

The large dugout canoe, fashioned from western red cedar, moved silently through the water. The ends of the canoe were slanted to give less resistance to currents and displayed beautiful carvings of various birds and animals.

White Shield's arm muscles flexed as he rhythmically pulled his paddle through the water. He was headed in the direction of Seattle, but that was not his destination. He was going to row on past it and across the Sound to Suquamish Indian country.

The more he noticed how fragile his grandfather's health was becoming, the more White Shield felt the urge to find a wife.

He hoped to marry and give his grandfather a great-grandchild before he passed on to the other side. His grandfather had so much to give. White Shield wanted his firstborn to feel that love as the child was held in the loving arms of his great-grandfather.

"His . . ." White Shield paused in his rowing for a moment.

He smiled as he whispered the words "his grandson."

Son, he then thought to himself.

Ah-hah, a son was what he desired first, and then a beautiful daughter.

But a son would be his first desire, for so many reasons. He looked forward to sharing the annual whale harvest with his son when the child grew old enough to learn the art of spearing the large water creatures.

Ah-hah, beyond the tranquil coves, pine forests, and stretches of white-sand beaches, was the vastness of the ocean. From November to May some twenty-one thousand gray whales came to the waters of this great Northwest Country on their journey north to the Bering

Sea. That was the time of whaling for his people. A time of a great sea harvest.

And in early spring, another sight to behold were the thousands of migratory shorebirds that stopped along Puget Sound en route to the Arctic tundra, their summer home. Along these shores the birds feasted on small fish, abundant eelgrass, and sea lettuce.

He resumed his rowing past coves and pine forests that were now tranquil after the storm that had come and gone so quickly.

He glanced toward land, at the dripping cedar and hemlock forest, clumps of sword ferns, glossy salal shrubs, huckleberry thickets, and mosses flourishing in brackish puddles.

He smiled as he noted how graceful and tall the cedar trees stood along the shore.

It was said that the cedar tree was the gift of life. Cedar contained a natural fungicide that resisted rot, an important factor in the wet climate along the Northwest coast. Its bark provided material for cradles and diapers for infants, as well as burial mats for the dead.

Some of the Skokomish people wore cedar bark tunics and rain hats, and used the bark for baskets and fish nets.

His eyes were drawn to his left, where he heard the haunting cry of a winter wren. Then he spotted a bald eagle surveying the coast from its perch high in a tree.

He smiled when he saw a cluster of high-step-

Cassie Edwards

ping shorebirds probing the sands for marine
morsels. His heart was filled with the beauty
that surrounded him.

And then his heart leapt and his paddle went
still again as he saw something that did *not*
please him.

His eyes widened in puzzlement when he saw
debris floating past his canoe . . . furniture,
parts of smokestacks from a ship, trunks, and
clothes.

He reached out and grabbed a piece of clothing that was twisted around a tree limb. He
brought it into his canoe and studied it. It was a
piece of woman's clothing, soft and silky to his
fingertips.

He let it fall from his fingers back into the
water as he watched other things float past. His
heart thudded hard within his chest as he realized there was only one way these things could
be floating in Puget Sound.

A ship.

A ship had been wrecked somewhere close by!

"Where? Where did the ship go down?" he
whispered, resuming his paddling. His eyes
were alert as he began scanning the banks of
the Sound.

The storm had probably caused the wreck.

No ship should have braved the monstrous
waves brought on by the winds of this recent
storm. But he was reminded that the storm had
come quickly, giving the ship's captain no
warning.

If someone *was* in the Sound, surely he or she could not have survived the pounding of the waves.

His heart skipped a beat and again he stopped rowing when he saw an ominous sight that made him feel sick to his stomach. Two portions of a ship were sticking up from the water near boulders that White Shield and anyone familiar with this stretch of the shore had always avoided.

But with the rain falling in blinding sheets, and with winds that whipped the waves into a frenzied state, no man, not even the most skilled at manning a ship or canoe, could stop his vessel from being dashed against the boulders. It was obvious that the ship had broken into two pieces. He doubted there were many survivors, if any.

"I must see if there are," he whispered, now moving slowly through the water, his eyes searching.

He imagined that white men had discovered the tragedy already and had scanned the land for survivors. All but one of Tacoma's hospitals had fallen on hard times. And Tacoma was closer to this spot than Seattle. The survivors would surely have been taken there.

He saw no one. Surmising that all survivors had been found, he turned his thoughts again to why he was traveling the waters of the Sound today. His heart was set on searching for that perfect woman to bring into his longhouse.

White Shield started to guide his canoe back to deeper water to avoid the debris that now seemed to be everywhere. Suddenly he stopped and stared.

His pulse raced as he looked at a woman who lay on the embankment, so still he was afraid that she might be *memaloost*, dead.

Wanting to do what he could, hoping that the woman might be alive, he rowed quickly to shore and beached his canoe among a scattering of rocks.

After making certain that his canoe was secure enough so that it would not float away in the Sound, he went to the woman and knelt down beside her.

As he reached a trembling hand toward her throat, to check for a pulse beat, he studied the woman. She was white with flawless features, her wet red hair framing a face of delicate loveliness. Although her skin was ashen and her lips a purplish color from her exposure to the cold water, she was still pretty. And her body was supple and slender, perfectly shaped, down to her tapering ankles.

Placing his fingertips to her throat, White Shield exhaled a breath of relief when he found the beat strong; she was in no danger of dying.

His fingers moved slowly up to her brow, swept her hair back and felt her scalp for signs of injury.

When he found none there, or anywhere else on her body, he assumed that she was unconscious because of the exhaustion she must have felt after swimming to shore through the horrendous waves brought on by the storm.

He took one of her tiny hands in his, flinching when he felt the coldness of her flesh. He had to work quickly now and get her somewhere warm.

He grabbed her up into his arms and carried her to his canoe.

He gently laid her on blankets that he always carried with him on his water journeys, covering her then with a pelt he also kept in his canoe.

He looked up the river toward Tacoma, and then looked in the direction of his village.

He concluded that his village was the closest of the two destinations and decided that was where he would take the woman. She needed quick attention, especially a warm fire to bring the color back to her lips and cheeks.

"*Ah-hah*, pretty woman, with intriguing hair of sunset color, I will take you to my home," he whispered, shoving the canoe back out into the water.

He climbed in and settled himself down on the seat where he could watch the woman.

Before he took up his paddle, he saw the woman begin to stir, and then she whispered something even though she was still unconscious.

Two names.

She had spoken two names.

She had said "Lexi" first, and then "Seth."

He moved to his knees beside her and leaned closer to her face.

"Lexi?" he said, his voice anxious. "Is that your daughter?"

His spine stiffened when he recalled the other name.

It was a man's.

Surely Seth was her husband.

White Shield did not understand this quick jealousy that had come to him like a slap in the face when she had said the man's name, for this woman was nothing to him.

She was a stranger.

A stranger who was in need of warmth.

Of friendship.

His eyes widened and his throat went dry when he saw her eyes slowly flutter open.

When he saw their grass-green color, everything within him knew that this would never be an ordinary woman to him. Although he knew that it was madness for a man to be instantly taken by the beauty of a woman, he could not help being drawn into a web that he knew was dangerous. She *had* spoken a man's name. She *had* spoken a girl's name.

That had to mean that she was already a part of a family.

Until this shipwreck, she had probably been the reason for a man and child to wake up each morning . . . to be with this beautiful woman.

And now?

Was she all that was left of that family?

Was she truly all alone in the world?

If so, he knew that he would not go to the Suquamish village, after all, anytime soon. He would concentrate on bringing happiness again to this woman.

Janice's eyes widened in horror, and panic seized her when she saw that she was with an Indian.

He was in the process of taking her somewhere in his canoe!

She had never had any dealings with Indians before. She just knew that most women were afraid of them.

She lay there, afraid to move, her heart thundering like wild claps of thunder in her chest, as the Indian continued to look down at her.

She was keenly aware of the shape of his long, muscular limbs and powerful chest, which were evident in his light garb.

Although he was intriguing to her, she knew that he had the power and strength to do anything to her that he pleased!

Oh, Lord, did he see her as his next conquest? Did he see her as a prize he would take to his village and show off to his warrior friends?

Would . . . they . . . each want a part of her?

That possibility sent stabs of fear through her consciousness. She was also terrified of being on the water again. And she was afraid that she would be taken so far away from where the ship had sunk that she would never find her daughter and brother.

Her eyes wild and desperate, she tried to sit up, but when her head began spinning, she knew that she had lost much of her strength in the recent ordeal, so much that her body was still too weak to allow her to fight off unconsciousness *or* the Indian.

As darkness fell all around her, she drifted off into unconsciousness, crying out Seth's and Lexi's names again.

White Shield reached for her and held her and rocked her when he saw that she was unconscious. He brushed her hair back from her eyes. "I saw much fear in your eyes when you saw me," he whispered. "I must prove to you that there is no reason to fear White Shield. I will even help you find your loved ones."

Ah-hah, seeing the love she felt for those she might have lost forever in the Sound's crashing waves made him realize that he must put foolish thoughts about her from his mind. She was a white woman with a white woman's fear of a man with red skin. It was sad that dark tales made up by evil whites could make the red man so disliked by so many.

It was because of such talk that so many wars had erupted between reds and whites, throughout the years.

With an empty feeling in the pit of his stomach, he rowed on toward his home.

He wondered how the woman would react when she found herself in the home of a red man. He had best keep his knives and weapons hidden until he could prove that she was with a friend, not an enemy with plans to harm her.

Chapter Four

*You are not wrong, who deem
That my days have been a dream;
Yet if hope has flown away
In a night, or in a day,
In a vision, or in none,
Is it therefore the less gone?*
                    —EDGAR ALLAN POE

In his longhouse made of cedar with its center posts supporting a gabled, tree-bark roof, White Shield knelt beside the woman, who still lay in a deep sleep. He had made her a thick pallet of furs and had placed her on them before a roaring fire in the tall stone fireplace at one end of the massive room. He had covered her with a soft blanket.

Since she had last spoken the names of those she must love with all her heart, and since she had looked at White Shield with such fear in her luminous green eyes, she had not again awakened.

There were no visible injuries on the woman, so White Shield decided there was not much he could do for her until she regained consciousness. Surely exhaustion had laid its claim on her.

White Shield reached a hand to her cheek. He smiled when he felt warmth there now instead of clammy coldness.

There was even some rosiness to her flesh. And her lips were no longer a purplish color.

Earlier he had called for his shaman uncle's wife, Snow Flower, to come and change the white woman into warmer clothing.

Being kind and gentle at heart, she had done as she had been asked. The white woman now wore a soft cotton gown.

White Shield had also asked Snow Flower to bring soup for the woman. When she awakened the warmth of food would help alleviate the inner chill that a fire and warm gown and blanket could not reach.

"White Shield, I have brought broth for the woman," Snow Flower said as she stepped up behind him. She wore a clinging doeskin dress, her dark brown hair hanging long down her back in one thick braid.

He turned with a start, for he had been in such deep thought that he had not heard her or his uncle, Sees Far, enter his lodge.

He rose to his feet and smiled at both of them, then reached a hand out for the heavy pot of broth, which sent out such a tantalizing, rich aroma that even White Shield's belly grumbled with hunger.

"*Mahsie*, thank you, Snow Flower," White Shield said, hanging the pot over the flames of the fire, so that it would retain its warmth until the woman was able to eat it.

"I thought broth would be better for the woman than soup," Snow Flower said. She knelt beside Janice and smoothed a hand across her pale brow. "She is such a lovely, tiny thing. It is a miracle that she survived the waves of the Sound."

White Shield nodded as he gazed at Snow Flower, and then looked at the white woman. They appeared to be the same age, which meant that the white woman must be past her twentieth year, for Snow Flower had just reached her twenty-second summer of life.

Like the white woman, Snow Flower was pretty and delicate.

He wondered if the white woman was as sweet and caring as his Aunt Snow Flower. She had stolen his uncle's heart the moment he had seen her at the Suquamish village.

And although his shaman uncle was much older than his new bride, the age difference did not matter to either of them. It was evident in their eyes that they loved each other deeply.

He looked at Snow Flower again and at the dress she wore. It was made of doeskin, soft to the touch and lovely to the eyes. He could see, in his mind's eye, how such a dress might look on the white woman. With her hair of flame, would it not contrast beautifully with the white of the dress?

"Nephew, I can see that much is on your mind," Sees Far said as he came and slid a comforting arm around White Shield's shoulder. "What happened today caused you to abandon your plans to go and seek a mate at my wife's people's village. Go now. Snow Flower and I will sit vigil at this woman's side. When she awakens, Snow Flower will spoon-feed her the broth and I will use words that will comfort her aching heart."

White Shield looked up at his uncle, who was revered by all the people of their Bear band. He was a man of holiness, as well as a doctor for his people, and his kindness reached inside everyone's heart like a beam of sunshine. Today he wore a plain floor-length robe, and his dark brown hair hung almost to the floor, thick and glossy from his wife having lovingly brushed it. In his eyes there was such kindness. He could often heal someone's pains by just looking at the afflicted one.

"Thank you, Uncle," White Shield said, again gazing down at the woman. He was touched deeply by the caring way Snow Flower caressed the stranger's brow with a damp cloth. "But now I have other things on my mind."

"This woman?" Sees Far said, slowly dropping his hand to his side. "You are so concerned over a stranger that you would delay going to seek a wife?"

"She is a person in trouble," White Shield said, nervously clasping his hands together behind him. "I must do what I can for her."

"And that has been done, has it not?" Sees Far said. "Nephew, do I see too much interest in your eyes? Do I hear it in your voice?"

"It is true that she has touched me as no other white woman ever has," White Shield said thickly, now uncomfortable under the close scrutiny of his uncle, who seemed to see clear through into his soul, where his heart beat differently than before. His fascination with this beautiful woman could not be denied. And he could tell that his uncle did not approve, for rarely did his uncle frown. He was frowning now. And White Shield knew why. It was because of the woman and his obvious interest in her.

"Did you not say that you heard her say two names?" Sees Far asked, his voice drawn. "Was not one of them a man's name?"

"*Ah-hah*, that is so," White Shield said,

uncomfortably shifting his feet on the wood floor beneath them.

"Then would you not believe that man was her husband?" Sees Far said, looking slowly at the woman. "She is of the age when a woman would not be without a husband."

"*Ah-hah*, that does seem so," White Shield said, frowning himself now as he looked down at the woman. He hated the pang of jealousy he felt at the thought of her already being married.

It was not like him to be obsessed by a woman.

The only cure for his obsession was to find the man named Seth. And the girl named Lexi. If he reunited them as a family, he would be forced to forget his foolishness.

Then he could resume his voyage to the Suquamish village and look upon the faces of the women there. Perhaps he would find someone who stirred his soul as this white woman had stirred it.

He turned quick eyes to his uncle. "I must leave now," he said, seeing a slow smile of satisfaction quiver over his uncle's thin lips.

"It is good that you will go now to the Suquamish village," Sees Far said, placing an arm around White Shield's shoulder again and walking him toward the door. "I do not believe you will have to look far to find the perfect woman for you. As you see, I found mine at the village where you are going to seek yours. She

47

has cousins. I hope you will look upon one of them with interest. It would be good for my wife to have a cousin with whom she can sew and talk while the responsibilities of shaman take me from our home."

"Uncle Sees Far, my journey to the Suquamish village must still be delayed," White Shield said, seeing disappointment enter his uncle's dark gray eyes.

"Where are you going if not there?" Sees Far asked, dropping his arm from around White Shield's shoulder.

"I will go to Tacoma now and see if anyone by the name of Seth or Lexi is among the survivors of the shipwreck," White Shield said. He turned and faced his uncle. "I am sure those who did survive were taken there. It is closer than Seattle."

Now understanding that his nephew was going to find this woman's husband, and perhaps her child, Sees Far smiled broadly. "This thing that you do is *kloshe*, good," he said, nodding. "If you find the woman's loved ones, and if they are able to travel, bring them back to our village. We will give them lodging until all is well again among them and they are able to resume their lives."

White Shield understood his uncle's eagerness for this woman's loved ones to be found alive. He knew that would bring an end to

White Shield's feelings for the woman. White Shield knew that was only true *if* the woman was married to the man she had cried out for.

He turned and gazed at the white woman again. Each time he saw her he was drawn more and more by her loveliness. If she was not married, he would look no farther than her in his search for a wife.

"Nephew, I sense that much is happening in your mind and heart. I fear that these changes are not in your best interest, or your people's," Sees Far said, his voice drawn. "One day you will lead. The woman at your side, your wife, will have many of her own contributions to make to our people. It is best that that woman's skin not be white."

White Shield turned with a quick jerk and gazed into his uncle's eyes. It was not like White Shield to do anything against his uncle's wishes, for Sees Far was not only his uncle, but also their people's beloved shaman.

But this was different. White Shield could not turn his feelings off and on just with a mere suggestion. If it was at all possible, he *would* have a future with this woman.

But first he must discover whether or not she was free to pursue.

"Nephew, I beg you not to allow yourself to think past doing what you can to help this woman," Sees Far said softly, placing a gentle

49

hand on his nephew's copper cheek. "You are a man of kind heart. Use it well, White Shield. Use it well."

White Shield swallowed hard, for it seemed that his uncle had read his thoughts.

And no, he would not allow himself to think past doing what he could to help the woman. He *was* a man of kind heart and would not wish for any man's death.

Not even if he was white and wed to perhaps the most beautiful and delicate woman in the world!

He gave his uncle a quick hug, then left the longhouse at a run.

After he was outside and some distance from his lodge, he stopped and sucked in a wild breath of air. Never before in his life had he been so torn about something.

He tightened his jaw and went to his canoe. He shoved it out into the Sound, then boarded it.

When he stepped over the blankets upon which the woman had lain, he reached down, plucked one up, and placed it against his cheek.

"Woman, you are now a part of my life, no matter what I find on my search today," he whispered, then rested the blanket across his lap as though it gave him a connection to her at this moment. Determinedly he paddled his way toward Tacoma.

Chapter Five

First vague shadow of surmise
Flits across her bosom young,
Of a joy apart from thee—
—RALPH WALDO EMERSON

As White Shield rowed onward toward Tacoma, he saw debris everywhere. Some was floating. Some was clinging to the banks, or tangled in piles of lumber along the shore . . . lumber that never made it to the saw mills after their huge cutting machines had been turned off due to the money crisis.

White Shield had heard tales of men shooting themselves over their financial losses.

Some had even jumped from the windows of high buildings.

He could not understand the sort of man whose courage could not withstand such losses. The red man had lost far more through the years as white men grabbed up their land, leaving little for the native inhabitants of this country. No Skokomish man that White Shield knew personally, or had ever heard of, had been so cowardly as to take his own life. The Skokomish held their heads high and forged onward, proving who was the better man in this world gone crazy with greed and selfishness.

As he approached Commencement Bay at Tacoma, he saw many canvas tents lined up along the wharf, displaying bold red crosses painted on the sides.

"The Red Cross," he whispered to himself as he paddled toward the rocky shore. He had heard about how the Red Cross was always there for whites in times of emergency. It was obvious to him that the one hospital that remained open in Tacoma did not have adequate room for the number of people thrown into the Sound when the steamer had dashed itself against the boulders.

He leapt from his canoe and beached it on the rocks.

His spine stiffened when he heard moaning, crying, and people yelling for help. He felt compassion for the people who had lost so much as a result of the shipwreck.

Then he turned and saw a face that was familiar to him . . . Doc Rose, with his shock of white hair, thick white beard, and black fustian suit.

His stethoscope hanging around his neck, and carrying his black leather bag, the elderly doctor was going at a frantic pace from tent to tent. A nurse dressed in white scampered alongside him.

White Shield increased his pace and caught up with the doctor. "Doc Rose?" he said, drawing the elderly man's deep brown eyes toward him as he stopped just before entering another tent.

"Good morning, White Shield," Doc Rose said, extending a hand that quivered from an ailment White Shield was not familiar with.

Doc Rose's head shook slightly, too, and he stood somewhat stooped, causing him to have to look up at White Shield at a strange, sideways angle.

"How did your people come through the storm?" Doc Rose asked. "You haven't come for me, have you, because some of your people were injured?"

White Shield saw a look of anxious hope in the elderly doctor's eyes, and he knew why. This doctor, whose heart was big and good, had always wanted to come to White Shield's island to care for the sick and elderly.

But his offer had always been rejected. White Shield's people wanted no part of the white man's medicine.

And Doc Rose knew that. Today he surely

Cassie Edwards

hoped that finally the Skokomish were breaking down that old taboo and were going to allow him to come and assist them.

"My people need no help," White Shield said. He placed a gentle hand on the old man's shoulders. "But White Shield thanks you again for offering. You are a *sikhs*, a friend, whose heart is good toward my people. Your kindness is appreciated."

"Then why did you single me out today and stop me?" Doc Rose said. He arched a thick gray eyebrow. "Many people were hurt today, White Shield, when the steamer sank in the Sound. It is a terrible tragedy."

"I saw the debris in the Sound," White Shield said. He nodded and dropped his hand back to his side. He looked past the doctor and again gazed at the long row of tents.

His insides tightened as he listened to the many cries for help and sobs caused by someone surely grieving over the loss of a loved one.

"That is what brought you here?" Doc Rose asked, turning and also looking at the tents, visibly shivering when he heard the mournful cries. He was one man who could do only so much. He had sent a messenger to Seattle to bring doctors back from there. Surely the animosity that he knew existed between the people of Seattle and Tacoma could be forgotten for the moment. They must all work together to help those people who were injured, or who had lost a loved one in the shipwreck tragedy.

"In a sense, *ah-hah*, that was what brought me to Tacoma," White Shield said. The doctor knew that since White Shield no longer worked in the capacity of forester, he rarely came into the city for anything. White Shield deplored the very reason this city had come to be.

Ah-hah, the Skokomish, Duwamish, and Suquamish had once shared the land that now belonged to whites. It was hard to stand on the soil where his people's homes had once stood, filled with children's laughter when food hung over the cookfire being prepared by their mothers.

Now buildings made of brick faced the Sound, their shadows a mockery of everything that once was Skokomish.

It was at times like this, when White Shield paused to think about it, that he regretted his dealings with the white man. He reminded himself that his role as forester had helped save many trees. That was what was important, not the fact that he had had to mingle with whites to make that possible.

Well, he wasn't a forester now, he thought to himself. He had no reason to mix . . . not until this moment. He *had* to find answers for the white woman.

Doc Rose turned his eyes back to White Shield. "White Shield, you were saying?" he asked, drawing White Shield from his deep thoughts.

"I came to inquire about a man named Seth,

and a girl, or woman, named Lexi," White Shield explained. "Do you know whether or not there are people with those names among the survivors of the wreck? I do not know their last names."

Being so rushed, Doc Rose did not take the time to inquire how White Shield knew those names, or why he bothered to ask about them. He had been kept from his rounds too long as it was. He pointed toward the hospital. "Go there," he said. "You will find a ledger in which all names from the ship are recorded."

"*Mahsie*, thank you. I will go there and see," White Shield said. He rushed away from the doctor. His heart was anxious to see if he could find the white woman's loved ones. Only by doing so could he proceed with his own life.

He *had* to forget her.

His uncle was right.

It was not in his best interest to have feelings for a white woman.

He was going to lead his people one day. He needed a strong, capable woman at his side. He needed such a woman to bear his children.

Sons should be in the image of their father, not born with a skin color that the father had learned to hate.

He must learn to detest this woman also.

White Shield was glad that he could read the list of survivors. He was educated enough to read, write, and count, but he had never gone to school. His grandmother had learned her skills from the wife of a trader long ago. She had patiently taught White Shield all that she knew.

Just as he reached the front of the hospital and started to climb the steep stone steps that would take him inside, White Shield was stopped abruptly when a man dressed in jeans and a plaid flannel shirt, and whose red hair hung in stringy, greasy wisps down to his massive shoulders, blocked his way.

"You git!" the man snarled, his buckteeth a contrast to his thick, bushy red beard. He leered at White Shield with narrowed, angry, dull gray eyes. "You have no place in a white man's hospital." He spat, all the while glaring at White Shield.

Then he stepped closer and brought his face near White Shield's. "Don't you know, savage, that your presence in a white man's hospital will contaminate the place?" he said, his lips forming a mocking smile.

White Shield knew this man very well. He was a beady-eyed lumberjack called Stumpy Jackson. He was named Stumpy because he had been born with one leg shorter than the other. This lumberjack was among those who had never approved of White Shield's role in choosing which trees should be spared the ax. He had always said that White Shield, not the failing economy, had cost the lumberjacks their jobs. White Shield knew that this beady-eyed man was *peshak*, bad.

Loathing this man so much, and knowing

that he was worthless even in the eyes of the white people of Tacoma, White Shield laughed mockingly and stepped around him. But he only got up one step before Stumpy grabbed him by the back of his hair and yanked.

White Shield stopped and doubled his hands into fists at his sides to keep from turning and hitting the man. He knew that white people welcomed an opportunity to imprison a red skin.

"Unhand him this minute!" Doc Rose shouted as he rushed up and stood beside White Shield. He placed his fists on his hips and glared at Stumpy. The lumberjack eased his hand away from White Shield's hair. "Stumpy, get lost. You're trouble. And there's enough trouble in Tacoma from the shipwreck."

His dignity somewhat marred, White Shield shook his hair back in place as Stumpy stamped away, mumbling and cursing.

Doc Rose sighed heavily as he gazed up at White Shield's six-foot height. "I apologize for that," he said. "But the business panic has left a few unruly cusses running around causing havoc we don't need in Tacoma. You were just a target for Stumpy's frustration. That's all."

White Shield knew better than that, but he didn't refute what the doctor said.

White Shield knew that Stumpy was a man he must keep an eye out for. Stumpy hated White Shield enough to kill him. More than likely, it would be by ambush, for that was the sort of underhanded thing Stumpy would do in order to achieve his vengeance.

"Come with me," Doc Rose said. He led White Shield up the steps. "I'll help you search for those names." He glanced over at White Shield. "What did you say the names were?"

"Seth and Lexi," White Shield supplied.

Doc Rose stepped up to a ledger that lay open on a sprawling oak desk.

White Shield's eyes poured over the pages as Doc Rose slowly turned them.

After turning the last page, Doc Rose closed the ledger and turned toward White Shield. "I'm sorry, White Shield, there are no such names listed here," he said softly. He arched an eyebrow. "Why are you interested? What are those names to you?"

White Shield sucked in a deep breath of air, looked nervously away from Doc Rose for a moment, then gazed into his dark eyes again. "I found a survivor," he said in a rush of words. "A woman. She mentioned the two names that I gave you. They must be very important to her, for she repeated them several times."

"If you know the names, then surely she told you who these people are to her," Doc Rose said guardedly. "White Shield, tell me about the woman. Is she injured? Should she be here under my care? Should I go to the island and see her?"

Panic grabbed at White Shield's heart. He

was afraid that he had said too much. He was afraid that Doc Rose might feel that he had a right to look into the welfare of the injured woman, even if she *was* on land that belonged to the Skokomish.

"She was not injured," White Shield said, his voice flat. "And she is being cared for. Your medicine is not needed. If she chooses to come to you, herself, then she will come. Until then, Doc Rose, she is doing quite well on our island."

Doc Rose kneaded his chin and looked more intently at White Shield. "If you say so," he murmured, slowly nodding. "I have never had any reason not to believe what you say. I know you well, White Shield, from our dealings while you were working for the lumber companies. You always stood back and did not interfere when I came to see to an injured lumberjack. You never questioned anything I chose to do, although I know that your people have your own ways of dealing with injuries. I always appreciated that, White Shield. As I appreciate your people caring for a white woman who is in trouble now."

Doc Rose placed a hand on White Shield's arm. "But if you *do* need my services, *if* you feel your shaman is not enough for the woman, you know that all you need to do is send someone for me and I will be there in the blink of an eye," he said thickly. "Understood, White Shield?"

White Shield nodded. "*Ah-hah,* understood," he said.

He respectfully waited for the doctor to remove his hand, then walked back down the steep steps, his thoughts even more deeply troubled since he had not found the woman's loved ones.

Now he had the wretched chore of relaying this news to her when she regained consciousness. He hoped that she had courage enough to accept the possible deaths of her Seth and Lexi.

He went to his canoe and turned the prow toward home. He was not aware of Stumpy Jackson watching him from the shore, swearing to himself to find a way to make the "savage" pay. No matter what anyone said, Stumpy knew White Shield was responsible for the loss of his job at the lumber company.

"One day, savage, one day I'll find a way to get back at you!" Stumpy whispered, doubling his hands into tight fists at his sides. "Oh, how I loathe the very sight of you!"

He turned and gazed at the hospital. He kneaded his brow as he wondered what had brought White Shield there.

Stumpy smiled wickedly. "This calls for an investigation," he whispered. He chuckled throatily as he hobbled toward the hospital.

Chapter Six

Trust no future, however pleasant!
Let the dead Past bury its dead!
Heart within, and God o'erhead!
—RALPH WALDO EMERSON

Feeling warmth all around her, relishing the comfort of the blankets in which she was snuggled, Janice lazily stretched out beneath them and yawned as she slowly awakened.

But as she opened her eyes and saw where she was, that she was not in the safe cocoon of her own bed in San Francisco, or her grandmother's cabin deep in the forest, her yawn turned into a low, anguish-filled gasp. Everything that had happened to her came back like a splash of cold water.

Sobbing, she closed her eyes, and in quick flashes, as though lightning strikes were illuminating her brain, she recalled everything that had happened.

The storm.

The winds.

The crashing of the waves!

And then she felt a deep pain inside her heart as she recalled that horrifying instant when she was thrown into the water and she had gotten a last look at her brother and daughter as they were swept away by the angry waves of the Sound.

The only thing that gave her some hope that perhaps Lexi had survived the tragedy was that Seth had been holding on to her for dear life.

But if Seth had died, so had Lexi!

And then she remembered nothing else except for a brief second when she had awakened and found herself in a canoe with . . . an . . .

"An Indian," she whispered.

She slowly raised herself on an elbow and looked around her. By the light of a fire in the huge stone fireplace, and a whale oil lantern on a table that sat against the wall opposite the fireplace, she saw that she was in a rugged-looking house.

Scarcely breathing, she looked more closely

around her. She was keenly aware of the smell of cedar and knew the lodge must be made of this lovely, fragrant wood. She saw that this one room was connected to others.

Pelts of various animals, colorful blankets, and ceremonial masks hung on the walls. Berries and fish hung to dry on the crossbeams overhead, under the rafters.

Beautiful blankets, woven in striking designs of cedar bark and the hair of the mountain goat, lay folded on a platform against one wall.

The chairs and tables were hand-hewn and crude.

The wooden floor, upon which she had been placed on a pallet of furs near the fireplace, had woven mats stretched across it.

Her eyes widened when she saw something else in the vague shadows of the room. It was a huge harpoon lying across wooden pegs that had been driven into the wall. She had read somewhere that whale hunters kept their precious harpoon heads in neatly made pouches of shredded bark.

She swallowed hard as she recalled seeing many whales in the ocean on her way north from San Francisco. They had been so awesomely beautiful, she couldn't see how any man could kill them. They had been like shadows passing in the deep, clear water.

Yet she knew the whales were used for many things that the Northwest Indians needed for survival, and she tried to understand their need to kill them.

There was a smell of spices in the air, and something else that made her stomach growl.

She looked quickly toward the fireplace and saw a huge pot hanging over the flames. She surmised that the delicious, tantalizing aroma was some sort of stew or soup simmering in the pot.

Then she looked elsewhere again and sat up. The one blanket under which she had lain fell in a heap around her waist as she gazed at her silk dress lying on a close-by trunk, her patent leather slippers sitting beside it.

She could tell that both had been ruined by seawater. The dress was a mass of wrinkles, and somewhat faded. The patent leather of her shoes no longer held a beautiful shine; it looked shrunken and drawn up like an old man's leathery skin drawn tight by weather and age.

She gasped, and her skin seemed to crawl when she saw that beside her shoes lay her underclothes in a heap, yellowed by the Sound's water.

"Who removed my clothes?" she gasped, paling as she glanced down and saw that she was now dressed in a soft cotton nightgown. Beneath it she wore nothing, which meant that who ever had changed her from her clothes to these had seen her naked body.

She paled when she thought of the warrior who had surely fished her out of the Sound.

She could not recall anyone being in the canoe with him.

Had he brought her to his home and seen to her welfare himself?

Or had someone been summoned—perhaps a woman?—to see that she was more comfortable in dry clothes and on a pallet of warm furs.

Or . . . had . . . his wife done it all?

But none of that truly mattered to her. Her thoughts went back to the tragedy caused by the storm. Because of the shipwreck, her whole world had been torn asunder.

Her loved ones had been swept away from her.

Had they survived?

Or was she faced with the same loneliness and despair that she had felt at another time in her life, when she had received word of the deaths of her parents?

Was it meant for her to be alone? Without her brother? Without her precious daughter?

"Oh, my dear grandmother," she whispered, sobbing as she lay back down amid the furs. "Oh, Mema, how *do* I tell you? You adored both Seth and Lexi. Will I be enough to help you in your sorrow? Only a year ago you lost your husband!"

Feeling totally drained and exhausted again, as though she had only moments ago fought the battle of the waves as she desperately tried to reach shore, alive, Janice closed her eyes, her sobs dying now to soft whimpers.

And then she heard a sound that made her

heart skip a beat and her breath catch in her throat.

The door.

Someone had just opened the door.

Oh, Lord, she was too afraid to look and see who it was.

If it was the warrior, what plans did he have for her now?

Was she his conquest?

Had he been kind to her only because he wished to keep her as his captive?

She had never had any dealings with Indians.

But she did recall stories of the atrocities that the white man was guilty of committing against the Indians of this country.

She couldn't see how any Indian could be kind to white people.

Not even to a vulnerable young woman who had just lost so much that was dear to her.

Would this man understand such a loss?

Would he even care?

She was afraid to know why he had brought her to his lodge.

Since whoever had opened the door still stood there, perhaps studying *her*, Janice took a deep breath for courage and slowly sat up and looked to see who was there.

Soft light poured into the dusky room from the open door. Janice's pulse raced when she made out the tall, lean figure of a man silhouetted against the light in the doorway.

Although she had been conscious for only a

short time in the canoe, it had been long enough for her to see the warrior and to remember much about him.

The man standing there, looking toward her, was that warrior.

She would never forget his long brown hair which hung down past his shoulders to his waist, nor his broad, muscled copper shoulders, nor his sculpted, sensitive-looking lips.

She could also recall his eyes, how deeply gray and mystical they had been as he gave her a look of wonder during her brief moment of consciousness.

And although she had been immediately afraid of him, she had seen his handsomeness and his noble bearing.

He stepped out into the light of the lamp, and she gasped when she again saw all of these traits.

In his eyes, she saw a concern that came with compassion and caring.

This gave her some hope that what she had earlier feared was wrong.

But she didn't have the chance to test that theory by openly questioning him. Suddenly someone else was there at the doorway. Her rescuer stepped aside and allowed this other man to enter the lodge.

He did not hesitate as did the younger warrior. He had long, graying hair, and wore a loose, flowing robe of some sort. He came and knelt down beside Janice, scrutinizing her closely.

"You are finally awake," Sees Far said, cautiously reaching a hand toward Janice to place it gently on her arm. He noticed that her hand was suddenly trembling and guessed how afraid she was to be there with strangers ... and not only strangers, but men whose skin was not of her own color, men who surely sent stark fear into her heart.

"Yes, and ... who ... are you?" Janice asked, her voice tight with fear. "Where ... am ... I?"

She looked past him and noticed that the younger warrior approached her slowly, so as not to frighten her.

But even though she was uneasy, she was also impressed by the younger Indian. With his six-foot height, broad shoulders, thick, sinewy neck, and luxurious, deep brown hair that he wore to his waist, he cut a striking figure. She continued to stare at his strong, determined face. He was perhaps the most handsome man she had ever seen.

And his eyes! They were bright and expressed intelligence, firmness, and decisiveness. Yes, he had a young man's hard, lean form, and an eagle's visage.

"My name is Sees Far," the older man said, bringing her eyes quickly to him. "You are safe here at my people's village. You are among *sikhs*, friends."

He drew his hand away from her when she suddenly grabbed the corner of the blanket and held it close beneath her chin. "I am of the Bear clan of Skokomish," he said. "I am their shaman. I . . . we . . . mean you no harm. You have been brought here by White Shield, my nephew, who is our people's sub chief. You were found unconscious. But that is the only harm your time in the Sound caused you. You are not injured, physically."

"I . . . wish . . . I were dead," Janice blurted out, turning her eyes away from both men as tears filled them again. "I have lost so much. I am not sure if I can bear it."

"You are too young to wish such things upon yourself," White Shield said, sinking to his haunches beside Sees Far, his muscles knotting and rippling, sharply defined by his leanness. "Tell me, white woman. What is your name? What was your destination when the ship was dashed against the boulders in the Sound?"

Hearing true concern in White Shield's voice, and glad that she now knew his name and tribe—from her grandmother's tales of the area she knew that the Skokomish were a friendly, non-warring tribe—Janice wiped her eyes dry with the backs of her hands and slowly turned and gazed into White Shield's dark, compelling gray eyes.

She scarcely noticed when the other man got up and left, leaving her alone with the younger warrior.

This Indian called White Shield was having an effect on her she never would have expected. The caring in his eyes and his gentle manner were making her trust him, yet she still felt threatened. These Indians, the Skokomish, had surely suffered at the hands of whites, as all Indians had.

Yet this warrior showed no resentment or hatred toward her, and *she* was white.

Her red hair made the physical differences between them very apparent. She had noticed that White Shield sometimes glanced at it. It seemed that her hair intrigued him.

"I was headed for Tacoma, to . . . to . . . be with my grandmother," Janice suddenly blurted out. "The waves, they . . ." Her voice broke. She covered her mouth with a hand, stifling a sob behind it.

"I can see that it pains you too much to talk about it right now," White Shield said, interrupting her. He glanced toward the pot over the stove, then looked at Janice again. "Let me bring you a bowl of broth. Surely you are hungry. You had a long, deep sleep. It must have been a long time since you have had nourishment."

Grateful that he understood the hurt it caused to speak of the shipwreck and her loss, Janice silently nodded, then took the wooden bowl filled with broth from him. She was very aware of his body when he stood up; his movements were as lithe as a panther's.

He poured cool clam juice in a wooden cup and handed this to her.

White Shield sat down before her and watched her sipping the broth from a wooden spoon and taking occasional drinks from the cup, her eyes only occasionally looking up and holding his. Every time they did, something within him took fire. He had been taken by her smallness and loveliness, by the soft way she spoke.

Her voice affected White Shield like the early warbling of birds in spring time. How wonderful it was to hear them after their long winter's silence.

So sweet!

So sincere!

So ready to spread joy throughout the land.

Yes, her voice was as sweet and lilting as a bird's.

She smiled as she handed him the empty bowl.

"It was very good," Janice said, then reached a hand out to his and stopped him before he refilled the bowl. "No, please. I have had enough."

When her hand grazed against his flesh, she felt the instant electricity that flowed between them.

Startled, she jerked it away. Their eyes locked again in a wondering stare.

She forced herself to break the silence, for she wasn't sure what was happening between herself and this Indian. But whatever it was, it felt beautiful inside her heart.

Even more startled than before by the way this woman affected him, White Shield sighed heavily and set the empty bowl aside. It seemed he had been mystically drawn to her. He felt as though he had known her in another time. She awakened something in him that he had never felt before.

"Did your wife make this broth?" Janice found herself asking. She felt a slight blush rush to her cheeks, and hoped that he didn't see it.

"No, I have no wife," White Shield said, his heart skipping a beat. She must be interested in him or she would not have asked such a question.

He started to ask her if she had a husband, and if his name was Seth, but she spoke again too quickly.

"My name is Janice," she said, extending toward White Shield a hand that was no longer trembling. Why should it? Before, her hands shook from fear.

Now there was no fear.

There was only a need to know more about this man.

White Shield reached out and accepted her hand in his, his heart soaring at the touch of her skin.

When he circled his fingers around hers, he believed he could feel her pulsebeat quicken. Certainly, his own heart was no longer beating at its usual pace.

Yet he had to fight this!

73

Surely she *did* have a husband, or was newly widowed.

"My full name is Janice Edwards," Janice continued. "My home is in San Francisco. But it was my plan to . . . to . . ."

Again she found it hard to think ahead to what she might discover, that her brother and daughter had died in the Sound. She found it hard even to talk about what her plans *had* been, for everything had changed in her life. Everything!

"White Shield is my name," he said, slowly withdrawing his hand when once again he saw tears in her eyes.

"I know," Janice said, wiping her nose with the back of her hand. "Sees Far, your shaman, told me. Remember?"

White Shield laughed nervously. "*Ah-hah*, I do remember now," he murmured.

"You spoke a word in your language," Janice said, lifting an eyebrow. "What was that word?"

"In the Skokomish language, I said the word 'yes' to your question," White Shield said softly. "I *do* now recall Sees Far telling you my name."

"Sees Far," Janice said, as though deep in thought. "He is a kind man."

She looked slowly around her, and then smiled at White Shield. "I have never been in a house such as this," she murmured.

"It is called a 'longhouse,' the lodge of my people's choice," White Shield said. "It is built of cedar. The walls' crevices are chinked with moss."

"It smells good . . . like the cedar used to line my closets back home in San Francisco," Janice said softly. "It always made my clothes smell fresh and clean."

"The cedar provides material for my people's canoes, houses, cooking boxes, ceremonial masks, clothes, and more," White Shield said matter-of-factly.

Then he smiled as he thought of something to say that might ease the tension the woman obviously felt while in his presence. "There is a legend about red cedar," he said. "Long ago, there was a good man who always helped people. When they needed food or clothes or tools, he provided them. When he died, a tree grew from his grave and that tree continued to give people what they needed. That tree is the red cedar."

"That is so interesting," Janice said, smiling. "I love legends. In my chest on the ship was a book of legends that I was reading on my journey to Tacoma."

She swallowed hard and then looked over at her discarded dress and shoes which had been ruined by the waters of the Sound. "Who else has been in your lodge?" she asked as she slid a slow gaze his way. "While I slept, who . . . removed . . . my things?"

"Sees Far's wife, Snow Flower," White Shield

said, nodding. "You are wearing her clothes. She also made this broth for you and brought it to my lodge to warm over my fire in anticipation of your awakening."

"I hope to meet her so that I may thank her for her kindness," Janice said, then searched his eyes with hers. "As I would now like to thank you for all that you have done for me. If not for you . . ."

She swallowed hard, lowered her eyes, then gave White Shield a sudden wild look. "Can you help me some more?" she cried. She reached a hand out to his arm and grabbed it in a desperate clutch. "Can you help me find my Seth and Lexi? Surely they are safe somewhere, as I am. Surely someone found them."

White Shield sensed the desperation in her touch and in her voice, and especially in her wide, wild eyes, and he wasn't sure what to say to her. He could not find it in his heart to tell her what he already knew, that their names were not listed among the survivors.

Perhaps her loved ones were alive, but their names had not been added to the register in Tacoma.

If so, it would be cruel to tell her what he had found when he arrived there.

He gently took her hand from his arm and held it. "I will do what I can to help you," he said, seeing a soft look of gratitude enter her eyes. "I will take you to look for them."

Filled with gratitude, Janice started to fling

herself into his arms and thank him but was stopped when an elderly man came into the lodge and stood in the light of the lamp.

Janice knew that this elder man must be related to White Shield, for he resembled him closely.

White Shield looked quickly up at his grandfather. He released Janice's hand as he started to stand up and give his grandfather a hug of welcome. He stopped and looked questioningly up at his grandfather, who was staring strangely at the white woman, as though he knew her.

White Shield glanced quickly at Janice. The lamplight revealed her full features.

Again he gazed up at his grandfather, who was now taking slow, shaky steps away from Janice, his eyes wide with shock.

White Shield rushed to his feet and reached a hand out for his grandfather, then dropped it to his side when Night Fighter made a quick turn and rushed from the longhouse.

Janice and White Shield exchanged wondering gazes.

Chapter Seven

This interval in every lifetime,
Infinite as it may always seem,
Will become only an intermission,
Temporarily suspending our dream.
       —MARY ANN WHITAKER

Leaving Janice standing in his longhouse, as stunned as he by his grandfather's strange behavior, White Shield rushed outside.

As his people stopped and stared, White Shield caught up with his grandfather and walked with him at a brisker pace than White Shield had seen his grandfather walk in many moons.

That puzzled White Shield anew, because he knew that his grandfather's reaction to the white woman had caused this renewed strength in Night Fighter's usually tired and aching old legs.

"Why, Grandfather?" White Shield asked, staring into his grandfather's faded gray eyes as he turned and glowered at him in a way that was very unusual. "What is there about the white woman that makes you behave unlike yourself? From your reaction, she must be someone you know. How can that be, Grandfather? If you knew her, would she not also know you? Would she not have spoken your name when she saw you in my lodge?"

Night Fighter still only stared into his grandson's eyes, then looked quickly away and lowered his gaze toward the ground. "I cannot talk about why," he said thickly, then turned away and hurried to his longhouse, leaving White Shield even more puzzled than before.

White Shield gazed at his grandfather's lodge. His grandfather's door was closed to White Shield. He tried not to allow this small gesture to hurt him. There was a purpose to his grandfather's every movement and action. He had to trust that Night Fighter had good reason now to avoid his grandson.

He turned slowly and looked toward his own lodge. He kneaded his chin as he wondered what sort of connection there could be between his grandfather and the white woman. It was apparent that she did not know Night Fighter or understand why he had looked as though he might have seen a ghost of his past.

Perhaps his grandfather had only seen something in her that reminded him of someone. But who? As long as he had known his grandfather, there had been no white woman in his life. There had only been his wife, someone loved by everyone who knew her.

Even now White Shield could see his grandfather's deep mourning for his wife, Winter Dawn, who only recently had died from a heart weakness.

Knowing that it was best to forget what had transpired between his grandfather and the white woman, since his grandfather had chosen not to talk about it, White Shield went back to his lodge.

When he stepped inside, he stopped and gazed down at Janice. She was on her knees, her silk dress draped across her lap, her one hand running slowly over it.

"The salt in the seawater took the color and ruined the fabric of your dress," White Shield said, gazing now into her eyes as she turned her gaze up to him.

He went and knelt down beside her, now looking at her shoes, which she had placed before her. They were also water-ruined.

"Everything else I own is surely at the bottom of the Sound," Janice said, swallowing back another urge to cry. "My trunks filled with my dresses and . . ."

She did not speak the word *jewels* aloud, for to do so would be to make this man suspect how rich she truly was.

"The storm claimed so much that was dear to me," she said, gently laying the dress on the floor beside her shoes. "Clothes and shoes can be replaced, but . . . loved ones . . . cannot."

"I will get you a change of clothes from my aunt, who is the same size as you, and then I will take you to Tacoma to search for those you have lost," White Shield said.

He was unable to stop himself from reaching over and stroking his hand through her thick red tresses as he swept some strands away from her brow.

"Your hair is like sunshine to the eyes and it is like silk to the fingers," he said. "It is like nothing ever before seen by my eyes, or touched by my fingers."

Touched deep inside her heart by how gentle he was toward her, Janice swayed in a near swoon.

She swallowed hard as her eyes met and held his.

He jerked his hand away, as though he also felt the strange current leaping from her flesh to his. She smiled nervously at him and then hurried to her feet and turned her back to him.

When she heard the soft sound of his feet and

81

then actually felt the heat of his breath on her neck, she knew that he was standing behind her, facing her. She closed her eyes and gritted her teeth in order to will herself to stop feeling these strange sensations brought on by this stranger, and not only a stranger, a man . . . an Indian!

"I did not mean to offend," White Shield said, his voice drawn. "It is just that your hair is entrancing. I could not help but touch it. I could have kept my feelings about it to myself. I apologize if I offended you. That was not at all my intention."

Janice felt a sudden urge to apologize to *him*.

But she knew that she could not tell him about her true reaction to his touch.

She especially could not tell him how his voice reached clean into her soul like a gentle, sweet caress, making her insides melt.

This was all new to her.

She had to learn how to cope with such feelings, especially toward a man who surely was only being kind to her because she had lost so much.

Once he reunited her with her family, she expected him to go on his way as though she had never existed.

She turned on a bare heel and gazed into his eyes. "Please don't apologize," she murmured. "There is truly nothing to apologize for."

She was fighting back her urge to reach up

and familiarize *her* fingers with the feel of *his* hair and his face.

She had to fight with every ounce of her being not to let him know how he affected her.

Never before in her life had she wanted to be held so badly by a man, or kissed.

She knew that if this man did hold and kiss her, she would be lost forever to him.

She would never want to be anywhere else but with him.

As it was, she forced herself to stand still and only look at him as she waited for him to accept her apology.

Seeing so much in her eyes, and feeling the strange, mystical connection between them, White Shield remained silent for a moment longer, aching to hold her and kiss her. He knew that it was wrong to allow himself to feel so much for a woman who probably had a husband and child. But nothing could erase the feelings from his heart. He was drawn to her so strongly, how could he ever forget these private moments with her?

He fought hard not to kiss her, for then he would certainly have cause to apologize, and he hardly ever placed himself in such an awkward position that he would have to apologize not once, but twice!

"I will go now," he blurted out, and turned and rushed from the lodge.

Stunned by the emotional tie that continued

to grow between herself and White Shield, as though it was their destiny to have met, Janice stood and stared at the closed door. She did not realize how long she remained there, motionless, until he appeared again, handing her not only a beautiful doeskin dress but also moccasins.

"I will leave while you change into these," White Shield said as he handed them to Janice.

Their eyes held for a moment again, and then again he was gone, leaving Janice with a racing heart and weak knees.

"What am I to do?" she whispered, feeling strange stirrings at the juncture of her thighs that she had never felt before. She knew that they were caused by this strange euphoria she felt while in White Shield's presence.

Here she was, alone and without her brother and daughter, and she was being overwhelmed by feelings for a Skokomish warrior.

Perhaps she had hit her head on something while being tossed into the Sound by the raging waves.

Perhaps she was never going to be the same person again!

Or was she falling in love for the first time in her life?

"Oh, what *am* I to do?" she whispered.

She sighed heavily as she laid the dress and moccasins aside long enough to pull the gown over her head.

She tried not to think about these new feelings, and instead focused on thoughts of Lexi and Seth. She tried to keep their faces in her mind's eye ... not White Shield's. She felt ashamed when he returned, over and over, his handsomeness and gentleness so appealing that she could not stop thinking about him.

"Seth ... Lexi ... Seth ... Lexi ..." she kept whispering as she dressed in the wondrously soft dress and moccasins.

Seeking a mirror in one of the other rooms, and a brush, and finding neither, she had to resort to using her fingers as a comb. She soon had her hair hanging in long, lustrous waves across her shoulders and down her back.

Recalling White Shield's reaction to her hair, she lifted one end and brought it around and gazed at it. "It is a pretty color," she whispered, smiling.

She had just never thought about it before.

Suddenly she was proud that it was different, especially because it had caused White Shield to admire her.

"White Shield ..." she whispered, the name like an elixir on her lips. She shuddered sensually.

Then, remembering that he was outside his own lodge, waiting for her to become presentable, she rushed from the inner room to the outer, and went to the door and opened it.

When he turned and gazed at her, she saw that he appreciated what he saw.

And she did feel special in the dress.

The moccasins were like nothing she had ever

worn before on her feet. They were like a soft caress.

But there was something more in how he looked at her this time. Although she had seen his interest in her before, this time he was without doubt giving her a look that men only gave women when they were sexually attracted to them.

It gave her a thrill, for this time she knew that there was no pretense in his reaction to her.

It certainly was not because of how much money he could get from marrying her!

White Shield had no idea whatsoever that she was from a wealthy background.

She lifted her chin and tried to force herself to forget that his eyes were making her feel so special and in love. All that was important now was to find her brother and Lexi.

"I am ready to go now," she forced herself to say, breaking the spell that had been weaving like a silken web between them.

"*Newhah,* come," White Shield said, extending a hand toward her.

She hesitated, then accepted it and walked with him, hand in hand, through the village.

When she felt eyes on her, she turned, and her heart missed a beat when she found Chief Night Fighter watching her from his open door.

She turned quick eyes up to White Shield. "Did you find out why your grandfather reacted so strangely to me?" she blurted out.

White Shield looked over his shoulder and

found his grandfather at his door, his eyes following Janice's each and every move. He ducked back inside when he caught his grandson looking his way.

White Shield's curiosity was aroused anew about his grandfather's behavior, yet he would not probe into something his grandfather obviously did not wish to talk about.

"No, I have no idea what there is about you that causes my grandfather to behave so oddly," White Shield said, his hand now on her elbow as he led her past the last longhouse of the village toward the water.

When he heard Janice gasp, he looked down just in time to catch her as her eyes closed and she drifted away into a dead faint.

Chapter Eight

Oh, I've been here, again and again,
Questioning reasons and dimensions,
Hoping to comprehend or perceive,
The meaning of this trying tension.
　　　　　—MARY ANN WHITAKER

When Janice heard White Shield's voice calling her as though from the depths of a well, she responded.

Her eyes fluttered open and she looked up at White Shield questioningly. She was on the ground, and her head was resting on his lap.

In his eyes she saw such concern.

She was touched deeply to know just how much he cared about her, how protective he was of her. For it was at this moment that she realized she must have fainted and that he had caught her and had cradled her head on his lap as he waited for her to awaken.

When she heard the waves lapping at the rocky beach, and realized that she was close to water again, she knew why she had fainted.

"Your village is located on an island?" Janice asked, rising slowly to a sitting position.

She shuddered as she realized that for her to get to Tacoma she would have to board White Shield's canoe to cross over to the other side.

"*Ahnkuttie*, long ago, my people's homes were on land where the trees grow tall and green near Tacoma," White Shield said.

He peered across the Sound, in the direction of Tacoma.

"My people's land stretched out along the Sound even where the city of Tacoma planted its roots," he said, glowering now as he looked over at Janice. "*Me-sah-chie*, treaties, wicked treaties, tore us from land beloved by the Skokomish and sent us over onto land the whites did not want . . . on an island where my people have flourished now for generations. It is our home, beloved by us all, but we can never leave behind us our bitterness at losing all that once was ours to whites."

"I'm sorry," Janice murmured, feeling ashamed that she was part of a community that cared so little for people whose skin color and customs differed from their own. "And I'm sorry for being such a bother. Surely you have duties you should be attending to instead of offering me, a white person, such kindness."

"I have told you before . . . you are not responsible for what others have done," White Shield said, his voice flat. "It is in the past. We were born into this selfish world, a world where white men are never content with the riches they amass. No, it never seems enough, whereas we Skokomish are proud of what we have, which is so much less."

Janice swallowed hard. She dreaded the moment when White Shield would discover that *she* was a part of that rich community. Would that discovery make him look at her in a different light? Would he see her as a rich brat who never wanted for a thing?

Or would he see her as someone who had little control over her own financial worth?

She hoped that he would believe her when she explained how she had been running from that wealth, how it blinded one's vision of who a person truly was.

"I feel foolish for having fainted again," she blurted out.

She forced herself to look at the water, and then slowly at the canoe.

She could not help it when she shuddered with dread. She knew that he must have seen the tremor of her body.

"I . . . just . . . hate thinking of going any-where . . . on water . . . again," she said shakily.

"I understand, but do not fear going in White Shield's canoe across the Sound," White Shield reassured her. "I have never capsized once, and I have manned canoes since I was a mere boy of five winters."

Her eyes wide with wonder, Janice looked quickly at him. "Truly?" she gasped. "You were made to master a canoe at that young age?"

Seeing her disbelief, somewhat amused by it, White Shield smiled. "I was not *made* to take canoes into the Sound, alone, at that age. I did it because I felt *man* enough to," he said, recalling the first time he had gone out, alone, in his father's elaborately carved canoe.

Heavy and long, the canoe had been hard for White Shield to maneuver as his tiny arms yanked hard on the paddle, but he had succeeded. He had proved to his father that he was a young man soon to become a mighty, muscled warrior. He had rowed back and forth in front of his parents many times before handing the paddle back to his father.

"Even at five?" Janice still marveled.

"I would have tried sooner, but my mother would not allow it," White Shield said, placing a hand at Janice's elbow to help her up from the ground.

He turned to her then and placed his hands at her waist and gazed down at her with true caring. "Are you now brave enough to travel in a canoe with White Shield?" he asked, his eyes searching hers.

"*Ah-hah,*" Janice said, smiling almost wickedly up at him when she saw the surprise leap into his eyes at her use of his language.

And then his dismayed look changed into a pleased smile.

Without hesitation he swept Janice up into his arms. As she clung around his neck he carried her to the canoe and gently placed her on the seat behind the one where he himself would sit.

As he slowly drew his hands away from her, their eyes momentarily held.

And then, as though someone was there drawing them mystically together, White Shield bent low and framed her face between his hands as he brought her lips to his.

Everything began spinning inside Janice's head as the kiss lengthened, his tongue probing between her lips.

And when one hand slid down and cupped a breast through the doeskin dress, she felt as though she might faint again, but this time from something so wonderful she doubted that she could define it.

White Shield, too, was lost in passion as their kiss deepened, and their hearts became forever entwined.

But forcing himself to remember why she was there in his canoe, and what he had promised to do for her, aching inside to know that a husband might even now be searching for her, White Shield yanked himself away from her.

Janice was shaken by the abrupt way he ended the kiss. She wondered if he had done so out of contempt for whites.

Should she be guarded in her feelings for him? There could never be anything between them if he carried a loathing in his heart for all whites.

But she could not deny how their eyes now held.

She could not even help it when she smiled and reached a gentle hand to his cheek!

White Shield was so affected by this woman, he now knew for certain that he could never love another, and that he would never travel to the Suquamish village to find a wife. If he could not have Janice, he did not want any woman!

"Again I apologize," he said thickly as she eased her hand from his cheek.

"Again you have no need to," Janice murmured, so in love she wished that she could shout it to the world.

But she knew, as did White Shield, that their love surely was not meant to be. It was just that they had been thrown together by circumstances that would just as quickly tear them apart when she got her life in order again.

He would do the same.

He would go about his daily life doing what he was accustomed to doing.

After Janice found Seth and Lexi, she would go on to her grandmother's cabin and do as she had promised.

But forevermore she would dream of White Shield.

White Shield stepped into his canoe. He was glad that his back was to Janice, for it disturbed him just how much control she had over him.

Every time he looked at her, he became foreign to himself.

And that kiss!

How could he ever forget that kiss?

He knew that Janice had put her whole soul into that kiss, as had he. It would be something that he would think about when they were apart, she doing her usual things with her usual people, and he, with his. As he gazed up at the stars at night he would always wonder if she was looking at them at the same time and thinking of him?

And even though he was concentrating on guiding the canoe across the Sound, and no matter how hard he was trying not to think of Janice, how could he ever forget the way she had responded to his kiss and how she had clung to him?

His insides melted even now as he remembered the feel of her pliant, slender body next to his. It had been like holding a feather, so weightless and beautiful, like those he had occasionally found floating in the Sound. He only wished that he could hold Janice now and never let her go!

As it was, surely he would soon be forced to say farewell to her. When she found her loved ones, she would no longer have a need for him. Her Seth would hold her in his arms and comfort her. It would be his lips that sent her heart into a sensual spinning. It would be Seth who would take her to his bed. . . . !

That final thought was too much for White Shield. He tightened his jaw and forced himself to pay attention to paddling across the Sound, but his thoughts were brought abruptly back to Janice when the canoe reached the debris from the shipwreck, and they saw the remains of the ship sticking like some ugly demon out of the water.

White Shield knew that Janice was surely reliving the tragedy all over again, experiencing the pain of her losses there again, like thorns thrusting into her heart.

He forced himself not to turn to her, for she had to get past her inner sorrow in her own way. If she did not have the strength and the will to overcome it, what could anyone else do for her?

His holding her was only temporary.

This loss, this emptiness she felt, might be forever!

It was something a person had to work out inside his or her own heart, or be lost in it like some dying soul floating endlessly in time, alone.

As White Shield continued to row past the debris, Janice gripped the seat so tightly that her knuckles turned white.

And as more and more debris now floated past, and she was thrown into that moment again when she was in the water, seeing Seth and Lexi taken away from her in the thunderous, crashing waves, she suddenly felt sick to her stomach.

She hung her head over the side of the canoe and retched.

White Shield heard her. He could not ignore her. And even though he felt that it was best for her to get past this grieving in her own way, he laid the paddle in the bottom of the canoe, turned on his seat, and reached out for Janice.

Her mouth now wiped clean of the stinging, outrageous bitterness that had come with emptying her stomach into the Sound, Janice moved into White Shield's arms.

She clung to him as he placed her on his lap.

He held her close to his heart while talking softly to her in an effort to try to ease the pain that had been awakened inside her heart again.

"I miss them so," she sobbed, clinging as she rested her cheek against his powerful chest. "I must find them, White Shield. I *must.*"

He only nodded, for to find them was surely to lose her, and he was not sure now that he could bear such a loss.

Still he reassured her again that he would do what he could to help her. Foremost was his desire to heal the pain in her heart.

"I am so glad that you hold no contempt for me as surely you must for other whites," Janice murmured, wondering again, though, why he had jerked himself away from her moments ago after they had shared such a wonderful kiss.

"There *is* contempt in my heart for whites, but there are some exceptions," he said, drawing her eyes up to him. "One day I shall explain how I became important to the white community and how I even found some friendships there."

"I want to know everything about you," Janice found herself saying, wondering at the surprised look in his eyes that her confession had caused.

Surely he knew the depths of her feelings for him!

How could he not?

She had not held anything back when they had embraced and kissed!

Did he believe that she had done that, as a ploy to assure his help in searching for her brother and daughter?

When a large limb crashed against the side of the canoe, the jolt of it sending Janice tumbling from White Shield's lap and sprawling onto the floor of the vessel, she began to giggle at how awkward she must look.

She was glad, at last, that there was a reason for some lightheartedness between them. Only moments ago she had felt so empty from grieving and loss.

Their eyes held as he helped her back up, but this time he saw that she was secure on her seat, not his lap. Then he sat down on his own seat with his back to her.

His long, brown hair lifting from his muscled shoulders in the breeze, he resumed rhythmically drawing the paddle through the water.

It seemed to White Shield that his each and every heartbeat spoke her name, over and over again, and he knew that nothing now would break the special bond that had formed between them these few hours they had been thrown together by fate.

He knew now that he could not ever say a final good-bye to this woman with hair the color of flames!

Ah-hah, he *would* find a way to be with her, even if it was by way of secret trysts! He smiled at the thought.

Chapter Nine

Voice your meaning,
Share all wisdom,
Catch my dream,
In your prism.
—MARY ANN WHITAKER

Even before White Shield beached his canoe on Tacoma's rocky shore, Janice's eyes widened with horror as she stared at the row after row of tents and realized why they were there. The tents had been erected on the lawn of the Tacoma Hospital, where there were not enough beds to care for the many victims of the ship wreck.

Her heart pounded anxiously as White Shield

Cassie Edwards

leapt from the canoe and dragged it onto the rocks as he beached it. Surely she would have to wait only a few moments more before she would find news of her daughter and brother.

But even if she did find them, just how badly had they been injured?

And what if she didn't find them at all in one of those tents, in the hospital . . . or at Seth's house?

Would that mean that they had not survived the accident?

Would she be forced to view their bodies and identify them as her beloved kin in the city's morgue?

Her thoughts scrambled by these awful possibilities, she did not even see White Shield step up to the side of the canoe and offer her a hand.

She continued staring at the tents, now almost too afraid to go and inquire about her brother and daughter, for fear that what she might be told would tear her heart to shreds.

"Janice?"

White Shield's voice broke through her terror. She looked quickly up at him. "I'm afraid," she said. "What if I . . . ?"

"Do not think the worst until you are certain that you have cause," White Shield said.

"Yes, of course you are right," Janice said, sighing heavily. She took his hand and stepped from the canoe.

Once on solid ground, he eased his hand from hers and they walked side by side up the slight

100

incline until they reached the tents, which stretched out in a long row before the hospital.

Janice was reminded of how she was dressed when people who were mulling around outside the tents turned and stared at her.

She looked quickly down at herself. Although she loved the deerskin dress and moccasins, especially the way they felt against her flesh, she knew that she must look peculiar in them.

But she would allow nothing to stop her, not even the people's rude stares, or their soft whispers. Janice held her chin high and walked onward toward the tents.

When White Shield saw Doc Rose exit one of the tents, he broke away from Janice and hurried to him.

When he reached him, he stopped him with a soft hand on his arm.

"Doc Rose, I have brought the woman I told you about to check on her kin," White Shield said softly. "She is well enough now to search for her relatives among the survivors."

Doc Rose didn't get a chance to reply. Janice had hurried up to White Shield's side and was studying Doc Rose. With his stethoscope around his neck, and with his black satchel at his side, he was clearly the city's resident doctor.

"Sir, I have come today to inquire about a Seth and Lexi Edwards," she blurted out, her cheeks hot from anxiety.

"Doc Rose," the physician said, extending a friendly hand for a shake. "Call me Doc Rose."

Janice smiled weakly, for she wanted to conclude these formalities and know if the doctor had treated her brother and daughter.

"Janice, my name is Janice Edwards," she said, giving him a quick handshake. "Doc Rose, *do* you know of a Seth Edwards? Or Lexi? Seth is twenty-seven. Lexi is . . ."

Before she could mention Lexi's age, Doc Rose stopped her. "White Shield?" he said as he looked over at him. "Didn't you tell this pretty lass that you have already been here to check on her relatives and found they weren't registered?"

Janice's eyes widened as she turned to White Shield. "Is that true?" she blurted out. "Have you been here? Did you come purposely to check on Seth and Lexi?"

"While you were in your deep sleep, *ah-hah*, I came and searched for your loved ones," he said, his eyes solemn, for she was soon to know the truth . . . that her kin were not here, nor had they ever been. "I knew of your concern for them. It was my hope to find answers that would please you. When I did not, I did not want to worsen your pain by telling you what I knew."

He swallowed hard. "Also, I did not tell you because I thought that you would have a better chance of finding the full truth about your lost ones than I," he said. He glanced over at Doc Rose, realizing that, in a sense, he had just insulted him by implying that the doctor would not cooperate fully with an Indian.

Tears filled Janice's eyes. She gazed for a moment longer at White Shield, touched that he had cared enough to come into Tacoma to try to find her loved ones. From the different things that he had said about his feelings toward whites, coming here must not have been an easy thing for him to do.

His willingness to overcome his qualms spoke volumes to her of how he felt about her.

And she would love him forever for it.

She turned slowly back toward Doc Rose. She blinked tears from her eyes. "Then you know nothing of Seth and Lexi?" she said, her voice breaking. "You have no answers for me? My Seth and Lexi aren't here? They are not among . . . the . . . survivors?"

"They are not among the survivor's listed on the register," Doc Rose said solemnly.

"Sir, would you allow *me* the chance to go over the names, myself, to check the register again?" Janice asked, her eyes pleading with the older man. She had been so wrapped up in her own problem that she had hardly been aware of the cries wafting from the tents, some from pain, others from grieving a death or a lost one.

But now, as Doc Rose took her gently by an elbow and began walking her past the many tents toward the one-storied brick hospital, she became keenly aware of the mournful sounds coming from the tents.

Again tears filled her eyes, for she had met

103

many of those people while traveling on the ship from San Francisco. She had to wonder who among those she had chatted with were among the dead, or injured, or bereaved. The faces of so many people flashed before her eyes, and she felt a deeper, intense sadness, for surely many of those she had known were now dead.

"Take the steps carefully," Doc Rose said, still gripping her elbow as they began walking up the steps to the hospital. "They are steep." He grumbled beneath his breath. "When I saw the plans for the hospital, I told them they should not have put it up so high on a hill." He sucked in a deep breath. "I am not ill, but I get winded each time I climb these damnable steps." He laughed as he glanced over at Janice. "I guess my added pounds are the real problem, wouldn't you say?"

Janice smiled awkwardly at him, for she was in no mood for small talk. She was moments away from searching the list of survivors. If Seth and Lexi weren't there, they had probably drowned.

The thought made her feel sick to her stomach all over again. She wanted to turn and run quickly away, so that she would not see the list.

But most of all, she wanted to still have hope!

"Well, young lady, finally, here we are," Doc Rose said, leading her and White Shield into the building where the desk sat with the open journal on it. "This is it?" Janice asked, her voice breaking as she glanced from the journal to Doc Rose.

Doc Rose nodded. He gestured toward it with a hand. "Now take your time," he said. "Go over each name until you've gone through all the entries. Perhaps the names you seek were overlooked."

White Shield could almost feel Janice's heart pounding as he stood beside her, for he could see the pulse beat in the vein in her throat and knew that her fear was mounting.

He waited with an anxious breath as her eyes poured over the entries. She turned each page anxiously eager to get to the other names.

And when she had no more pages, and no more names to read, White Shield wasn't sure what to do, for he understood that Janice's hopes had been shattered.

He wanted to pull her into his arms and comfort her, yet with Doc Rose there, a witness to a red man holding a white woman, he forced himself to just stand there and wait to see what Janice's next move would be. He would not leave her alone to grieve.

He still wanted to offer her help if he could.

"Lord, you were right," Janice said, her voice drawn, her heart aching. "They aren't there."

"Let me at least reassure you about one thing," Doc Rose blurted out. "They are not among those who were taken to the city's morgue, for I checked, myself, after White Shield came inquiring about your kin."

Janice sighed deeply. "At least I have that to be thankful for," she said softly. "That gives me some hope that Lexi and Seth are still alive. Perhaps, like myself, they were able to get to shore and were not injured enough to go to the hospital."

Yes, she still had one more place to look. She still had *some* hope left of Seth's and Lexi's survival.

"Doc Rose, sir, can you direct me to St. Helen's Street?" she asked. "Seth might be at his home. Lexi might be with him. Please give me directions to St. Helen's Street."

After Doc Rose gave Janice the directions she needed, White Shield accompanied her on her search. She was impressed by the city, with the greenery of the forest pressing in upon it from three sides. The wooden streets were flanked by sidewalks built up on wooden stilts. Beyond the business district where she and White Shield were now walking, she could see the city's houses. They were similar to those back home in San Francisco, with their spindles, jigsawed brackets, and band-sawed cresting atop the roofs.

Some displayed Gothic windows with art glass transoms and fancy shingles. She saw many round towers, topped by minarets that looked like candle extinguishers.

Some houses were painted a variegated brown up to the belt course and finished up above with various shades of red.

As they walked on through the business district toward the beautiful homes, Janice was puzzled by the inactivity of the city. There were no fancy horses and carriages on the streets, nor were there any beautifully dressed women coming and going from the shops.

In fact, there were boards over many of the windows.

On Merchant's Row, even the largest, tallest building was boarded up.

All banks but one had boards nailed across their windows.

During their last days in San Francisco, she and Seth had heard some gossip about problems in Tacoma, that some bankers were having trouble.

But believing it was just rumors, possibly created by jealous Seattleites, she and her brother had paid no heed to the gossip. They were too involved in preparing for their trip north. They had found it difficult to hire someone they could trust to maintain the San Francisco mansion, so that when they returned the expensive paintings, silver, and plush furniture would still be there.

Once they did finally find a reputable married couple who vowed to keep things as they were, Seth and Janice had been anxious to get on their ship, especially Seth, who missed his wife.

Seth had always felt secure in his investments, proud of them. Knowing that her brother was an intelligent man, Janice trusted his choice of stockbrokers and stocks.

She had purposely distanced herself from such talk. Her brother was the one who loved boasting of his riches. Janice could care less. She had her grandmother's love of simplicity . . . she hungered to live in the forest in her grandmother's cabin!

As for Seth, while they were out at sea these past two weeks, he had enjoyed his time with Janice and Lexi so much, business had been the farthest thing from his mind.

Sweet Lexi had been so wide-eyed and filled with questions about the ship and everything in it. The last time she had been aboard a ship she had been forced to stay down below with her mother and father, who were on their way to San Francisco, hoping to find work with a wealthy family.

When her parents had died from dysentery before they even arrived at San Francisco's shores, Lexi had been placed out onto the street, alone, to fend for herself.

Yes, the voyage was made sweet and wonderful for little Lexi this time. And she had eaten the best foods and had slept in the finest bed on the ship.

And Janice had had such wonderful plans for Lexi's future. All those plans were like ashes now, unless luck was with her and she found the child and Seth safe and sound at his fabulous home.

Yet as she came to St. Helen's Street and saw that most of those houses had been vacated, she knew that something terrible must have happened. She started to turn to White Shield to ask him if he knew anything about it, but stopped when she saw that she had come to Seth's Victorian mansion.

She stopped and stared, for it was exactly the way Seth had described the house to her. It looked like a fancy three-storied Mississippi riverboat with its white latticework gingerbread trim. Its porch reached across the entire front where white wicker rockers rocked slowly in the breeze. Beautiful lacy, sheer curtains hung at the many windows. Flowers flanked the walk that led to the front steps.

Janice could not wait any longer. She broke away from White Shield and ran up the steps to the porch even though she was not anxious to meet Seth's shameless wife, a woman he had swept away from "Opera Alley," that byway of mystery where the ladies of the red-light district lived.

Janice still couldn't believe that her brother could have married a whore that she had taken from a brothel after falling in love with her at first glance.

She was afraid that the woman had married Seth only for his money and the respect she would get from having such a fine husband.

Janice was not one to speak her mind when no one had asked for her opinion, so she had made herself accept her brother's choice of women.

But it had been difficult. This woman wasn't only a prostitute; she also wanted to flaunt herself on the stage . . . longed to star in one of those new cinema productions that were fast sweeping the country.

And Seth could help her in that respect, too. It was no secret that he had always dreamed of opening an opera house in Tacoma, where actors and actresses would perform in stage shows.

Forcing herself not to think any more about why the woman had gone after Seth, Janice knocked on the door and breathlessly waited to meet her sister-in-law for the first time.

She prayed that Seth and Lexi were there, well and healthy and happy to see that Janice was alive, too.

The door swung open. Janice found herself face to face with a beautiful woman in a lovely turquoise voile floor-length dress that was fetchingly flounced.

Seth had told Janice that his "precious" Rebecca went for plumed hats and smart carriages. Since she had become Seth's wife, she was now a fancy dresser and was always clad in the finest of clothes and the most ostentatious of jewels.

Except for the lack of jewels today, this woman fit Seth's description. She had jet black hair and blue eyes—strong Teutonic features with a prominent nose and wide mouth.

Seth had said that Rebecca could be regal as she swept into a room, or she could tell the latest off-color joke with a twinkle in her eyes.

Seth had also said that there wasn't a man about town who didn't know her.

And there wasn't a woman in the area who didn't despise every breath she took.

But today Janice was seeing someone who was neither haughty nor self-confident. She saw a woman whose eyes were swollen from crying and whose stomach was quite swollen . . . with child!

Janice grew pale. Her insides tightened as she stared at Rebecca's stomach. Seth hadn't told her about the pregnancy!

Oh, Lord, what else had he not told her? Janice worried to herself.

When Rebecca finally spoke, Janice's heart sank.

"Have you come with news about Seth?" the lovely woman asked anxiously. "Please, please tell me that my beloved Seth is alive!"

Janice now knew that neither Seth nor Lexi was there!

Chapter Ten

Nature's loom,
Weaves veils,
Omens and Dreams,
Winding trails.
—MARY ANN WHITAKER

Tears filled Janice's eyes, yet she knew that she had to keep her composure. She could see the anxiousness in Rebecca's eyes as she waited for Janice's response to her question about whether or not she had come with news of Seth.

The way Rebecca wrung her hands so desperately, the way she almost begged with her eyes to hear good news, made Janice hesitant to tell her the truth.

Rebecca's pregnancy worried her. She hoped that the shock of hearing about Seth's disappearance would not harm the child.

Although this was the child of a woman who had a colored past, it was Seth's child, and Janice's niece. Being an aunt was something she had thought about often, for she loved children so much, and she would adore her brother's child!

"Tell me," Rebecca cried when Janice paused to get the courage to tell her the news. "Surely you have come about Seth. Have you seen him? Is he all right?"

It was surprising to Janice that Rebecca had not seemed to notice Janice's Indian attire, or even White Shield, who stood at the foot of the steps, giving Janice a private moment to ask her questions about her brother. She seemed absolutely absorbed in Seth's welfare.

"I *am* here about Seth," Janice finally said. "But not in the way you would hope."

"No!" Rebecca cried. Tears rushed from her eyes as she covered her mouth with her hands. "He's dead! You've come to tell me that he's dead!"

Realizing that she had taken the wrong approach, Janice quickly reached a hand out and gently touched Rebecca on one arm.

"I truly don't know where Seth is," Janice murmured. "Rebecca, I'm Janice. Seth's sister. I came today to see if you have received word of him."

She looked over her shoulder and gave White Shield a weak smile. He still stood patiently, waiting for the right time to join her. She could tell that he wasn't close enough to hear what was being said. After these strained moments between herself and Rebecca were over, she would introduce White Shield.

Rebecca slowly lifted her face up from her hands. She gave Janice a searching stare, then gazed into her eyes. "You . . . are . . . Seth's sister?" she asked, her voice breaking.

"Yes, I'm Janice," she said, trying to hide her own pain over not finding Seth at his home. Now where could she look? If he was well, this would be the first place he would go, for *he* knew the condition of his wife—that she was quite big with child.

"Then . . . where . . . is Seth?" Rebecca asked, her voice breaking. "He was supposed to be with you."

"Rebecca, the steamer we were on was dashed against boulders by a sudden storm. My brother and I, and my daughter, were separated," Janice said, hating to have to explain the tragedy to anyone, because then she had to relive it. "The last time I saw Seth, he . . . he . . . was being carried away from me in the waves. He . . . had . . . Lexi in his arms. I have not seen either of them since."

At that news Rebecca seemed to fall apart. She flung herself into Janice's arms. "Everything is going wrong," she cried out. "Seth is missing, the bank has foreclosed on our house. Seth has lost everything, even his dream of the opera house, and he might never even know. If he is dead . . ."

"Don't think that way," Janice said as she tried to reassure Rebecca, even as she was having a hard time grasping everything herself.

And then came another blow that made Janice's knees almost buckle beneath her. . . .

"And that is not all that has happened in your family," Rebecca sobbed as she eased herself from Janice's arms and gave her a pitying look.

"What else could there be?" Janice asked, her voice thin and drawn.

"Your grandmother Hannah died three days ago and was buried only yesterday," Rebecca said guardedly. She openly winced when she saw how that news made Janice's body stiffen, and then tremble.

"Hannah's lawyer has padlocked your grandmother's log cabin until you or Seth come to claim it," Rebecca said. She wiped tears from her eyes. "They won't even let me go and stay there today after my eviction, which I expect at any moment. I even had to sell my jewels to put food on the table these past several days."

Janice's head was spinning from all that Rebecca had revealed to her. The news that her grandmother was dead hurt worse than the knowledge that she and Seth had lost everything in the financial crash. Money could be regained. A precious grandmother could not.

But because Rebecca was so distraught, Janice knew that *she* had to be strong. Janice knew that Seth would want her to look after his pregnant wife. And Janice would, if only for the sake of Seth's unborn child.

"Rebecca, go and gather up your belongings," Janice said hoarsely. "We will go to my grandmother's cabin. We will live there. And I will do everything I can to find Seth and Lexi."

As Rebecca went into the house to get her things, Janice went to White Shield. "It seems my entire world has been turned upside down," she said, swallowing back a sob. "Not only are Seth and Lexi missing, but my family has also lost everything in the financial crash. And not only that, my beloved grandmother died and was buried only yesterday."

She turned and gazed at the house, and then flung herself into White Shield's arms. "My brother wasn't there, White Shield," she sobbed. "My brother Seth . . . might . . . be *dead*. Also Lexi. I am not sure if I can live with the loss. I loved them both so much."

White Shield embraced Janice as she clung to him and sobbed out her grief to him. He was stunned to now know that what he had thought all along wasn't true.

Seth was not her husband!

He was her brother.

That meant that she was a free woman, a woman free to love!

His insides stiffened when he thought about

Lexi. She was Janice's daughter. That meant that Janice had surely been married before.

But that truly didn't matter to him. She was free now. He would accept her daughter as his, if Janice agreed to become his wife.

Now he felt free to hold her. And she felt so good in his arms.

He only wished that he could erase her pain.

He wished that he could find her brother and daughter so that the world could be sweet for her again.

And then there was her grandmother. There was no way he could erase the pain of having lost her. Only time could do that.

Janice stepped away from White Shield. She wiped tears from her eyes with the backs of her hands as she turned and looked up at the house. Then she turned back to White Shield. "Rebecca is getting her things," she murmured. "We are going to go to my grandmother's house. We will live there. Perhaps Seth will find his way back there, if I don't find him first."

Then she recalled that Rebecca had said the cabin was locked. She was glad that no one had been able to go inside and vandalize it. She realized it would be difficult for *her* to go inside and see all of her grandmother's things. It would make her mema's absence all the more real.

"I will accompany you and Rebecca to the cabin," White Shield said thickly. "I will make certain you are safe there before I leave. During these times of stress, men can become crazy. Two women traveling alone might be in danger."

"Thank you, thank you," Janice said, moving into his arms.

She reveled in the comfort his wonderfully muscled arms gave her, and even more. For the first time in her life she was in love. And if he cared for her as much as he seemed to, she knew that it had nothing to do with wealth, for she had just told him that her family had lost everything.

That meant that she was now poor.

Poor! she thought to herself. All of her life she had resented how people treated her because of her money. They did not seem to see her when they looked at her, but dollar signs instead.

Now it would be different.

She would not be different, though, for she had never flaunted her riches, nor treasured having them.

Now she could truly live free of the burden wealth placed on one's shoulders.

Janice stepped away from White Shield. She looked up at the house again. "I must go inside and see if Rebecca is all right," she said. "She now knows that her husband might not have made it through the shipwreck. It might be too much for her."

"I will go with you," White Shield said, taking her by the hand.

Hand in hand, they went up the steps, and

even before they went inside, Janice could see the heavily carved newel posts through the beveled glass of the front door.

And when they stepped inside the door, they both stopped and gazed at the beauty of the home. Although the bank had foreclosed on the house, the furnishings were still there, untouched. This mansion even outshone her family home in San Francisco. The floors of the entry foyer were Genoese marble. A winding staircase swept up both sides of the foyer to the upstairs.

From the hall one could pass from the drawing room to the library between columns made in imitation of twisted rope, under a design of turned spindles.

White Shield followed Janice into the parlor.

Immense, exotic tapestries that entranced the senses with the flash of gold and silk hung from the walls, which were paneled in rare, dark woods.

There were gilt and glass curio cabinets, lavish furniture upholstered in rich fabrics, a baby grand piano, many velvet chairs and settees.

Her brother had obviously taken many pains to make this home exquisite for his wife. He had not left one thing undone.

It made Janice sad to know that if her brother survived, he would soon discover that he had lost much that was dear to him.

Janice felt eyes on her and turned to gaze up at White Shield.

Cassie Edwards

He must realize that Janice had been a part of the affluent community he despised. If she explained to him that she had never enjoyed such riches, would he truly believe her? Had seeing all of this changed his feelings for her?

"Isn't it beautiful?" Rebecca said, coming to stand beside her as Janice continued to gaze quietly into White Shield's eyes. "Seth did it all for me. He . . . he . . . told me that he was making up to me for all the wrongs I endured in my life before I met him." A sob caught in her throat. "Until only yesterday I was staffed with liveried servants, including a stately butler and his housekeeper wife, several maids, a footman, and an errand boy. Now I have none of them. I had to send them away."

Having only half heard Rebecca, Janice reached a hand to White Shield's arm. "I believe I know how you are feeling," she murmured. "I . . . I . . . know how you feel about the rich white people who took so much from your people. Yes, it is true that I am from a wealthy family, but that should not condemn me in your eyes. I have never enjoyed the life of the affluent. I . . . was . . . coming north to live a simpler life with my grandmother. I had so looked forward to living in the forest in her cabin. . . ."

Feeling guilty for having made Janice feel as though she had to apologize for her status in life, White Shield took her hand and smiled down at her. "Say no more," he said softly. "No matter how you are accustomed to living, you are a woman of heart." He gave Rebecca a frown, then smiled at Janice. "You are not like those who like to be rich. That sets you apart from them."

When Janice heard Rebecca clear her throat behind her, she realized that she hadn't introduced Rebecca to White Shield yet.

An alarm of sorts went off inside Janice's head when she saw Rebecca smiling what might be a seductive smile at White Shield.

Janice was forced to recall how Rebecca had made her living prior to marrying Seth. It would not surprise her at all to see Rebecca flirt with every man she met.

"This is White Shield," Janice said warily. "He found me unconscious after the shipwreck. He took me to his home. There he fed me and gave me dry clothes. He also gave me something else. *Hope.* He has offered to help find Seth and Lexi."

Rebecca nodded. "I have heard your name spoken among the lumberjacks who frequented the brothel," she said to White Shield, speaking openly of the brothel as though she was not ashamed at all of having worked there. "Some admired you . . . some hated you."

"I am aware of the mixed feelings of whites toward me," White Shield said stiffly. "I ignore them all, for what I did, I did solely for the good of my people."

"Yes, I'm sure you did," Rebecca said, her eyes holding White Shield's a moment longer. Then she turned to Janice.

"Poor little Lexi," Rebecca said, tears in her eyes again. "Orphaned so terribly before you found her and took her in, and now this?"

White Shield's eyes widened. He now understood so much. The child had not been born to Janice. Janice had taken her in and given her a home.

When the child was found, he hoped to take not only Janice into his home, but also her daughter. They could be a family.

"I hope we will find Lexi when we find Seth," Janice said, swallowing hard.

"We *must* find Seth," Rebecca said, a quick sob catching in her throat. "I do love him so."

Wanting to believe that, wanting to believe that she had not seen flirtation in Rebecca's eyes a moment ago when she had been talking with White Shield, Janice reached a hand out toward her sister-in-law. "I hate to leave, but we must," she said. "Are you all right? You are so pale."

"I'll be all right," Rebecca said, lifting the tail of her skirt and going out into the foyer. "I . . . I . . . am much stronger than I might appear to be."

Janice sighed as she gazed up at White Shield. "I think I might have some problems figuring her out," she said, laughing softly. "My brother has married a woman of many colors, wouldn't you say?"

"Scarlet is the color I think of when I think of

this particular woman," White Shield said, laughing throatily.

"Shame on you," Janice scolded, trying not to laugh, because she knew that she would be laughing at her brother's wife.

They left the room together and went over to Rebecca, who was looking into the study, her eyes wide as she gazed at something.

Janice stepped up beside her and looked into the study herself, then took a step away, gasping.

"Isn't it just too horrible?" Rebecca said, visibly shuddering.

"That looks like . . . a . . . mummy," Janice gulped out, glad when White Shield came to her other side and slowly slid an arm around her waist. His eyes were also locked on the strange sight in the study.

"Yes, that's what it is all right," Rebecca said, sighing. "It's something Seth bought only a day before he left for San Francisco. He was going to give it to the Museum of Art when he returned."

"Whom did it belong to?" Janice asked, still gawking at the strange thing wrapped in a ragged, filthy sort of twisted tape.

"A lady here in Tacoma," Rebecca said. "A Mrs. Allen Mason. Her husband was a civic developer who spent a fortune journeying to far climes. He recently sent his wife this Egyptian mummy."

Rebecca turned her eyes to Janice. "Mr.

Mason arrived home just in time to realize he had lost everything because of what has happened here in the Northwest," she murmured. "Mrs. Mason has recently joined him back East, trying to make a new start after losing so much here."

"One by one the rich have fallen," Janice murmured, wondering how Seth would take the discovery that he had lost everything.

"It's time to go," Janice said, gently taking Rebecca by an elbow.

Rebecca sniffled and nodded as she left the house with Janice and White Shield. Janice felt that this was a turning point in her life, that the existence she had once known would never be again, especially if her brother had been taken from her forever!

Chapter Eleven

Unknown rhythms,
Still the night,
Enchanting . . .
Peace . . . quiet—
—MARY ANN WHITAKER

Although the house and furniture now belonged to the bank, as well as the fancy carriage Rebecca had loved, she had managed to hold on to a means of transportation.

White Shield went to the stable at the back of the mansion and prepared the old mare and the wagon for the trip to Janice's grandmother's house in the forest.

Janice came to him and ran a hand down the

old horse's withers. It seemed the last insult to her brother that someone had exchanged one of his finest steeds for this old horse whose bones stuck out as though it had not been fed in weeks.

She was not even sure if it had the strength to pull the wagon.

But for Rebecca's sake, Janice knew that this horse and wagon were the best way to travel to her grandmother's cabin. She doubted that Rebecca could get very far on foot without sinking to the ground in exhaustion.

"Are you going to be all right?" White Shield asked, as he gazed intently at Janice. She had become so quiet since leaving the house.

"I just wish I could close my eyes, and when I opened them again, everything would be as it was the day Seth and I left San Francisco," Janice said, swallowing hard. She turned to White Shield. "I did not get the chance to say good-bye to my grandmother." She lowered her eyes. "Or to Seth and Lexi. Lexi was only ten. It would be so unfair if her life has been cut short at such a young age. She had so much ahead of her. Like everyone else, she had dreams."

She laughed softly. "One day not long ago she even mentioned something about wanting to be a movie actress when she grew up," she said. "I thought that was so sweet. A movie actress . . ."

Her voice trailed off as she was overwhelmed by emotions that almost broke her heart.

"Do not lose hope for your brother and

daughter," White Shield said, placing a finger beneath her chin and gently lifting it so that his eyes could look into hers. "Until you know for certain you will never see them again, never give up hope of finding them. I promise you this: I will do everything within my power to help you."

"But you have your own duties to see to," Janice said, deeply touched that he was placing her concerns before his people's. "You are sub-chief. Surely you should be among your people performing the duties required of you."

"Do you not know that today, and even tomorrow, my duty is toward you?" White Shield said thickly. He smiled slowly when he saw a look of wonder in Janice's eyes. "Until you need my assistance no longer, I am here for you."

"I don't know what to say," Janice said, her eyes searching his. "That you would do this for me . . ."

"How could I not?" White Shield said, now placing his hands at her waist. He drew her next to him. "You know as well as I that there is much between us that is *kloshe,* a word in my language that means 'good.' A tragedy brought us together. Let us now, together, find a way to lessen the hurt caused by that tragedy."

"I cannot help but love . . ." she began, then stopped and turned with a start when she heard someone step up behind her. She knew that she was blushing as she stared into Rebecca's wide, puzzled eyes. Although Rebecca must have bedded many men of varied colors, it was obvious that she was shocked by the feelings that were obvious between Janice and a Skokomish sub-chief.

"I have things on the porch that need to be placed in the wagon," Rebecca quickly said, as she looked from Janice to White Shield. "White Shield, could you get them for me?"

After he left, Rebecca turned pale and grabbed at her stomach. "Lord, no," she gasped out. "I . . . felt . . . a pain. It can't be."

"The baby?" Janice said, hurrying to place an arm around Rebecca's waist to steady her. "You aren't going to have the baby early, are you?"

"I'm not certain what I am supposed to feel when it is time for the baby," Rebecca said, giving Janice a wavering stare. "I . . . I . . . never did go to any doctor. Because of my work at the brothel, most shun me. It's as though I am beneath their notice."

"That's horrible," Janice gasped. "I met Doc Rose. He is such a kind old man. Surely you were wrong to think he would not sympathize with you and help you with your pregnancy."

"I did not want to chance being hurt again," Rebecca said, wincing when another pain shot through her abdomen. "It does hurt, you know, to be treated like a nonperson."

"Yes, I imagine that would be terrible," Janice said softly. "How are you feeling? Have the pains let up?"

"I had one more," Rebecca murmured. "That's all. Now they seem to have stopped."

"Thank goodness for small favors," Janice said, sighing heavily.

"I'm sorry to have worried you," Rebecca said, clearing her throat nervously as she shook her thick black hair back from her ivory-pale face. "I'm all right. Truly I am."

"It is time to go," White Shield said as he came up to them with an armload of Rebecca's belongings. "I will bring the rest of your things back to the wagon."

"Thank you, White Shield," Rebecca said, swallowing hard. "Your kindness toward me is truly appreciated."

Recalling that he had referred to her as a "scarlet woman" only moments ago, White Shield glanced guiltily at Janice, who smiled weakly back at him, proof that she was thinking the same thing.

Janice sighed and wondered if she could ever get used to having Rebecca as a sister-in-law.

But for the child, she *must* accept Rebecca and her past, for hadn't Seth loved her? Surely he had seen something that Janice could not see. Perhaps in time *she* would understand why Seth had put his trust in the woman, enough to bring her into his family.

"I'm anxious to get to Mema's house," Janice said softly as she tried to put Rebecca's past life from her mind. "Although she won't be there, at least I will feel her all around me."

"I love the nickname that you and Seth gave Hannah," Rebecca said softly. "Seth told me that it was he who first called her that . . . when he could not pronounce the word 'grandmother.'"

"Yes, and our grandmother was the one who told him that he could call her Mema. Then, when I was born, that was what she was to me, also," Janice said, walking toward the wagon, watching how beautifully While Shield's shoulder and arm muscles flexed as he picked up one thing and then another to place them in the back of the wagon.

"I was told by the bank president that everything but a few personal things must stay with the house," Rebecca said, tears filling her eyes as she watched the last of the boxes put in the wagon. "Seth is going to hate it when he realizes what he has lost. Each piece of furniture was chosen by him. Each piece of crystal, china . . ."

"My brother is a strong person, and when he returns and sees what's happened, he will accept it and go on with his life," Janice said, smiling at White Shield as he came and helped Rebecca onto the seat of the wagon.

Janice climbed up by herself and placed herself on the seat between Rebecca and White Shield so that she could be next to White Shield.

Not a word was said as the horse and wagon pulled away from the beautiful mansion.

Janice placed a gentle hand on Rebecca's arm when she saw the other woman turn and give the house a last look over her shoulder.

"It's only a house," Janice murmured. "There are many more important things to worry about, Rebecca, than a mere house. There's Seth. There's Lexi." She swallowed hard. "There is the fact that I have recently lost one of the most precious people on this earth, my grandmother."

"Yes, I know," Rebecca said. She rested her hands on the huge ball of her stomach. "It's just that so much has happened so quickly."

"We had heard rumors that there was some sort of money crisis in the Northwest, but neither Seth or I ever imagined it could be this disastrous," Janice said, slowly shaking her head. "We were caught up in Lexi and making her voyage enjoyable. The last time she was on a ship, it had been horrible for her. We didn't want her to think of that time. And until the storm came and tore our lives asunder, we were successful in making Lexi's trip something like a dream."

"I wish I could have met her," Rebecca said. "Seth told me so much about her."

"Do not speak of her in the past tense," Janice said, shuddering visibly. "She *is* alive, *somewhere*, and so is Seth. We just have to be patient until we find them, or . . . until . . . they find us."

"Do you think Seth will know to come to your

grandmother's cabin when he finds our house abandoned?" Rebecca asked, tears again filling her eyes. "I wanted to be there for him. I should have stayed. Surely the people from the bank wouldn't have kicked a pregnant woman out onto the street."

"We are doing what is best for us all," Janice murmured. "And, yes, I believe my grandmother's cabin will be the first place Seth will look when he discovers no one at his house."

"The cabin is locked up," Rebecca blurted out. "I told you it was padlocked. Your grandmother's lawyer has the key. How can we get in once we arrive there?"

In all the turmoil of the past hour, Janice had forgotten that Rebecca had said Mema's cabin was locked up.

She thought for a moment, then turned to Rebecca again. "Where does my grandmother's lawyer reside?" she asked. "We will go to him and get the key."

Rebecca swallowed hard. "When I spoke of your grandmother's lawyer, I should not have said he *has* the key," she murmured. "I should have said he *had* it. You see, he too, lost everything in the financial crunch. I received word only yesterday that the man shot himself."

Janice went pale at the thought. "Shot himself?" she said weakly.

"Many white men have taken their own lives due to their losses," White Shield said thickly.

"How horrible," Janice said, visibly shuddering. She had not thought about how devastating all of this must be to men who worshipped "the mighty green," living each day so they could amass more money and brag about it.

She thought of Seth, and wondered how he might have reacted if he had been in Tacoma at the onset of the crash.

He was a strong man. But was he strong enough?

She wished that he had been more careful when purchasing his mansion. If he had paid for it in cash instead of saving his funds to invest in the stock market, at least his house would still belong to him.

But she had trusted his judgment. Until now, his decisions had been sound ones.

She wondered now how he would react when he arrived in Tacoma and discovered that his home and belongings were no longer his.

She wondered just how long Rebecca would stick around. She was no longer the wife of a rich man. She was perhaps even poorer than she had been while working at the brothel.

"We need no key to get you into your grandmother's lodge," White Shield said reassuringly. "I will pry the padlock off the door."

He looked over at Rebecca. "Give me directions to the cabin," he said tightly.

Rebecca rattled them off to him, then became quiet and stared straight ahead.

"I am stunned by everything that has happened," Janice said. She glanced over her shoulder at a lone man on horseback in the road behind them.

When he made a sharp turn right, onto another street, and was lost to sight, she soon forgot him. White Shield snapped the horse's reins and they left Tacoma behind, traveling now on a single worn lane through the forest. Finally Janice saw a huge cabin a short distance away through a break in the trees.

"There it is," Rebecca said, pointing toward the cabin. "There's your grandmother's cabin."

The sight of it took Janice's breath away, for never had she imagined her grandmother's cedar log cabin being so large. It was apparent that although her grandmother had ached to return to the forest to live, she had not been able to turn her back entirely on the way she had grown accustomed to living . . . in a grand manner. The two-storied, grand log cabin must have been everything her grandmother could have ever wanted.

Tears came to Janice's eyes as she gazed at the boarded-up windows. She was recalling all of the letters that she had received from her grandmother, about how happy she was at her cabin, how she adored living amid the huge trees, and being near the forest animals.

She had written to Janice how she loved waking up each day to the sounds of the birds singing their morning songs. She had written that if there were a heaven on this earth, she had found it.

And Janice could see now why her grandmother had felt that way about her home. Now that the horse and wagon were stopped directly before the cabin, Janice could hear the birds singing in the high treetops all around her.

She could see squirrels at play, some even hopping along the roof of the cabin, as though it were theirs.

Then she saw a movement at the right side of the cabin. It was a deer and her fawn walking leisurely through the forest next to the house, stopping trustingly to chew at a few leaves hanging low from branches swaying gently in the breeze.

"It's so beautiful here," Janice said, sad that she would never be able to share this with her grandmother.

Oh, how she would have loved to have sat on the front porch with Mema. It reached across the entire front of the house.

A porch swing swayed in the wind at one end.

Yes, together she, her grandmother, and Lexi could have enjoyed the wonders of nature.

But, sad as it was, that was something that would now happen only in her dreams.

Unless she eventually found sweet Lexi. She would sit in the swing with her child and tell her everything about Mema.

She would bring Mema alive inside the child's heart, for Mema and Lexi had grown close.

Lexi had cried her eyes out when Mema had left San Francisco for her new home in Tacoma.

Janice pushed these sorrowful thoughts from her mind and focused on the present as she waited for White Shield to help Rebecca down from the wagon, then slid across the seat and welcomed his arms as he also helped her to the ground.

She hesitated before going up the steps.

She watched White Shield and Rebecca go to the door, and waited while White Shield used his knife in an attempt to pry the lock off.

When Janice finally went up the steps, she felt her grandmother's presence. It was as though Mema was there, watching, waiting to hold Janice in her loving arms.

When White Shield finally got the lock off the door, she scarcely breathed as he slowly opened it. Rebecca was the first to enter. And then Janice went with White Shield across the threshold.

She squinted as she tried to see things, but there wasn't enough light coming through the boarded-up windows.

"I'll light a lamp," Rebecca said. She felt her way through the room and went to a table, where she quickly lit the kerosene wick of a beautiful lamp.

As the fire's glow filled the dark spaces of the room, Janice gasped. She saw many things that were familiar to her from their home in San Francisco.

Fighting back tears, she went around the

room touching things precious to her grand-mother: her hand-stitched needlepoint uphol-stery, a tall grandfather clock, her grandmother's victrola, her player piano, a leather photo album, and the rag rug on the floor, which her grandmother had made patiently out of clothes she had grown tired of.

Janice lit another lamp and carried it with her into the dining room. A beautiful gilt armoire was filled with linens and flatware.

She quickly recognized her grandmother's favorite chintzware tea collection.

The dining table was only large enough to sit six, for her grandmother had said that she would have no one visit besides family.

Leaving that room, Janice stepped into a hall-way that led to many rooms.

She went into the first bedroom and became choked with emotion when she saw more of her grandmother's beloved things.

She went to the massive oak bed and slowly ran a hand over the cotton crocheted bed-spread, and then moved to the foot of the bed and ran her hands over the velvet of a patch-work quilt folded there, a quilt that her grand-mother had made from her fancy gowns.

She turned and moved around the room, her fingers softly touching the lacy scarf on the bureau.

She went to the closet and opened the door.

She set the lamp aside as she sorted through

her grandmother's clothes. Her grandmother's favorite French perfume still clung to them.

It was a diversified wardrobe of both cotton and silk.

There were several travel skirts and blouses, leather boots, and pretty patent-leather slippers.

And then something else caught Janice's eye. An embroidery hoop was still in place on a pillowcase her grandmother must have been embroidering just prior to her death. The needle with thread was still thrust into the pillowcase close to where her grandmother had been sewing initials on it.

Knowing that this might have been something her grandmother was working on the very day she died, tears filled Janice's eyes as she took the embroidery work down.

As she held it out to see whom Mema might have been making the pillowcase for, she was taken aback when she did not recognize the initials. They didn't belong to anyone in her family.

Who else could her grandmother have had in mind while embroidering the pretty blue initials on the case?

Janice slowly ran her fingers over the mysterious initials as she read them.

"N. F.," she whispered to herself, an eyebrow arching. "Who on earth did she know with the initials N. F.?"

But that was quickly forgotten. She lurched and dropped the embroidery work to the floor when she heard a lone gun blast outside the cabin, soon followed by many others.

She was seized by panic when she could actually hear the bullets ricocheting off the boarded-up windows of the bedroom.

Her heart pounding, Janice ran from the bedroom, recalling now that her grandmother had written to her about the lumber barons in the area trying to force her off her land so that they could cut her trees. They had even offered top dollar, but she had stubbornly refused.

Surely those who were shooting at the house were connected somehow with the lumber companies.

Just as Janice reached the living room, Rebecca went into hysterics. "It was gunfire that downed Hannah!" she screamed, her eyes wild. "No one is safe in this place. I thought the financial crash had spelled the downfall of the lumber barons! Why are they shooting at us now, when they don't even have money to buy Hannah's house? And why shoot at us? Wasn't it enough that they murdered Hannah?"

"My grandmother was murdered?" Janice gasped out. "I thought she died from natural causes. I . . . I . . . was coming to take care of her because she was ill. I thought her illness had claimed her life. Now you are telling me that she . . . was . . . murdered?"

"Yes, and just like her, we're going to be murdered!" Rebecca screamed. "Why did I come here? Why? I was wrong to believe the lumber barons would stop their vengeance against Hannah. They must blame everyone related to Hannah for not allowing them to cut the trees on her property. We're all going to be killed!"

Janice just stood and stared at Rebecca, then realizing that the gunfire had stopped, she ran with White Shield to the door and hurried out onto the porch just in time to see the gunman ride off.

Both Janice and White Shield got a good look at the man as he looked over his shoulder and laughed boisterously, then rode off at a hard gallop.

"Stumpy Jackson," White Shield growled out. He clenched his hands into tight fists at his sides. He was recalling Stumpy's insulting behavior at the hospital, and other times when the redheaded weasel had threatened him in one way or another.

White Shield silently vowed to himself to find the lumberjack and stop him, but not now. He had the women's welfare to see to. He knew how frightened they both were.

Rebecca ran to the door and grabbed Janice's arm, her fingernails digging into the flesh as she looked at her with wild eyes. "I can't stay here," she cried. "I have the child to think about!"

Seeing Rebecca's desperation, and touched by the woman's concern for her baby, Janice was uncertain what to do. She wanted to stay at her grandmother's house. She didn't want to be forced to give up something her grandmother had died for. And if Seth was still alive, he would come directly to this cabin when he discovered that his home had been taken from him.

And Lexi!

Oh, Lord, surely Seth would have Lexi with him.

White Shield saw how torn Janice was and how afraid Rebecca was. "You both would be welcome at my village," he said, drawing their heads around. "I know of a vacant longhouse. You can make residence there."

Rebecca turned to Janice and grabbed her arm, her fingernails digging into her flesh painfully. "We should go with White Shield," she cried, her eyes wild. "We can come back to the cabin when it's safer, or when Seth shows up and can protect us."

Janice looked slowly around the room. She still felt her grandmother's presence. She hated to leave but knew she had no other choice. It wasn't safe here. At least not at this time. Later, perhaps. When Seth was there to keep men like Stumpy Jackson in their place.

Yet she hated giving in to threats.

She gave Rebecca a soft look, knowing that for now she must put everything from her mind except for finding a safe shelter for her brother's very pregnant wife.

Chapter Twelve

Desperation, impatience,
Deep within her silent cries,
Doesn't matter, no one hears,
While faintly silence dies.
        —MARY ANN WHITAKER

"Janice, *please* let's leave this place," Rebecca said. "This cabin is too isolated. Don't you see how easy it was for that man to shoot at us? He knew that we are too far from anyone for his shots to be heard."

"Yes, I know that we must," Janice murmured, thankful for White Shield's invitation to go to his island with him. Along with all of her other belongings, Janice had lost her traveling money in the Sound. She didn't have a cent to her name to pay for room and board at a hotel.

Janice turned to White Shield. "Are you certain your people will not resent our presence there?" she asked, her voice drawn.

"Did you see resentment in my people's eyes when you were there before with White Shield?" he asked thickly.

"This is the best way, you know," he went on. "You can stay at my village for as long as you wish."

Tears of gratitude filled her eyes, and Janice gave White Shield a lingering hug. "Thank you," she murmured, clinging. "Without you, I am not certain what I would do. You are giving me courage to go on."

"Your courage is within you because of yourself, not because of someone else," White Shield said. He stepped away from her and smiled into her eyes. "You are a woman of much courage and strength. You will survive this. Your future and what you will do with it patiently await you."

She smiled and nodded as she went to a desk that was positioned against the far wall. "I can't give up hoping that Seth is all right and that he will eventually show up here at Mema's house," she said, opening drawer as she searched for paper. "I shall leave my brother a note telling him where he can find us."

She looked quickly up at White Shield. "Do you think he will know about your island?" she asked softly. "Where it is?"

"All people of Tacoma know of the Skokomish island," White Shield said dryly. "And even why my people live there instead of land now occupied by whites. *Ah-hah*, he will know where to look for you."

Hearing the bitterness in White Shield's voice, Janice was again reminded of how his people had been tricked by hers.

She was thankful that although his people had been forced to move they now loved their island home and had no wish to leave it.

"Hurry, Janice," Rebecca said, looking nervously toward the door. "That gunman might return. He . . . might . . . even bring others with him the next time and make certain he killed us, instead of just frightening us."

Janice nodded just as she found a small tablet, with a pencil beside it, in the bottom drawer.

Taking them out, she placed the tablet on the top of the desk and hurriedly wrote Seth a note, explaining where she and Rebecca were.

She signed the note, softly kissed it, then laid it on a table just inside the door beside a lamp, where Seth would surely see it the moment he came into the room and lit the lamp.

She touched the note one last time, hoping that the next person who touched it would be her brother, then left the cabin with White Shield and Rebecca.

Rebecca clung to Janice's arm and looked wild-eyed in all directions as White Shield secured the door.

Once that was done, they all boarded the wagon again and turned back toward Tacoma.

As they rode off, Janice shuddered when she gazed over her shoulder and saw the marks over the windows that had been made by a madman's bullets.

She wondered whether the maniac who had done the shooting today was the very one who'd killed her grandmother. She glanced over at White Shield. She knew that he had recognized the man. He had even spoken his name . . . Stumpy. Stumpy Jackson.

Through White Shield, she would find the man and see that he was brought to justice for the crime of killing one of the gentlest people who ever walked this earth.

Then she thought of something else.

"White Shield, what can I do with the horse and wagon while we are at your island?" she blurted out. "I don't want to part with them altogether and I have no money to pay for boarding them."

"I know a man who will care for them," White Shield said, smiling at Janice. "He is someone who lives on this side of the Sound, who has come through the financial crisis with a smile.

He is Harvey Brave Eagle, a half-breed whaler, who makes his living harvesting whales during whaling season. He does not need Tacoma's money. He takes his products into Canada to sell. They use much whale oil in Canada."

"Why would he be willing to help me?" Janice asked softly, as Tacoma came into view through a break in the trees.

"He would be doing it for me, a man to whom he owes a debt," White Shield said, chuckling beneath his breath.

"What sort of debt?" Janice asked, raising an eyebrow as she gazed into White Shield's dancing eyes.

"As whites might say, I fixed him up with a wife," White Shield explained. "One of my cousins. She is as beautiful as the stars in the heavens. She has made him a fine wife, and a wonderful mother to their five children."

"Five . . . children . . . ?" Janice gasped. Rebecca's eyes widened at that comment.

"And the sixth should be born any day," White Shield said, nodding.

Janice laughed softly. "I'm not sure you should go to him to collect on your debt," she said. "He might run you off. Did he plan on getting six children in the bargain?"

White Shield's smile turned into a frown. "You speak as though you do not favor children, yet you have a daughter," he said, his voice drawn. "Do you not take having children seriously enough to mother more than one?"

"I was only jesting," she blurted out. "I love children. I hope to have many."

She breathlessly awaited his response and was relieved when she saw his lips quiver into a smile.

"Such a woman as you *should* have many children," he said.

"I hope to," she murmured. "I do love children."

Then she smiled at him. "You said that your friend is a whaler," she murmured. "Is he among those who hunts huge whales and uses harpoons to catch them?"

"That is so," White Shield said, nodding as he guided the horse and wagon down the long, narrow lane. "Harvey Brave Eagle is a master of the art of harvesting whales. He is one of the men who stands in the bow of the canoe who thrusts a harpoon into the whale."

"I saw a harpoon in your lodge," Janice said softly. "Are *you* a whaler?"

"That is not my full-time occupation, no," White Shield said as he glanced at her. "My duties to my people keep me mostly on land. The leader of a whale hunt must prepare for months, purifying himself and praying to the whales to swim toward the village after it is harpooned. A whaler is admired by all. His occupation is both strenuous and dangerous."

"Are whales that important to your people?"

Janice asked, glad to have something else besides worry to occupy her mind.

"Whaling is important, but it is not all that keeps our people going," White Shield said. "Still, a whale kill provides a whole village with blubber and oil for a year, as well as bone for tools and weapons."

They both grew silent as White Shield led the horse and wagon onto a brick street that led almost straight downward to the Sound.

Janice clung to the seat with all of her might as the mare strained backward against the harness to keep the wagon from running away as it traveled the steep slope. From time to time one hoof or another would slide dangerously on the slick bricks.

But finally the street leveled off and they were once again passing the many tents, listening to the water of the Sound slapping gently at the rocky shore.

Shivers ran up and down Janice's spine as again she heard people crying, the sad sounds wafting from the many tents.

She was glad when they reached White Shield's canoe. They worked quickly to place Rebecca's belongings into the canoe, then soon were making their way across the Sound in the huge, carved vessel.

"I will take you to the longhouse where you will make your home while you are among my people," White Shield said when they landed. He helped Janice from the canoe, and then Rebecca. "I will come then for your things. It is important first to get you settled in the longhouse."

He looked from one to the other, then looked solemnly at Janice. "You both need rest," he said. "Also food. I will see that you get everything you need to make your stay here comfortable."

Janice flung herself into his arms and hugged him. "I shall never forget this," she murmured. She eased from his arms and smiled up at him. "But I think you are growing tired of hearing me thank you, aren't you?"

"Just remember this, pretty woman, no thank yous are ever necessary for anything I do for you," he said thickly. He looked over at Rebecca. "Come. I will take you and Janice to your lodge." He glanced down at her abdomen. "Your child needs rest, also."

"Yes, the terrible things that have happened recently have surely not been good for my baby," Rebecca said, placing both hands on her tummy and softly patting it. "But I've done the best that I could under the circumstances."

"And I am sure that is good enough," Janice said, trying to reassure her. She reached a hand out for Rebecca.

Rebecca smiled weakly, then took Janice's hand and walked with her as White Shield led them up from the embankment into the village of longhouses.

Janice was stunned that although two white women were being brought into the village, one obviously very pregnant, the people continued with their daily routine, only a few stopping to glance their way.

The children were the most interested. They came up and gave Janice a big smile, then gazed in wonder at Rebecca's large belly.

"She will soon be having a baby," Janice quickly said, glad that the children were being friendly. "Who of you have baby brothers or sisters?"

"I do," one small boy said, then others chimed in.

"Run along," White Shield said as he gestured with a hand toward the children. "Go and see if your mothers or fathers need your help."

Giggling and laughing, the children scampered away.

Janice smiled, then swept an arm around Rebecca's waist and hurriedly ushered her along.

When they finally reached the longhouse in which they would be staying, White Shield opened the door and Janice and Rebecca went inside.

They stood back in the shadows and waited as White Shield lit a whale-oil lantern, then knelt down before the fireplace and started a fire.

He then stood up and looked from Janice to Rebecca. "You are safe here," he said softly. He gazed intently at Rebecca. "You have a place to rest now so that your child will be born healthy."

Rebecca nodded and looked toward a thick pile of pelts and blankets that he had already prepared for her. She smiled at White Shield, then went and stretched out before the fire.

Janice drew a blanket over Rebecca, then went into White Shield's arms. "I think she'll be all right," she murmured. "And so will I."

"As I have already said, I think you should rest, also," White Shield said, placing a finger beneath her chin and bringing her eyes up to meet his. "There is a bed in the other room. Go. Sleep while I bring everything from the canoe, and then go to my uncle's house to tell Snow Flower that food, clothes, and kindness are needed."

Before Janice had a chance to respond, White Shield swept her up into his arms and carried her to the bed.

Before he placed her on it he lowered his lips to hers and kissed her.

Janice's insides melted. She slid an arm around his neck and returned the kiss with ardor, then sighed heavily when he lowered her from his arms onto the bed.

"How do you expect me to rest after that?" Janice said, her eyes twinkling. For the moment all sadness had left her mind.

White Shield's eyes twinkled as he gave her one last gaze, then turned and left the room.

Janice stretched her arms above her head,

yawned sleepily, then pulled a blanket up over herself. In a matter of moments she was asleep, a smile on lips that still tasted of the man she loved.

Chapter Thirteen

By a route obscure and lonely,
Haunted by ill angels only.
    —EDGAR ALLAN POE

Janice awakened with a start when she heard
Rebecca suddenly cry out in pain.

Having been wrenched from a deep sleep,
Janice was momentarily disoriented.

Her eyes wide open now, she slowly sat up
and looked around. Everything that had happened came back to her like a flash of lightning.

Exhausted and emotionally drained, she had
slept so soundly that it had been as though
these past days had been swept from her consciousness.

But as she looked around the small room, mixed emotions overwhelmed her.

It pained her deeply to think about Seth and Lexi.

But then there were those sweet moments with White Shield that brought gentle peace to her heart.

The sound of Rebecca crying out in pain again made Janice start.

"Rebecca!" she whispered, scurrying from the bed.

Still wearing the wondrously soft moccasins and doeskin dress, Janice hurried into the main room of the longhouse.

She went pale when she saw Rebecca stretched out on the pallet of pelts, clutching at her belly. The pain that she was experiencing was evident in her eyes as she turned and gave Janice a look filled with panic.

"Janice, the baby!" Rebecca cried, sweat pouring from her brow. She winced and gritted her teeth. Moaning, she turned to her side and drew herself into a fetal position. She closed her eyes as another pain swept through her abdomen.

"Lord, no," Janice said. She hurried over to Rebecca and dropped to her knees beside her.

"Help me," Rebecca moaned, her eyes opening. In them was terrible fear. "I can't have the baby. Not now. And, oh, Lord, not here. I'm afraid. I don't want a medicine man telling me how I should have my baby."

"But you said that you didn't go to Doc Rose, either," Janice said, truly not knowing what to do since Rebecca didn't have a doctor she trusted.

"That was then, this is now," Rebecca cried. She clutched at Janice's arm. "And surely Doc Rose would look past my reputation for the sake of the child. I must try, Janice. Please help me. I'm afraid the baby is coming soon."

"What if you have the baby before we get across the Sound?" Janice said, shivering at the very thought of having to get in a canoe again, much less be responsible for getting Rebecca safely across the Sound all by herself before the baby was born.

"We must take that chance," Rebecca said. She clutched at her abdomen with trembling fingers, groaning when another pain grabbed her.

"You might be having false labor pains," Janice suggested. "Try to relax, Rebecca. Remember the other time when you had pains? Maybe these will go away, also."

A tantalizing smell of food wafted toward Janice from a huge pot hanging over the slow-burning flames in the fireplace. It hadn't been there before she had fallen asleep. That had to mean that while she was sleeping, White Shield had returned with the food, and had then left after seeing that both she and Rebecca were asleep.

She was touched deeply by his continuing care for her, and now for Rebecca, too.

She only wished that things could be different . . . that Seth and Lexi were safely home and Rebecca had had her child.

Only then could Janice feel free to love White Shield.

Until things were righted in her tumultuous world, she could not think of her self. Too many other lives were in peril.

"Janice, I'm scared," Rebecca sobbed, reaching out to grab Janice's hand. "I've never seen anyone have a baby before. I don't know what to expect. I . . . don't . . . know how."

"Take some deep breaths and try to will those pains away," Janice said, twining her fingers around Rebecca's.

She was seeing now why Rebecca had stolen Seth's heart.

This woman was beautiful, sweet, and very vulnerable.

Janice had to smile to herself when she recalled that her brother had said Rebecca could tell off-color jokes like any man.

Yes, there must be a dark side to Rebecca, Janice thought to herself. She had worked in a brothel, and anyone who did that for a living *had* to be hard, for surely it took a lot of nerve to raise one's skirts to strangers and take money from them by pleasing their sexual urges, no matter how twisted those urges might be.

"Janice, what are we going to do?" Rebecca cried, drawing Janice's eyes back to her.

"Have the pains lessened any at all?" Janice asked.

She raised a hand to Rebecca's brow and gently caressed it.

"Yes, thank God, somewhat," Rebecca said. She swallowed hard. "Do you think they *are* false pains? Do you think they will go away? If only the baby will wait until Seth comes home so that he can be with me when I have his child."

"I wish he was here now," Janice said, her voice breaking.

"But he isn't," Rebecca said, her lower lip turning down into a childish pout. She closed her eyes as she fought back tears. "I do love him so, Janice. He . . . is . . . my life."

She opened her eyes and put both of her hands to her belly. She smiled weakly up at Janice. "This child?" she said, her voice breaking. "Because of it my life has changed."

"What . . . do . . . you mean, because of the child your life has changed?" Janice asked.

Was Rebecca married to Seth only because of the child?

Had she been pregnant when she married him?

Oh, Lord, how would he even know if the child was his?

"Seth gave me hope for the future when we met and fell in love. But the child?" Rebecca murmured. "It has made my life complete. Hav-

157

ing both Seth and the baby will be something like a dream come true for me. Those terrible nights at the brothel, when I was forced to please men, I put my mind far from what I was doing and thought of a white knight in shining armor rescuing me. I dreamed of a child born of our love."

She smiled sweetly at Janice. "And the day I met Seth, when he saved me from being run over by a horse and buggy on the streets of Tacoma, I knew that I had found my knight," she murmured. "Seth and I fell in love so quickly, Janice. He was able to overlook my shameful past and take me as his wife."

"Yes, Seth has always had a very big heart," Janice murmured. "He would be able to accept things other men might not. He is a special man. And if he truly believed that you had been thrown into a brothel by circumstances that you had no control over, he would be the sort to want to rescue you from that life."

"Yes, he understood when I told him about my stepfather's abuse, and how I ran way from home because I felt my life threatened after my mother died and I was left alone with that terrible man," Rebecca blurted out. "Serena, the owner of the brothel, was the only one who had mercy on me when she found me homeless on the street. I am forever in her debt."

Janice had no chance to reply. Rebecca was grabbing her belly as another pain swept through it.

"Was that pain worse than the others?" Janice asked softly, relieved when it did not last as long as the others.

"No, not as bad," Janice said, sighing heavily. "Perhaps I will be able to wait for Seth. Just perhaps . . ."

Janice looked around her for a basin of water, finding none. Surely when White Shield had arrived with the food and found both Janice and Rebecca in a sound sleep, he'd decided not to go for water until he found them awake.

When she spied an empty wooden basin on a table, she moved quickly to her feet.

"Where are you going?" Rebecca asked, her eyes following Janice.

"I'm going for water," Janice said, grabbing up the basin. "I won't be gone for long."

As Janice saw it, she had no choice but to get Rebecca across the Sound to have the baby with the help of Doc Rose. Janice could not believe the friendly old man would ignore Rebecca's plea for help, especially with the life of a newborn baby lying in the balance.

"Yes, that's what I must do," she whispered, following the shine of water into the trees where a stream crept snakelike through the woods. "I have to get her across that dreadful Sound."

She tried to block out her fear of water but knew that it would always be there to haunt her. It would only fade away once she found her loved ones.

The farther she went into the forest, the more nervous she felt. She called on her courage to run deeper into the dark, dank shadows; the stream was now only a few feet away.

She stopped with a start and her knees went instantly weak when a man leapt out from the shadows, leering at her. In his hand was a thick-bladed knife.

There was just enough light filtering through the leaves of the trees overhead for Janice to recognize the intruder. It was the very man who had fired at her grandmother's cabin.

"Yeah, you recognize me, don't you, missie?" Stumpy said. "Yep, it's me, Stumpy Jackson. But don't be afraid. I haven't come to hurt you. I wouldn't want the wrath of the Skokomish to come down on me for harmin' you, you pretty thing. I've watched you with White Shield. I've seen how suddenly that sub-chief is so protective of you."

"You know that White Shield is going to search for you until he finds you, don't you?" Janice found the courage to say.

"Well, I have a little surprise for *you*, missie," Stumpy said, slowly inching his knife closer to Janice's abdomen. "There's been no love lost between me and that savage for some time now." He laughed throatily. "I've been tryin' to find a way to get back at him for what he did."

"What do you mean?" Janice asked, surprised at the courage she had found to stand there with a man who held a knife on her. "What did he do?"

"I don't have time to get into that," Stumpy growled. "Just like I don't have time to stand here jawin' with you. I know White Shield is out for my hide. I don't hanker for him to take it from me just yet."

"Than why are you here so close to his village?" Janice asked warily.

"I've been watchin' it for a chance to talk to you," Stumpy said. He slowly lowered his knife to his right side. "I don't mean you no harm, just like I didn't mean you no harm when I shot at the old lady's cabin. I just wanted to put a bit of fear into your heart after I heard you were the granddaughter of the old lady I grew to despise. When I saw you and the savage together it gave me the opportunity to kill two birds with one stone . . . scare *you*, and intimidate White Shield." He chuckled and his eyes narrowed. "And it worked, didn't it? I spooked you good, didn't I?"

"You are a fool to believe that White Shield will allow you to get away with your orneriness much longer," Janice said, placing her fists on her hips. "I'm not certain what started your spat, but I do know that White Shield is not the sort of man who will stand for it."

"Like I said, I didn't come here to jaw about White Shield," Stumpy grumbled. "I've come here with a message for *you*." He smiled crookedly. "I've got ways of findin' things out, you know, like you are Hannah's granddaughter and that you lost your brother and daughter in the shipwreck, and that you've been searching for both of 'em." He leaned his face closer to hers. "Ain't I right?"

Janice's spine went stiff, for she was almost afraid to hear what this man had to say next.

Yet surely he could not be believed. He seemed filled with the devil, through and through.

And was he really only trying to scare people with his bullets?

Or had he missed by accident?

But even though she knew that a man such as he rarely told the truth, Janice found herself anxious to hear what he had to say, because it was obviously about Seth and Lexi.

"Yes, I've been inquiring about my brother and daughter," Janice said warily. "What does that have to do with you?"

"I know where the child is," Stumpy said. "She's at a Haida village. It's a half day's canoe trip from here. I'm here to take you to the child. But I must be promised payment. I know about your brother and how rich he is. You must be rich, too."

"You . . . truly . . . know where Lexi is?" Janice asked, her pulse racing. "You have seen her?"

"I saw her and even spoke with her, myself," Stumpy said. He smiled wickedly when he saw the hope and anxiety in Janice's eyes. "Promise payment. I will take you to her. You will be reunited with her."

"I just can't believe you've truly seen her," Janice said, all the while she was desperately hoping he *had!*

"I saw her, that's for certain," Stumpy said. He reached a hand out toward Janice, rubbing his thumb and forefinger together. "Give me the promise of payment. I'll take you to 'er."

"If you truly know Seth, then you should know that Seth is now no richer than you, and *I* have no money to pay anyone for anything," Janice blurted out. "Not even to pay you to take me to sweet Lexi."

Stumpy's eyes narrowed, and then he shrugged. "Okay, I'll do it without payment for now, but I know Seth, and I know that he is a clever, imaginative son-of-a-bitch who will find ways to get rich again," he drawled out. "When Seth *does* have money, *then* you can pay me. Or you can hand over that fancy cabin in the forest to me now, as payment."

Again he shrugged. "I ain't in no hurry," he said, chuckling. "I'll give you time to think about which way you want to pay me for my services. But you must go with me now, and alone. I want no more trouble from White Shield. If he knew I was anywhere near, he'd sniff me out like a dog. Because of our difference in opinion over lumbering, we've developed bad blood between us. If the savage dies before me, I'll be the first to dance on his grave."

That made a shiver ride Janice's spine.

She didn't know whether or not she could believe this evil, filthy man, who might have even sent the fatal bullet into her precious grandmother's body. Perhaps this was a ploy to get her alone far from the Skokomish village.

Above all, she needed to get back to Rebecca.

But if he was telling the truth and she *could* be taken to Lexi, how could she chance *not* going with him?

Yet instinct told her not to go anywhere with this vile man. He was surely lying to her. Or else why would he be so willing to take her to Lexi when she had not promised him any sort of payment?

Dropping the wooden basin to the ground, Janice turned and began running quickly away from him, breathing hard, afraid that at any moment he would catch up with her and tackle her. Once she was on the ground, at his mercy, surely he would sink the knife into her belly.

She wondered if she was living the very last moments of her life.

She flinched when he shouted at her and called her a stupid bitch, threatening that she would be responsible for whatever happened to the little girl.

"Stupid woman!" he continued to shout at her. "The Haida ain't kind to their captives, especially female kids whose skins are white!"

Janice smiled with relief when she caught what he had said about the child's skin being white, for that gave him away. That proved that he had made the whole thing up, for anyone who knew anything about Lexi knew that her skin was not white . . . that she was of Chinese heritage, not American!

Stumbling through the thick brush, relieved to see the backs of the longhouses only a short distance away, Janice went onward, then ran on into the longhouse assigned to her and Rebecca, panting, and with sweat streaming from her brow.

"Janice!" Rebecca cried when she saw Janice's condition. "Oh, Janice, what happened?"

"I'm truly so lucky," Janice said, breathing hard as she fell to her knees beside Rebecca. "That vile man! I am so lucky that he didn't force me to go with him. Oh, Lord, I am so fortunate that he didn't kill me on the spot!"

Janice turned her head toward the door when she heard footsteps approaching outside.

She stiffened and felt a quick panic grab at her insides. What if Stumpy had decided to follow her? What if he was going to kill her no matter what happened to himself afterward?

What if he had decided to put his fear of White Shield from his mind in order to get at Janice?

Scarcely breathing, she watched the door.

Chapter Fourteen

And long shall timorous fancy see,
The painted chief, and pointed spear,
And Reason's self shall bow the knee
To shadows and delusions here.
                    —PHILIP FRENEAU

When Chief Night Fighter entered the room, Janice's breath caught in her throat.

She could hear Rebecca's gasp of terror behind her, and Janice understood her sister-in-law's fear. She also saw the strange glint in the old chief's eyes, which seemed to look clean into Janice's soul.

And never once did his eyes stray from Janice. As he stepped inside the door, a blanket draped loosely around his bent shoulders, Janice wanted to back away from him.

But feeling the need to show bravery in the presence of this powerful Skokomish chief, she stood her ground and waited for him to reveal why he was there, singling her out with his searching eyes.

He picked up a lamp from a table and, taking it to Janice, held it close to her face, studying her. She could hear Rebecca sobbing behind her. Janice wasn't sure if her crying was from intense fear or from labor pains that had begun again in earnest.

But feeling that it was still best to stay put and wait for the chief to reveal his reasons for being there, Janice didn't move an inch.

She could feel the heat of the lamp against her flesh as Chief Night Fighter held it there, his eyes closely scrutinizing her.

"What do you want of me?" Janice finally blurted out.

She found his eyes now locked with hers as he lowered the lamp back down onto the table.

"Why are you looking at me so closely?" Janice said, this time more warily. "Do I remind you . . ."

He interrupted her. "You are not to question a Skokomish chief, but to do as commanded," he said, his voice deep and full of authority.

Eyes wide, Janice nodded.

"Tell me your full name," Night Fighter said. He reached out a hand and slowly moved his fingers over her facial features which were so familiar to him.

"Janice," she choked out. She was dying a slow death inside as his wrinkled fingers traced the curve of her chin. "Janice Edwards."

By the way he jerked his hand down to his side, and by the way he looked at her even more intently now, as though her name had struck a chord of recognition inside his heart, Janice was even more puzzled than before ... but strangely enough, she was less afraid.

"Tell me your grandmother's name," Night Fighter demanded, clasping his hands together behind him.

"I had *two* grandmothers," Janice said, wondering why he would ask such a thing as that. "Do you want to hear both their names?"

"*Ah-hah,* say them both aloud to me," Night Fighter said, his eyes narrowing. "Now. Speak them now."

She told him her mother's mother's name, which caused no response or interest in his eyes.

But when she spoke Hannah's name, she was stunned to see how he flinched, as though someone had slapped him.

"Your grandmother did have the name Hannah?" Night Fighter said with difficulty, his eyes wavering and with tears shining in their corners.

"Yes, as I said, her name was Hannah," Janice said, her heart lurching at his obvious recognition of the name. "You did know my grandmother, didn't you? I could tell by your reaction to the name that you . . . somehow . . . must have known her."

Janice's lips parted in a slight gasp when Night Fighter turned suddenly and quickly left the longhouse.

Shaken by what had just transpired between herself and the chief, Janice was afraid now that he might have somehow had a bad experience with her grandmother during the short time Mema had lived in her cabin. Although sweet and fragile, Janice's grandmother was the sort of person to speak her mind, and had even been known to threaten people who got in her way with her rifle. If she had somehow had a confrontation with the elderly chief, and had ordered him off her property with her firearm, Janice might be in danger, herself.

"Janice, we've got to get off this island," Rebecca said, holding her belly as she slowly sat up on the pelts. "I saw the chief's strange behavior, his reaction to Hannah's name. I hadn't thought to tell you before, but Hannah's cabin was built on the very strip of land where the Skokomish village once stood. Perhaps when Chief Night Fighter heard about the cabin, he went to it and had an argument with Hannah. If so, neither you nor I are safe here. Especially since he now knows that Hannah was kin to you."

"But wouldn't White Shield have known about such a problem?" Janice asked, arching an eyebrow. "When we all arrived at the cabin, did you see him react in any way?"

"No, but perhaps his grandfather had not told him about his confrontation with your grandmother, especially since it seems as though she got the best of the old chief," Rebecca said. She placed one hand at the small of her back, using the other to push herself to her feet. "No. I don't think a man like Night Fighter would tell anyone, especially a grandson, about a woman besting him."

"I imagine you are right," Janice said, turning to stare at the closed door.

"Janice, we have no choice but to return to the cabin," Rebecca said, now standing. She ran her fingers through her hair as she swept it back from her face. "Although it frightens me to death to live in that isolated cabin without the protection of a man, it is surely a safer place than here where that chief behaves so strangely toward you."

Janice spun around and faced Rebecca again. "I don't know, Rebecca," she said somberly. She went to Rebecca and gently took her hands. "I don't know what is best for us now. It seems that we are in danger no matter where we are."

"I don't want to be at the mercy of Indians," Rebecca said, visibly shuddering. "I was raised on tales of their atrocities ... of scalpings, rapes, and oh, things even worse that I cannot say aloud."

"Don't you know that much of that nonsense was made up by white people who, themselves, were the true monsters?" Janice murmured. "So much that has been said about Indians is hogwash."

"But still, Janice, I don't want to stay here, not after seeing how strangely the chief is behaving toward us . . . toward *you*, especially," Rebecca said. She slid her hands free of Janice's and reached down to grab a blanket. "Let's go now while we have the chance."

She looked at her bags of belongings, then at Janice. "Between the two of us we can get the bags to the Sound," she said, her voice breaking. "We can steal a canoe. Come on, Janice. Each moment we delay might bring us closer to becoming captives of the Skokomish. Please? Let's go. Now. The cabin is the better of the two evils."

"Yes, I guess so," Janice said, sighing.

It pained Janice deeply to think of leaving the island without first telling White Shield. If he took their departure the wrong way, she might never see him again.

Yet she could not deny being afraid of Chief Night Fighter. If he hated Janice's grandmother, surely he would hate Janice, as well, for being blood kin to her.

Janice looked past Rebecca and gazed at the

171

Cassie Edwards

door, then looked at Rebecca again. "Soon it will be dark," she murmured. "It's only dusk now. But it is dark enough for us to sneak around to the back, and then go to the Sound through the forest. With luck, no one will be there. If someone is, we will just have to wait until the coast is clear to steal a canoe without being caught."

Her fear of the water made her insides recoil of the thought of being at its mercy again as Janice and Rebecca paddled across to the other side.

And then again, there was White Shield. She had fallen hopelessly in love with him. Yet she knew that it was an impossible love. Their two worlds would always be colliding.

And now, worst of all, there was his grandfather. It was apparent that there had been some sort of bad blood between White Shield's grandfather and Janice's grandmother.

That alone would make it impossible for anything to come of the feelings that were so evident between White Shield and Janice.

"I wonder where he is now," she whispered, wondering if she might run into him as she tried to flee his village.

If so, how could she explain her actions?

How could she explain something that she was not so sure of herself, for down deep inside her heart she believed that anything could be worked out if someone loved someone enough.

But for now, she had to follow her instincts and leave this island.

And to hell with her fear of the Sound. The waters of the Sound surrounded the land upon which she would be living, and she must learn to regard it as an ally, not an enemy.

"Rebecca, you carry the lightest bag," Janice said, nodding toward it. "I shall carry the other, heavier one."

Rebecca was visibly trembling.

"We have no choice, Rebecca," Janice said. She gazed at Rebecca's tummy, then looked into her eyes. "Have the pains stopped altogether?"

Not wanting to give up the chance to leave this place, Rebecca lied, reassuring Janice that she was all right. The pains were sharp when they came. And she could feel her stomach tighten with them, which meant that she *might* be in labor.

"Are you certain?" Janice asked, moving closer to Rebecca. "I don't want to have to deliver a baby in a canoe in the middle of the Sound."

"I'll be just fine," Rebecca said, forcing a smile.

Janice sighed, then slowly opened the door and peered outside. No one was near and she saw no one looking her way.

She searched for White Shield among the clusters of men who stood talking in groups, and saw no sign of him. No doubt he thought that she and Rebecca were still resting. If so, he had no idea that his grandfather had paid Janice and Rebecca a visit.

"Janice, what's the delay?" Rebecca whispered behind her. "Do you see someone? Isn't it safe to leave now?"

Janice looked up at the sky. It was just growing dark. There was no more time to waste. She certainly didn't want to cross the Sound during the black of night!

"Come on," Janice whispered back. "But keep watch on all sides of you. If you see someone looking our way, tell me."

Rebecca nodded.

They sneaked from the longhouse and rushed behind it toward the Sound.

No one was there to stop them when they chose a small canoe, which was obviously built for a woman's use.

They placed their bags inside the canoe.

Janice helped Rebecca inside and placed a blanket around her and across her lap.

Then, swallowing back her fear of the water, and forcing herself not to think of the tragedy it had brought into her life, she dragged the canoe out into deeper water, then climbed aboard.

Recalling how White Shield used his paddle to make the canoe go, she lowered the paddle into the water and sent the canoe out into deeper water.

As the sun set along the far horizon, sending off sprays of pinkish light across the heavens,

Janice looked over her shoulder at the island that she was leaving behind.

She wondered what White Shield's reaction would be when he found her gone.

Would he be offended and forget her?

Or would he care too much for her to let things die between them? Would he search her out and question her about why she'd fled without telling him?

Forcing herself to stop thinking of him, Janice sighed and watched the distant shore as she paddled her way toward it.

She wasn't sure what her next move should be.

Since the storm, she had learned to take each moment as it came, praying that the future would be better than the past.

She did not want to lose hope, that was certain.

Already she missed White Shield with every fiber of her being!

"Where are you now?" she whispered to herself. "Are you thinking of me?"

Chapter Fifteen

Mine and yours;
Mine, not yours.
Earth endure;
Stars abide—
—MARY ANN WHITAKER

Having gone back to Tacoma while Janice and
Rebecca were resting to inquire again about her
brother and daughter, White Shield walked
toward the longhouse where he had left the
women soundly asleep.

Only a short while ago the still night had
come down like a cloud. A silvery full moon
splashed its white light over the towering trees
of the forest, and his village. The breeze was

NAME: _____

ADDRESS: _____

_____

_____

TELEPHONE: _____

E-MAIL: _____

____ I want to pay by credit card.

__ Visa   __ MasterCard   __ Discover

Account Number: _____

Expiration date: _____

SIGNATURE: _____

*Send this form, along with $2.00 shipping
and handling for your FREE books, to:*

Historical Romance Book Club
20 Academy Street
Norwalk, CT 06850-4032

*Or fax (must include credit card
information!) to:* 610.995.9274.
*You can also sign up on the Web
at* www.dorchesterpub.com.

Offer open to residents of the U.S. and
Canada only. Canadian residents, please
call 1.800.481.9191 for pricing information.

If under 18, a parent or guardian must sign. Terms, prices and conditions
subject to change. Subscription subject to acceptance. Dorchester
Publishing reserves the right to reject any order or cancel any subscription.

gentle and warm as it blew in from the Sound. A loon cried its eerie song from somewhere along the shore, its echo sounding as though another bird were there, responding.

As White Shield came up to the longhouse door, he hesitated a moment. If he had come with good news for Janice, he would eagerly go to her.

But as it was, with her brother and daughter's whereabouts still a mystery, he was debating whether or not to tell her where he had been. Surely she had begun to wonder about him, for he had been gone for some time now.

He had not left a stone unturned this time.

Expecting her and Rebecca to be awake, he was puzzled that he heard no conversation coming from inside the lodge. Although the women's voices were soft and sweet, he should be able to hear them through the door.

They were so tired, perhaps they are still asleep, he thought, idly shrugging.

He opened the door.

The lodge glowed warm with lamplight and the light from the fire, but the moment he stepped inside, his heart skipped a beat. There was no sign of either woman.

He took another step into the longhouse, scarcely breathing so that he might hear their voices coming from one of the other rooms, and he still heard nothing but stillness and the continuing cry of the loon outside the lodge. He knew then that he had returned to an empty longhouse.

He was confused about why they were gone, and where they might be.

As he turned and gazed at the open door, where the moonlight swept through like a pale ghost, he wondered if they might have gone to sit by the Sound to talk.

Yet, no, that could not be so. He had just been at the Sound. The moon's glow would have revealed them there, sitting or standing, and he had not seen them.

He turned with a jerk and stared at the quiet, empty spaces of the lodge again, his mind still swirling with confusion over their disappearance. When they had arrived there, they'd seemed content enough about their lodging, especially Janice. She had seemed to welcome the solace and comfort of the lodge after a day filled with painful moments.

But now she and Rebecca were gone.

He sighed with frustration, then his breath caught in his throat, and his eyes widened with discovery when he thought of something . . . some*one* . . . who might be the cause of their fleeing the safety and shelter of the lodge.

"Grandfather!" he whispered harshly. How could he have forgotten his grandfather's strange behavior upon seeing Janice? After White Shield had left the island, could his grandfather have gone to Janice and said something to her that frightened her?

"I must go to him and question him," White Shield said, turning abruptly on a heel and leaving the longhouse.

When he reached his grandfather's lodge, the door was open, which was usual for him on a moonlit night. His grandfather had recently told him that the moon's glow reminded him of his wife, for it was during a full moon that he had asked Winter Dawn to marry him those many moons ago.

Now when the moon was full and bright, his grandfather felt as though his beloved wife was there, sitting with him.

Stepping inside his grandfather's longhouse, White Shield found Night Fighter sitting with his head bent, asleep, before his lodge fire, a blanket draped around his shoulders.

White Shield started to turn around and leave, but his footsteps, although light as a panther's, had awakened Night Fighter.

His grandfather did not speak his usual words of welcome, and White Shield could see by the look in his eyes that something was haunting him.

"Close the door for me, grandson," Night Fighter said, lifting a hand and motioning toward the door with it. "The moon's glow troubles me tonight."

Puzzled by that, White Shield closed the door.

179

"Now tell me why you are here," Night Fighter said, his jaw tight. His old eyes turned from White Shield and now looked into the lapping flames of the lodge fire.

"Grandfather, the white women are gone from their lodge," White Shield said thickly. "You know that I noticed your response when you saw Janice Edwards, yet you have not told me why you reacted so."

When White Shield saw that the question caused his grandfather to flinch—his lips drawn into a tight, narrow line—and to ignore White Shield as though he was not there, White Shield knew there was something about Janice that troubled him.

"Grandfather, you have always spoken openly with me about everything," White Shield said. He moved closer to his grandfather and sank to his haunches beside him. "What is there about Janice Edwards that makes you grow silent now while I am here questioning you about her?"

White Shield became unnerved by his grandfather's continued silence. "Grandfather, are you responsible for Janice leaving the island?" he blurted out. "Did you say something to her?"

When his grandfather continued to ignore him, White Shield started to leave, but instead, he resolved to continue questioning his grandfather. "Grandfather, what *is* your connection with Janice?" he asked warily. "It was obvious when you saw her that you recognized something about her. What was it? She is new to this area. You could not know her!"

Still his grandfather refused to talk. He sat stoic and tight-jawed as he stared into the dancing flames of his fire.

Sighing with frustration, White Shield gave his grandfather one last lingering stare, then hurried back to the longhouse where he had last been with his woman. They had even kissed.

When he still found no one there, he was certain that the women *were* gone, and not only from the longhouse, but also the island. White Shield ran from the longhouse and went to his canoe.

He paddled hard across the Sound, beached his canoe, then set out at a trot for Janice's cabin.

When he finally arrived there, he stopped and stared when he saw that the boards at the front of the cabin had been removed and the windows were filled with the soft glow of lamplight.

He looked upward and saw smoke spiraling from two chimneys, one from the fireplace, and the other one surely from a cook stove in the kitchen.

His pulse racing, he crept up the porch steps and and gazed through a window.

His heart leapt when he saw Janice sitting in

a comfortable chair beside the fireplace, absorbed in a strange-looking book.

His gaze shifted.

Rebecca was lying on the sofa directly before the fire, an afghan pulled up over her and her gaze locked on the fire.

His gaze shifted again.

He now saw a rifle resting against the chair in which Janice sat.

He smiled, for although it was obvious that she had reconsidered and had chosen to live in her grandmother's lodge, she was wise enough to know that she needed protection. She had surely taken the firearm from her grandmother's gun cabinet, which he now saw hanging on the wall on the far side of the room.

He started to go to the door, to question Janice about why she had chosen not to stay at his lodge, but as he turned, he tripped on a piece of wood that had rolled from the chopped logs that had been piled on the porch, against the house.

As he lost his balance, he fell against the stack of wood, causing those at the top to roll off. An avalanche of logs crashed to the wood flooring.

He winced when he realized that Janice must have heard the noise. It would surely frighten the women. He could picture Janice grabbing the rifle.

He hoped that she looked before she fired.

Startled, her heart thumping like claps of

thunder inside her chest, Janice laid the photo album aside on a table. Rebecca sat straight up, her eyes wild as she stared at the door.

"Janice, who could be out there?" Rebecca said, clutching the afghan up to her chin.

Janice looked over at Rebecca and saw just how frightened she was.

Janice was no less afraid. She realized now that she had been premature to remove any of the boards from the windows.

But she had felt penned in by them. Being claustrophobic, she had to be able to look outside when she wanted to. She realized now, however, that anyone who came to spy on her and Rebecca could look right in.

And the worst of her fears had happened. She and Rebecca were no longer alone. Someone was outside on the porch. He had stumbled over the stack of wood. It could even be Stumpy Jackson.

"Shh!" she whispered to Rebecca as she placed a finger to her lips. "I'll go and see who's there."

"Janice, oh, Janice, be careful," Rebecca whispered, trembling.

Janice nodded.

Her knees weak with fear, Janice grabbed the rifle and hurried to the door.

She opened it, but didn't go out onto the porch. She stood in the doorway, holding the rifle steady before her.

"Whoever is there, show your face," she screamed. "Or I will come out shooting!"

"It is I, White Shield," he called out, remaining hidden in the shadows until he felt it was safe to step out into the open.

As soon as she heard White Shield's voice, Janice breathed in a deep sigh of relief and lowered the rifle to her side.

She rested the firearm against the wall and rushed out to the porch.

When White Shield stepped into view, and his eyes met hers, she stopped and gazed at him. Then, feeling so relieved that he was there, she ran to him and flung herself into his arms.

"I'm so glad it was you," she said, reveling in the protective strength of his arms. "I . . . I . . . thought it might be . . ."

She stopped short of saying Stumpy Jackson. She decided to leave what had transpired between herself and Stumpy unsaid, for she had already dismissed what he had said about Lexi as a lie.

White Shield slid his hands down to Janice's waist and eased her away from him. He held her at arm's length as he gazed deeply into her eyes. "Were you afraid that it might be my grandfather who had followed you here?" he asked, his voice drawn. "He *is* the reason you left the island, is he not? Did he give you cause to be afraid of him?"

"No, I'm not afraid of him, but I did not feel

comfortable staying on the island after he came and questioned me about things that I do not understand," Janice said. "White Shield, he demanded to know my grandmother's name. When I told him, there was recognition in his eyes. I am almost certain that, somehow, he knew my grandmother, or else why would he be acting so peculiar while in my presence? Why would he question me like that?"

"I am as puzzled as you are by my grandfather's strange behavior," White Shield said, slowly dropping his hands away from her. "When I saw that you were gone, I went and questioned my grandfather. He acted as though I was not there." He stopped and sighed. "That is not like my grandfather. He has always been open to me. In a sense, he has been my best friend."

"It makes me feel eerie, somehow," Janice said, visibly shuddering. "It was as though the ghost of my grandmother was with me when your grandfather was questioning me."

Rebecca came to the door. "White Shield, I'm so glad it's you and not someone intent on harming me and Janice," she said softly. She placed a hand on her tummy and smiled weakly at Janice. "Janice, I'm going to bed. I . . . I . . . still . . . don't feel so good."

"But the pains have stopped," Janice said. "That's all that's important, isn't it?"

Rebecca sighed heavily. "I'm just so relieved

that it was White Shield who came tonight, not some stranger who would take advantage of two defenseless women," she said.

White Shield smiled at Janice, then gazed down at Rebecca. "From what I saw, you seemed quite well protected," he said, chuckling. "Your sister-in-law seems determined to keep strangers from your doorstep."

Janice smiled awkwardly, for she did not want to tell either one of them that she knew not the first thing about firearms. She had never even fired one.

In fact, she wasn't certain if she had the rifle loaded properly.

She would have been afraid to fire it if she had been forced to. She was afraid that the bullet might explode in her face!

But as long as seeing a weapon aimed at them was enough to frighten off most men, Janice believed she could keep herself and Rebecca safe from intruders.

"Rebecca, if those pains resume, please let me know and I will go for Doc Rose," Janice murmured.

Rebecca nodded, then left Janice and White Shield alone as she went back inside the house.

"Come with me?" White Shield asked, his eyes searching Janice's. "There is a close-by stream. From there you can see the front door of the cabin. Let us go and sit beside it in the moonlight and talk. We can keep watch on the cabin from there."

Janice glanced at the door, then up at White Shield, then closed the door and left the porch with him.

When they reached the creek that ran ribbon-like through the forest, Janice sat down with White Shield on a thick bed of moss.

"I went back to Tacoma and again searched for answers about your brother and daughter," White Shield said. "I bring you no good news. I still found no one who knows of the child or your brother."

"You must have been there when Rebecca and I left the island," Janice said, feeling guilty now for having left without waiting to tell White Shield. All the while she was plotting to leave the village without his knowing, he was in Tacoma doing things for her.

"When I brought food to you and found you both asleep, I decided to go and try to find answers for you," White Shield said. "Then, when I returned and you were gone, I did not know what to think."

"I'm sorry I didn't wait to tell you that we felt we should leave," Janice murmured, lowering her eyes. "But Rebecca seemed frantic over your grandfather's behavior. She felt threatened." She looked slowly up at him again. "The baby was all that I could think about, White Shield. And Rebecca was having pains . . ."

He slid a hand gently over her lips. "Say no more," he said softly. "That was then. This is now. We are together again, are we not?"

Janice eagerly nodded.

"That is all that is important, is it not?" he said thickly, looking deeply into her eyes.

Janice nodded again.

"Then say no more about it," White Shield said.

"Thank you for caring so much," Janice murmured. "And I feel that I will see my brother and daughter again. I will never allow myself to believe they are dead. God is surely looking out for them, and in time, we will be reunited."

Then she reached over and grabbed one of White Shield's hands. "Listen," she said in a whisper. "Hear that strange sound? It sounds like a bird, yet I've never heard anything quite like it."

"You are hearing the song of a loon," White Shield said, listening as well.

"I have heard people say 'crazy as a loon,'" Janice said, laughing softly. "Now I see why. That bird call is the strangest I have ever heard."

Her heart melted when White Shield placed his hands on her cheeks and turned her face to him, his lips moving toward hers.

And when he swept his arms around her and lowered her to the ground, his lips on hers, everything but the love she felt for this man was blocked from her consciousness.

She had not realized just how explosive a kiss could be, or how quickly she could get undressed, until she was spread out silkenly nude on the bed of moss. White Shield blanketed her with his own naked, muscled body, sending a sweet warmth she had never known before throughout her, especially her heart.

His fingers went to the juncture of her thighs, and he began caressing her where her heart seemed centered, causing her head to spin with pleasure. A small, nervous part of her cried out that they should stop before they went too far.

But another part of her, who loved a man for the first time in her life, and who felt safe in his arms, won. Her whole body yearned for what he was giving her.

His kiss was now soft, sweet, and deep, as he ran his fingers over her body, stopping to cup her breasts, his thumbs circling her nipples.

As though she had made love many times before, Janice seemed to know how to respond to each new awakening of her body.

And when she felt the part of him that had swollen with his own needs probe gently where she ached so sweetly, she knew somehow to open her legs to him.

When his manhood pushed ever so gently into her folds, spreading her open as though she were a flower opening to the beckoning rays of the sun, Janice sucked in a wild breath of pleasure.

He slid his mouth from her lips and whispered into her ear. "I will be gentle," he said, sensing that this woman was a virgin. "But should it hurt too much, tell me. I shall stop and ready you some more, or I shall stop completely, if that is what you ask of me."

Her heart pounding, not sure of anything at this moment, except that she loved White Shield with all her heart, and that she wanted him so badly she ached, Janice reached a hand to his cheek.

"My love," she murmured. "I am ready. Please? Please make love to me."

He smiled down at her with passion-hot eyes, then smothered her outcry of pain with a fiery kiss as he pushed himself into her.

And then he stopped and waited for her reaction, smiling to himself when her hips began to move, in an invitation for him to continue with his lovemaking.

Janice gave herself up to the rapture as White Shield's lean, sinewy buttocks moved.

She sighed and closed her eyes dreamily when he swept his mouth down and showered heated kisses over her taut-tipped breasts.

White Shield's hands slid beneath Janice and lifted her closer so that he could fill her more deeply with his heat, moving slowly now, with acute deliberation.

Ecstatic waves of pleasure rushed through him with each thrust inside her.

And when he felt the flames growing higher

and hotter inside his loins, and he knew that he was near to exploding, he buried his face between her breasts and groaned throatily.

Feeling new sensations flooding her that were so incredibly sweet, Janice slowly tossed her head back and forth, moaning.

Aware that his strokes were growing faster, moving deeper, deeper, and frantic with need of something she could not even define, Janice reached down and lifted his face so that their eyes could meet.

"I have never experienced such bliss," she said, her voice strangely husky. "I . . . have . . . never felt so alive."

Her body turned to liquid as he swept a hand down her body. He caressed her where she throbbed, yet did not slow down his rhythmic thrusts within her.

She closed her eyes and let the heat of passion sweep her away on clouds of ecstasy, then cried out when something even more beautiful happened inside her. It was as though she was flooded with sensation, which momentarily swept away all consciousness of time, place, or worries.

It was so beautiful, she felt as though she were floating above herself.

She was only vaguely aware of his body responding to her overwhelming moment of rapture, trembling and quaking against her.

Overcome with a feverish heat, his body on

fire with euphoria, White Shield tightened his arms around Janice. He held her against him as he pumped hard into her, then fell away from her, breathing fast, yet totally fulfilled as he came down from that wondrous plateau of release.

Then he reached for Janice and cradled her close, pleased that she had received pleasure, as well.

And this was only the beginning. After she found peace in her life again, he would take her as his wife. He would not let his grandfather's attitude toward Janice stand in the way of his own happiness, not even if he had to go against his grandfather's wishes for the first time in his life.

"It was so wonderful," Janice whispered, her hands running slowly up and down his back. "I hope you don't think badly of me for . . ."

He rolled away from her and lay on his side facing her as she turned toward him. "Do not ever think that what happens between us is anything but good," he said reassuringly. "It was meant to be, just as the stars were meant to be in the heavens."

"But I should have waited," Janice said, sighing.

"Did not the moment help you forget the pain inside your heart?" White Shield asked, brushing fallen locks of her hair back from her face.

"Yes, oh, yes, and I shall never forget it," Janice murmured. She smiled weakly. "I can't see myself as a loose woman like my sister-in-law once was. For me you are the first man . . . and . . . for certain, the last."

"I will marry you soon," White Shield said, hoping that would help erase whatever shame she might be feeling for having been with a man before marriage vows were spoken.

He turned on his back and looked heavenward. He swept a hand out and gestured toward the sky. "Tonight we *were* wed," he said softly. "To each other! Beneath the stars, the moon, the entire heavens!"

Laughing softly, loving the way White Shield was trying to help her overcome the shame she felt for having given herself to him so easily, Janice moved closer to him and cuddled against him. "I thee wed," she murmured. "My love, I take thee as my husband. The stars, the moon, the sky are our witnesses."

Chuckling, finding this moment so precious, White Shield swept his arms around her. "I take thee, Soft Sky, as my wife," he said, gazing into her eyes as she looked quickly up at him.

"You called me by another name," she murmured. "Why?"

"It is a name that fits you," he said, then lowered his mouth to hers and kissed her.

Soft Sky, she thought to herself, loving the name, and feeling oh, so blessed for having been given this wondrous moment with the man she adored.

And she *did* feel as though they were married. The vows spoken between them were no less important than those which they would share on their wedding day.

She only hoped that her brother and daughter could be there to witness their true marriage!

Chapter Sixteen

I could follow him,
Always and forever,
If he beckoned me.
—MARY ANN WHITAKER

Now dressed and sitting quietly next to one another beside the stream, they put off saying good-bye. Janice sighed contentedly, leaning against White Shield as he held her close, his arm around her waist.

"If only Seth and Lexi were safely home, this would be the most precious moment of my life," Janice said, turning her gaze up to White Shield. "I never thought it could be possible to love a man as I love you. And that you love me as much . . ."

He leaned down and brushed her lips with a kiss. "*Ah-hah,* I do love you," he said, then gazed again into her eyes. "You are like a miracle in my life, for it was only recently that I decided that it was time for me to search for the woman who would make my life complete."

"How is it that you have only now decided to include a woman in your life?" Janice asked softly. "You will make such a wonderful husband, *and* father. I have never met a man who was so gentle, caring, and compassionate."

She snuggled closer. "And handsome," she said, smiling wickedly up at him. "Surely everywhere you go women's eyes follow you."

"If so, I have not been aware of it," White Shield said.

"Of course you are being too modest," Janice murmured. "Tell me, White Shield. Why have you put off being married?"

"For so long I was occupied with other things," White Shield said, his voice more serious. "I was wrapped up in being a forester. It was my job to keep the lumber companies from stripping the entire forest of its trees in one fast sweep. But now that the lumber companies are no longer in business, I can pursue other interests in my life. It is time now for me to choose a woman for my lodge."

His smile faded. With a haunted look in the depths of his eyes, he looked out across the water. "And there is my grandfather's health," he said, swallowing hard. "I am not certain how much longer he will be a part of my life."

He then looked quickly at Janice again. "I would like to see a child of mine in my grandfather's arms," he said thickly. "I would like for my grandfather to feel the joy of being a great-grandfather."

"Again you think beyond self and consider others," Janice said softly. "Your grandfather is so lucky to have you as a grandson. And he must be special, himself, to have evoked such qualities in you."

"*Ah-hah,* it is my grandfather who molded me into the man that I am. He became both mother and father to me when my parents died," White Shield said.

He scooted around and faced Janice. He took her hands and gazed into her eyes. "Now tell me more about *you,* why *you* are not married," he said. "Surely it is not because you have not had endless opportunities. How could any man not want you?"

"Yes, I have had many suitors, but none of them stirred my heart into loving him," Janice murmured. "Only you have done that, White Shield. Now I know why I could not allow myself to love. *You* hadn't come into my life yet."

She decided not to tell him that she had never trusted a man enough to allow herself to fall in love with him.

Cassie Edwards

She could never be certain that her suitors loved her, not her money.

But now was different. White Shield was different from most men. Everything about him spoke of his honesty.

"There were many men before me?" White Shield said, his eyebrows arching. "But tonight it was proven that I was the first, sexually."

Janice blushed, then laughed softly. "I didn't mean to imply that any of those men . . ."

She laughed nervously. "What I mean to say is that although many men paid notice to me, I did not return the attention," she blurted out, now feeling the need to explain things she just decided to omit.

"You see, White Shield," she said softly, "I could never take any of those men seriously. My family was very affluent. In San Francisco we lived in one of the most elaborate houses on Nob Hill. When my parents died, their wealth was divided between my brother and me. It is because of that wealth that I felt suspicious of the men who paid attention to me. I never knew if it was for my money, or *me*. So I just paid no attention to any of them."

"No man would discount your loveliness and want you only for your money," White Shield said in a scolding fashion. "I want you because I love you. It matters not that you might have all of the money in the world."

"Even so, it is good to know that you weren't aware of my money when you fell in love with

198

me," Janice said. Then she laughed softly. "And it's good that you love me for myself, for I don't have money now. When my brother became suddenly poor because of financial adventures gone awry, so did I, for as I said, our wealth was equally shared."

He drew her into his arms and held her close. "My Soft Sky, do you not know that by knowing you and having your love, I feel like the wealthiest man in the world?" he said thickly. "And for me, the white man's dollars are not signs of true wealth and prosperity. How one's heart reacts to another reveals the true worth of things."

So in love, so glad to know that White Shield loved her so much, Janice clung to him. She felt guilty for feeling such glorious joy, for all she had to do was think about Seth and Lexi and she was torn apart all over again at not knowing how they fared.

She was beginning to wonder if she ever would.

A sudden rush of tears spilled from Janice's eyes. "I miss Lexi and Seth so much," she murmured, a sob catching in her throat. "How can two people just disappear like that? There is no trace of either of them. Why? Oh, why did it have to happen?"

White Shield placed gentle hands on her shoulders and eased her away from him so that their eyes could meet and hold. "I will go beyond Tacoma tomorrow in my search for

Seth and Lexi," he said thickly. "Would you like to join me?"

Janice wanted so badly to say yes, but she remembered Rebecca and the pains that she had been experiencing. "I can't," she blurted out. "I haven't told you yet, but my main reason for leaving your village so abruptly was because of Rebecca. She went into labor. I . . . I . . . thought she was ready to have the child. I felt the need to get her closer to Doc Rose."

"Because she did not trust my people's shaman," White Shield said, his voice dry.

"No, she didn't," Janice said softly. "But please don't take offense. She doesn't trust Doc Rose either, but she decided that she would rather use his services than your shaman's. It was her decision. She's the one having the baby. I had to do what she felt comfortable with."

"It is understandable," White Shield said, nodding. "I only hope that you do not feel the same about my people's shaman as Rebecca. Soon you will be a part of not only my life, but my people's."

"I will trust everything that has to do with you," Janice reassured him. "You don't know how much I want to please you and be the wife that you desire me to be."

She reached a gentle hand to his face and looked adoringly at him. "I especially want your people to accept me into their lives," she said softly.

She paused, then said, "But, White Shield, as long as your grandfather is acting so mysterious about me, how can I be expected to relax while in his presence? And won't your people pick up on his feelings about me? Won't that make them resent me? I know how they revere your grandfather."

"In time my grandfather will reveal why he has behaved so strangely in your presence," White Shield said. "He and I share everything. When he feels it is the right time to explain his behavior, he will. And then I shall share it with you."

"But until he does, should I stay away from your village?" Janice asked, raising an eyebrow. "What if he doesn't even want me there? There is something about me that truly troubles him."

"Again, in time, I will know what that is," White Shield said. "Until then, let us not think about it. There are other things that are more important. Your brother and daughter. I will search tomorrow and with luck bring answers to you about them."

"Good news, I hope," Janice said, gripping his hands as together they rose from the ground.

He swept an arm around her waist and walked slowly back toward the cabin. When they reached the steps, he stopped and held her at arm's length as he gazed down at her. "One day I will not say good-bye when it is time for us to go to our beds," he said thickly. "They will not be separate beds. We will sleep in one another's arms. To think of waking up and seeing you every morning is something that makes my heart swell with joy, for soon this will be so."

"I wish it were now," Janice said, moving gently into his arms. She clung to him as though it were their last time together. "Please be careful as you go from place to place, alone. If anything happened to you . . ."

He put a hand beneath her chin and lifted it so that their eyes met and held. "I have been faced with danger from the moment I took my first breath of life," he said thickly. "White men have hated my people from the beginning of time. Why? No one will ever truly know. It is just something that we have learned to live with."

"I never knew it was that bad," Janice said, visibly shuddering. "Now that I do, how can you love me? How can you *trust* me?"

"I have been taught survival skills that the eagle is born with," White Shield said. "Those skills have brought me into my twenty-eighth year. I know who to trust." He reached a hand up and twined his fingers through the thick tresses of her hair. "You? Soft Sky, I knew that you were put on this earth for this warrior. Fate brought us together."

"I want to smile at that word *fate*, for I do love you so, and I am so glad that we were brought together to love one another, but it is also 'fate' that swept my brother and daughter from my life in the tumultuous waters of the Sound," Janice said, swallowing hard.

"Love, faith, and hope will bring you together again, but it might take time," White Shield said. "I will do everything within my power to see that you do not have to wait too long."

"Thank you," Janice murmured, then melted inside when his lips came to hers in a deep, long kiss.

He eased her away from him, gave her a soft smile, then was lost from view in the depths of the dark forest.

"Please keep him safe," she whispered as she gazed heavenward.

After she was inside the house and had the door locked, Janice turned to go to the bed that she knew had been her grandmother's. She stopped when she found Rebecca sitting on the floor in front of the fire, seemingly lost in thought.

"Rebecca, are you all right?" Janice asked as she went and knelt down beside her. "I thought you were going to bed."

Rebecca turned and Janice saw tears in her eyes.

"Are you in pain again?" Janice asked anxiously.

"In a way, yes," Rebecca said, wiping tears from her eyes with the back of a hand.

"It's not the baby?" Janice said, sitting down on the floor beside Rebecca.

"No, but I ache so for Seth," Rebecca said, tears filling her eyes again.

"I know," Janice murmured, reaching over to lay a gentle hand on Rebecca's arm.

"No, you don't," Rebecca said, swallowing hard. "Not really. No one but Seth knows my true feelings."

"Would you feel better if you shared those feelings with me, as well?" Janice asked, searching Rebecca's eyes and seeing true pain in their depths.

Rebecca nodded, then opened up and told Janice all about the brothel, how she'd hated it, and how ashamed she was ever to have been a part of it.

"I still can't believe that Seth believed in me so much that he took me away from that life of sin," Rebecca said, her voice breaking. "And now there is to be a baby. Do wonders never cease?"

"Rebecca, if there were so many men in your life before Seth became a part of it, how can you know for certain that the baby is my brother's?" Janice blurted out.

This had been troubling her from the moment she had seen that Rebecca was pregnant. How could she not worry about the possibility of the child belonging to another man? Rebecca had taken so many men to her bed!

A look of shaken trust crossed Rebecca's face and Janice realized that she had spoken out of turn. She was filled with regret.

"I apologize," she said. "Truly I am so sorry

for having said that. It was wrong. I . . . surely . . . wish I hadn't said that."

"But you did, didn't you?" Rebecca said, renewed tears flooding her eyes as she silently turned her head away from Janice.

Chapter Seventeen

Breezes in the tree tops,
Gentle, like your touch,
Sand between my toes,
I miss you so much.
—MARY ANN WHITAKER

In the early light of a new morn, the tension between Janice and Rebecca was like a tightrope ready to snap. Needing food, as well as an excuse to get away from the cabin for at least a little while, Janice had left and had just arrived on the waterfront to dig for clams.

Before she left the cabin, though, Janice had forced the rifle into Rebecca's hands, telling her that she had to protect herself in Janice's absence.

Janice would never forget the look of horror in Rebecca's eyes as she had stared at the rifle, then dropped it to the floor as though it were a hot coal burning her hand.

Only after she was certain that Rebecca understood the true danger of being alone in the cabin, especially since her pregnancy made her even more helpless and vulnerable, did Janice leave.

She stopped now and gazed at several Skokomish children as they chatted and laughed among themselves while they dug clams.

Janice was there for the same reason. She had paid keen attention when White Shield had told her about the Skokomish children digging and selling clams to the half-starved populace of Tacoma.

It was only by chance that clams were one of Janice's favorite meals. She had gone often to restaurants on the piers along San Francisco's waterfront to eat them.

But never had she dug any for herself, nor cooked them. At this moment she felt almost as helpless as those people who had lowered themselves to existing only on clams because they no longer had money to pay for the delicacies of the rich.

Janice knew that most of the rich people felt

that it was beneath their dignity to dig clams, especially with people whose skin color did not match their own.

But Janice had never behaved like most rich people. She was proud of her ability to mix with all kinds of people, especially now that she loved White Shield.

Had she been one of those uppity, pursed-lipped, diamond-bedecked women she knew in San Francisco, who held their noses in the air when they passed by an Indian on the streets, or a Chinese person, she never would have allowed herself to fall in love with a Skokomish warrior, or adopt her precious Lexi.

Tears filled her eyes at the mere thought of Lexi. Watching the children made her absence even more painful.

Oh, how confused and afraid the child must be! What was she doing? Janice wondered desperately. Was she being treated decently?

Oh, did her heart ache for Janice as much as Janice's ached for her?

Was . . . she . . . even alive?

A tug on the skirt of her doeskin dress brought Janice out of her deep, troubled thoughts.

She looked down and found a Skokomish child, a girl dressed in a pretty, beaded doeskin skirt and blouse, with moccasins embroidered with matching beadwork, standing beside her with a basket full of clams.

"White lady, I know you," the child said, smiling as she dropped her hand away from Janice.

"You are White Shield's lady friend. That makes you *my* friend. What are you doing here?" She glanced down at the wicker basket that Janice held at her right side. Then she looked up at Janice again. "Have you come to dig clams?"

Janice was deeply touched by the sweetness of the child, and by her trust.

Janice was especially moved that the little girl showed no resentment of her friendship with the child's sub-chief. The child wore her dark brown hair in a long braid down her back. Her deep gray eyes were full of life and laughter. And the dimples in the cheeks of her round face were adorable.

It made Janice want to reach down and take her into her arms, but she knew that would be too impulsive.

"*Ah-hah,* I have come to dig clams," Janice murmured. She bent to a knee before the child. "But I don't know how. Do you think you might teach me?"

The child's eyes widened and she gasped with surprise. "You spoke a word in my people's tongue," she said. "You said *yes* in Skokomish. How do you know to do that?"

"White Shield taught me," Janice murmured, smiling.

"If White Shield can teach you to speak our language, then I shall be the one to teach you to dig clams," the child said, pride shining in her eyes. She reached a hand out for Janice. "Come. I will show you now."

Janice was lost, heart and soul, to this child when her tiny hand went so trustingly into Janice's. Janice stood and began walking with her down the beach, toward the other children, who had stopped their chatting and digging to stare in wonder at her.

"My name is Pretty Fawn," the child said, smiling up at Janice. "And I know your name. You are called Janice."

"Yes, I am Janice, but I am also called Soft Sky by your sub-chief," Janice said proudly.

Then Pretty Fawn smiled. "*Ah-hah*, the name fits you well," she said. "Yes, it is a good name. But it would be, if White Shield chose it."

"You love him dearly, don't you?" Janice asked, stopping just before reaching the others, who had resumed their digging.

"As though he were my very own father," Pretty Fawn said, her voice breaking. She hung her head. "My father died while on the whale hunt. My mother has never remarried."

"I'm so sorry," Janice said. She gently touched the child's arm. "If she is as beautiful as you, though, she will marry again. You will have a father again."

Pretty Fawn wiped a tear from her eyes and smiled up at Janice again. "*Ah-hah*, she will, but she loved Father so much, she will not be smiling back at men for many sunrises," she said, with what seemed the intelligence and insight of an adult.

Pretty Fawn fell to her knees in the sand. She

gazed up at Janice. "Come now and I will show you how it is done," she murmured, but she had hardly begun before Janice was back on her feet staring at something else.

Pretty Fawn's eyes followed Janice's gaze. When she saw that Janice was looking at White Shield, Pretty Fawn leapt to her feet and ran toward White Shield's canoe, which he was now beaching on the shore.

When Pretty Fawn reached White Shield, Janice watched as he lifted the child and swung her around and around, her giggles filling the morning air with sweetness.

But Janice was troubled by the way White Shield kept looking at her with an odd expression, instead of joining in the laughter and merriment as the other children clamored around him, begging to be swung around next.

Seeing his love for children, how he was patient enough to give each child a turn, Janice imagined him with their own children. He would be such a wonderful, caring father. She would adore watching him with them.

And they would have the best of teachers in him.

That was important, for he would be teaching their children all of the Skokomish customs.

She would, in a sense, be a student, as well, for she would never tire of knowing something new about his culture.

Finally the children left White Shield and resumed their digging. Pretty Fawn joined them

Cassie Edwards

now, as though she knew that Janice needed to be alone with White Shield. Clam digging with Janice could come later.

"Come and let us sit away from the noise of the children," White Shield said, taking Janice's hand, leading her away from them.

He glanced down at her basket, and then looked into her eyes. "You have come to dig clams?" He asked, his demeanor still somewhat withdrawn and very much unlike him.

Janice was afraid to ask him why there was not the usual peace in his eyes. He was definitely troubled by something. He had not come to tell her anything good.

"Pretty Fawn was getting ready to show me how," Janice said, nodding. "She is such a dear child."

"Of all of our people's children, she is most precious to me," White Shield said, looking over his shoulder at Pretty Fawn. "Black Lance, her father, was my best friend. While whaling, a harpoon flipped backwards as he tried to fire it. He died instantly."

"How horrible!" Janice gasped. "How very horrible."

"For many moons he was mourned by my people," White Shield said, now guiding Janice toward a strip of sand that reached out into the Sound, where rocks and seashells had washed up.

"You seem to still be mourning Black Lance,"

212

Janice said, following his lead as he went out onto the strip of land.

"I shall always feel the loss inside my heart," White Shield said as he gestured toward a place in the sand where it was less rocky. "Let us sit here. I have something to tell you."

By his mood, she was afraid to hear it. If he had brought news that Lexi or Seth were dead, she wasn't sure how she could stand it. Her eyes searched his as he paused, then reached out and held her hands.

"I have been searching today for answers about your loved ones," he said thickly. "I finally have some news of the child."

Janice's heart pounded. Her throat went dry, and her knees were weak with fear, for she knew that if the news was good, he wouldn't be so withdrawn and guarded.

"No, don't tell me that she's . . . she's . . . dead," Janice said, jerking her hands away from his, placing one over her mouth to stifle a sob of sorrow.

"I should have begun in a different way," White Shield said, taking her hands again and holding them. "I did not mean to alarm you. The news is not all bad. It's just not exactly what you want to hear."

"Tell me," Janice blurted out, her heart pounding. "Tell me what you *did* find out."

"Word was brought to me that a small Chinese child by the name of Lexi is with the Haida

Indians," White Shield said softly. "It has to be your daughter. But there is no news about your brother."

"No news about Seth?" she said, swallowing hard.

Then what he had said about Lexi sank in. She flew into his arms. "Oh, Lord, she is alive!" she cried. "My daughter is alive!"

Then her heart skipped a beat.

She eased from his arms. "What Stumpy Jackson said was true, after all," she murmured.

"What about Stumpy?" White Shield asked, raising an eyebrow.

In a rush of words Janice told him what had happened, and how she had thought that Stumpy was lying to her.

"And he said the child was white," Janice explained sighing. "I believed that what he'd said about Lexi was a lie. I suspected it was a trick to lure me into going with him. You see, he told me that I must go alone with him to the village."

White Shield kneaded his chin thoughtfully. "*Ah-hah*, it *might* have been a way to lure you away, but it is true that a child is with the Haida, whether or not he knew that she was Chinese," he said. "I have heard it from a reliable source and caution must be used in going to get the child. Although there is no more actual warring between the Haida and Skokomish, our two tribes remain wary of each other. The Haida brought death to our people often in the past. We, in turn, brought death to their villages."

"Then does that mean that I will have to go alone to their village to get Lexi?" Janice asked, gulping hard at the very thought of entering the Haida village without White Shield's protection.

"It is time to make peace with the Haida," White Shield said. "I have already sent an envoy ahead to the Haida village with the message that I wish to have council with Chief Blue Rain."

He softly gripped her hands. "I will leave as soon as I receive word that it is all right for me to go there, but it is best that you do not accompany me," he said. "I will be able to achieve my goal much more quickly if I go alone."

"But it will be better for Lexi if she sees me," Janice murmured. "You will be no more than just another stranger to her."

"When she hears me mention your name, and I let her know that you are waiting for her, she will know that it is not an enemy who speaks of such things to her," White Shield reassured. "Soft Sky, resume what you are doing today. Be patient a while longer. I will return soon with the child, and at least then half of your sorrow will be behind you. I hope we will soon receive word of your brother Seth. Then your entire heart will be mended. It will then be free to beat only for me, your future husband."

"Yes, yes," Janice said, again flinging herself into his arms and hugging him.

He held her for a moment longer; then, after she picked up her basket, they went hand in hand from the sandbar.

As they approached the children, Pretty Fawn rushed toward them with a basket filled to the brim with clams.

"Soft Sky! Soft Sky!" Pretty Fawn cried, beaming up at Janice. "These are for you. You do not have to dirty your hands or dress digging clams. I have done it for you."

Touched deeply by the child's kindness, Janice knelt and took the basket. She gazed at the huge pile of clams, then reached a gentle hand to Pretty Fawn's cheek. "There are so many and I have no coins with which to pay you," she murmured.

"These are gifts from Pretty Fawn," the child said, proudly glancing past Janice and into White Shield's eyes as he stood watching them.

"You are so sweet," Janice murmured. "I truly appreciate your kindness."

Pretty Fawn and White Shield exchanged smiles, then the child gave Janice a quick hug and ran to join the others.

"I do believe you have found yourself a friend," White Shield said as Janice rose to her feet and stood beside him.

"She is Lexi's age," Janice said, watching the child laughing with her friends. "Lexi is the one who will truly profit by this friendship. It will give me such joy to see those two young, beautiful girls develop a close friendship."

Janice gazed down at her empty wicker basket, then looked at Pretty Fawn again.

She walked away from White Shield and went to Pretty Fawn. "Please take my basket as payment," she murmured. "It is quite large. It should hold many more clams than the basket you are used to carrying."

"It is mine to keep?" Pretty Fawn asked, her eyes wide with excitement.

"Yes, yours to keep," Janice said, then glanced up at White Shield as he came and stood beside her.

"I will go now," he said, reaching a gentle hand to her cheek.

Janice nodded. She watched him board the canoe, and continued watching him as he departed on his venture of the heart.

"Our people are so proud to have White Shield as our sub-chief," Pretty Fawn said, drawing Janice's eyes down to her. "He will one day make a great *head* chief."

"*Ah-hah*, he is a very special man," Janice said, smiling as once again she gazed into the distance and could still see White Shield pulling his paddle rhythmically through the water.

"Where is he going?" Pretty Fawn asked, shielding her eyes with a hand as she peered into the distance to see White Shield.

"To get my little girl," Janice said, her voice breaking.

Pretty Fawn turned quickly and looked up at Janice. "Your . . . little . . . girl?" she asked, her eyes filled with wonder. "You have a little girl?"

Janice smiled down at Pretty Fawn, then picked up the end of the child's long brown braid. "Her name is Lexi. She is your age," she murmured. "And I love how your hair is worn so much, I am going to braid Lexi's hair in the same manner."

"I will have a new playmate?" Pretty Fawn asked excitedly.

"*Ah-hah*, you will have a new playmate," Janice murmured, then drew the child into her arms and hugged her. She only hoped that she wasn't being premature with her promises to this sweet child, for if by chance it wasn't Lexi at the Haida village, she did not want the chore of telling this lovely child that she would have no new friend after all, at least . . . not . . . yet.

She prayed to herself that she was wrong to doubt that Lexi would be returned to her today.

She must never allow doubts to win over hope!

Chapter Eighteen

Early morning's light,
Across the window panes
Dances with rhythm,
Like an endless kaleidoscope.
    —MARY ANN WHITAKER

Seth Edwards stirred in his sleep, then awakened with a start when he realized where he was, and why. After drifting in and out of consciousness since his arrival at the hospital in Vancouver, British Columbia, he had fully awakened a day ago.

Now he opened his eyes and looked slowly around him again, everything coming back to him like a splash of cold water in the face. In this room of white, where sheets smelled sterile and bleached, and where the white iron bed on which he lay stood next to a window where he could gaze out and see the blue of the sky, he could not hold back tears as he recalled the last time he had seen Janice. She had been fighting to stay above water after falling overboard into Puget Sound. Desperately clinging to Lexi, he had been dragged away from Janice by the current.

The last he saw of the child was when a monstrous wave crashed over them.

Since then, he had been living in a black void of unconsciousness.

But now that he was fully awake and could think things through, he came to the conclusion that both Janice and Lexi were surely dead.

Moaning, he closed his eyes and slowly tossed his head back and forth as he remembered everything that had been told to him after he had regained consciousness.

A doctor had come to him and told him that he had been alone when he had been found.

He had been rescued by a British steamer on its way to Vancouver. He was in the water, unconscious, floating, his body somehow tangled in the limbs of a log, which had kept him afloat, saving him from drowning.

He had been plucked out of the water that day by the steamer's captain and crew.

As the doctor explained things to him, Seth

had remembered where he had been at the time of the shipwreck.

Far into Puget Sound between Tacoma and Seattle.

To have floated so far from the Sound, and out to sea, where the British ship had found him, God had to have been with him that day, perhaps saving his life for some purpose. But he had lost so much in the accident, he almost resented being saved himself, no matter why.

"I must find Janice and Lexi," he whispered, determined to leave the bed and the hospital today. Too much time had been wasted as he slept beneath warm blankets. To think of Lexi and Janice out there somewhere, possibly cold, alone, and . . .

No! he cried to himself. He would *not* think about their being dead! They were alive!

And by God, he *would* find them.

Always a determined man who stopped at nothing to achieve his goals, especially goals that had to do with his family, Seth tried to move his legs.

Then he moaned throatily when he discovered, as he had upon his first awakening yesterday, that he no longer had control of his legs.

They were like two dead weights attached to his body.

Partially paralyzed since the accident, he was lifeless from his waist down.

When Seth heard footsteps enter the sun-splashed room, he opened his eyes again and looked quickly toward the door.

A tall, thin man dressed in white, stood there. His hair was cropped short above his collar line, and combed to perfection, his narrow, thin, freckle-speckled face and dark eyes friendly as he smiled down at Seth. Seth remembered him from yesterday. He was the doctor who had explained Seth's condition to him.

He had also had the task of telling Seth that as far as anyone knew, of the three members of his family, Seth had been the only one to survive.

He had given Seth some hope, at least about his legs. Dr. Adams had told Seth that it was between Seth and his Lord as to whether or not his legs would be useful again. From all they could tell, there was no true reason he couldn't walk. Apparently, the reason his legs weren't cooperating with him was not exactly physical, but instead, psychological.

The doctor had explained what he believed had happened. The moment Seth had realized that he might have lost his sister and niece in the tumultuous waters of the Sound, he had felt guilty for having survived himself, perhaps so guilty that he had willed his legs not to work as a way to punish himself.

"And, young man, how are you today?" Dr. Adams asked, picking up a stethoscope from the table beside the bed.

The doctor's reference to Seth being a young man, brought a smile to Seth's face, for the doctor was not even as old as Seth's age of thirty-five. He knew that the doctor could hardly be more than twenty-five. He realized that Dr. Adams had made this particular reference to lighten up their conversation. He had to know that Seth was worried to death about his loved ones.

"Has any word been received yet about Janice and Lexi?" Seth asked, his smile fading quickly.

"No, no word," Dr. Adams said, slipping the stethoscope around his long, thin neck.

Those words tearing Seth's heart to shreds, he swallowed hard and turned his eyes away from the doctor.

He flinched when the coldness of the stethoscope came in contact with the flesh of his chest as the doctor lifted the pajama top and placed the instrument there to carefully listen to one lung, and then the other.

Waiting until the doctor was finished, and the pajama top was covering his chest again, Seth turned slow eyes to the doctor again. "Were there *any* survivors of the wreck?" he asked thickly.

"I called Tacoma General Hospital and inquired for you," Dr. Adams said, sighing as he sat down on a stool beside the bed, his eyes locked with Seth's. "They checked the register of those who had been brought to the hospital. Neither your sister's name nor Lexi's were on that list. I tried to get Doc Rose to the phone, to talk to him personally, but seems he's being kept busy around the clock, taking care of the survivors."

"Then there *are* more survivors than myself," Seth said, relief flooding him to know that. And if there were so many, just perhaps not everyone's names had been registered.

He *had* to get to Tacoma!

He would never be convinced that his sister and sweet niece were dead until it was absolutely proven to him that they were!

He placed his hands under his legs and lifted them toward the side of the bed but groaned when he realized there was still no sensation whatsoever in them. He knew that it was useless to try to leave the bed.

"Rebecca," he whispered, somehow having pushed her into the deeper recesses of his mind while he was worrying about Lexi and Janice.

He gave the doctor a pleading look. "Can you bring me a telephone?" he asked softly.

"There are no phones at our hospital that can be taken from room to room," Dr. Adams said, rising from the stool.

"I need to call my wife," Seth explained. "I've got to reassure her that I'm all right."

"Give me your number," Dr. Adams said, pulling a tablet and pencil from the inside pocket of his white jacket. "I'll be glad to call them for you."

Seth reached a quick hand out for the doctor, desperately grabbing hold of the tail of his jacket. "Don't tell her that I can't walk," he begged, his eyes wild. "She's pregnant. I don't want to shock her into a miscarriage."

"I'll tell her that you're doing fine," Dr. Adams said, nodding. "I'll tell her that you just need some more rest and then you'll be home soon. Is that all right?"

"Yes, yes, that's good," Seth said, easing his hand away from the doctor. "Could you do it now, then return and tell me how she took the news?"

"I'll be glad to," Dr. Adams said, nodding. He turned on a heel and walked from the room.

Seth again tried to move his legs, only to fall back onto the bed in sweaty exhaustion.

He closed his eyes and rested for a moment, then again opened his eyes and watched the door for the doctor's return.

When Dr. Adams came back into the room, Seth noticed that he wasn't smiling. That caused all sorts of thoughts to swirl in his mind. Had his wife had a miscarriage already due to not knowing whether or not her husband had survived? Or . . . had she had the baby too early for it to survive?

"Well?" Seth said, pushing himself up on an elbow. "Did you talk to Rebecca?"

"No, there was no answer," Dr. Adams said, frowning. "In fact, Seth, the phone has been disconnected."

"What?" Seth said, his eyes widening. "What do you mean . . . disconnected?"

"The operator said that number is no longer

in service," Dr. Adams said. He held out a newspaper. "Maybe this is the reason?"

He pointed to the headlines as he gave the newspaper to Seth. "I got through to the hospital all right when I called them, but service to many telephones has been interrupted due to the sudden crisis in Tacoma," he explained.

A nurse rushed into the room, saying there was an emergency in another room. Dr. Adams hurried out after her, leaving Seth with a pounding, fearful heart as he read the headline over and over again.

A financial crash?

Suicides?

Businesses in Tacoma had closed down?

Seth was so stunned by the news, he felt as though his entire world had been taken from him.

First his sister and niece.

And now this?

To become poor overnight due to someone's mismanagement of funds and wild fluctuations in the stock market?

"Have . . . I . . . lost everything?" he cried, the newspaper fluttering toward the floor as Seth released it from his trembling hand. "My family? My legs? My . . . fortune?"

He closed his eyes and tried to fight back the picture of his pregnant wife and where she might be at this moment.

Destitute?

On the streets?

Or . . . had she sought shelter in that damnable

whorehouse because she had nowhere else to go?

"Mema," he whispered, sighing as a trace of hope came into his tear-filled eyes. "Surely Rebecca went to Mema's. Mema has grown to love her. She'll protect her until I can get home to her."

Finally able to think more clearly, Seth regretted not paying much attention to the whispers of bank failures in the Northwest while he was in San Francisco. But he had never thought that anything like this could happen to Tacoma. He had thought that Tacoma's economy was solid.

"How could this have happened?" he whispered, running his lean, long fingers through his reddish-brown hair in frustration. Tacoma had become the boomtown of the Northwest, even surpassing Seattle.

"Oh, Lord, what of my home?" he whispered, his heart sinking as he thought of his dream of opening an opera house, which was also gone now. Although he had had money in the bank, he had financed his home in order to be able to use his wealth in other places, especially investing in the stock market, where he planned to double his money in no time flat!

He had even transferred all of his funds from San Francisco's banks to Tacoma's!

Could it truly be that all he had left was his mansion on Nob Hill in San Francisco and the jewels, artifacts, and paintings he and Janice had left there?

A sudden thought came to him. Rebecca! He had always wondered about her love for him. Had she truly married him only for what his money could give her? Now that it was gone, had he also lost her?

He did not even try to fight off the blackness that engulfed him, grateful for any reprieve from reality. He fell into a dead faint.

Chapter Nineteen

Not so the ancients of these lands—
The Indian, when from life released,
Again is seated with his friends.
                              —Philip Freneau

White Shield beached his canoe in the shadow
of four tall totems that lined the shore. The
Haida had carved their village out of the forest
along Puget Sound far downriver from White
Shield's Skokomish island.

He stepped back from his canoe as many
heavily tattooed Haida warriors appeared out
of the shadows of the dense forest, their spears
grasped tightly in their hands.

White Shield didn't feel threatened by them.

The warrior that he had sent to this island to request council with Blue Rain had returned and said that permission had been given. He knew that the Haida warriors were only there as a silent warning to White Shield: Although he was allowed to enter their village, the Haida were still wary. The Haida and Skokomish had been enemies for so long, it was impossible to put their history behind them as though it had never happened. It was only normal that the Haida would be looking at White Shield with much suspicion in their deep-set gray eyes.

And White Shield looked at them with the same wariness. He had been orphaned at a very young age by the Haida.

But as White Shield had been told the full story of what had happened those many years ago, he had learned that his Skokomish people had achieved their vengeance. The Haida had paid a terrible price for the attack on the Skokomish village. Their own village had been attacked in return. Blue Rain, the young chief of this village, who was the same age as White Shield, had lost his own parents in this attack.

Since then there had been ambushes here and there between the two tribes. Even as recently as five years ago a council such as the one he planned with Blue Rain today would have been out of the question.

As it was, both White Shield and Blue Rain were trying to place their animosities behind them as best they could, or as much as could be expected of men who had lost their parents because of the feud.

White Shield looked past the warriors and saw Chief Blue Rain walking toward the waterfront, himself, to personally welcome White Shield to his village.

White Shield's warrior had taken word back to him from the Haida chief that Chief Blue Rain now wanted more than an uneasy peace between himself and White Shield. He wanted friendship; more could be accomplished among the Indian populace if all the tribes of this vast Northwest country worked together as one.

"Welcome, White Shield," Blue Rain said, stopping now to stand before White Shield, a blanket draped around his broad, muscled shoulders. White Shield's gaze went quickly over him. Besides the colorful blanket, the Haida chief wore only a breechcloth and moccasins, proudly showing off his body, which was heavily tattooed with various designs of forest animals and birds, the eagle being most prominent.

White Shield glanced up at the totems. The carvings on the totems matched the tattoos on Blue Rain's body. The eagle at the top of the totem, carved in the exact likeness of this majestic bird, seemed so alive, it looked as though it were only perched there and would soon take flight into the blue heavens above.

White Shield's gaze was brought back to Blue

Rain as the Haida chief stepped closer. "I received word from your messenger that you wish to have council with me," he said. "You are welcome to my village. It is good that you feel safe to beach your canoes on Haida land. I would hope that it is the beginning of an enduring, mutual trust. I hope that should I want to come to your island for council, I would feel safe to beach my canoe on land that belongs to you."

"*Ah-hah*, you would be welcome," White Shield said, although he was somewhat hesitant. His long brown hair fluttered in the gentle breeze. He also wore only a breechcloth and moccasins today.

But he wore no blanket around his shoulders. The autumn sun was too welcome to hide his body from it, for soon snows would be upon their land, and jackets would then be required.

"Come with me to my lodge," Blue Rain said, gesturing with a hand toward his large longhouse, which sat back from the other smaller ones.

Smoke spiraled from two chimneys, one on each end, and a young brave and girl stood just outside the door, their eyes intent on White Shield as he now approached them with Blue Rain.

White Shield knew them as the chief's children and he was glad when they showed no animosity toward him, but instead offered wide smiles of welcome.

"My son and daughter," Blue Rain said, going to stand between them, a hand resting on each of their shoulders.

A beautiful tattooed woman stepped from the lodge, a loose buckskin dress revealing that she was with child.

She stepped forth and offered a friendly handshake to White Shield.

"My wife, Morning Sunshine," Blue Rain said, smiling proudly at her as she stepped up to his side, her daughter quickly taking one of her hands, while the son took his father's.

"And your children's names are . . . ?" White Shield asked, trying not to show his envy of someone his own age having such beautiful children, and another one on the way.

In his mind's eye he envisioned himself as a father, with his own children, and in his mind's eye, he saw Janice standing at his side as his wife.

Strange how suddenly he saw the girl that would be born of their love—a child with white skin, in Janice's likeness, while the son would be in his.

He smiled to himself, for it would please him if it did happen that way. How could he ever resent a child whose skin was not of his own color if the child looked like her mother?

"Raven Feather is my daughter's name and my son goes by the name Three Eagles," Blue Rain said, proudly looking from his daughter to his son.

Then he nodded to his wife. "Take the children to play in the sand while I have council with White Shield?" he said, more in a questioning way than as a command; obviously he respected his wife.

"Come, children," Morning Sunshine said, taking both their hands as they ran, giggling, with her toward the Sound.

Seeing the children brought something else to White Shield's mind besides fantasies of having his own children.

His reason for being here on the land of the Haida: Janice's child.

Her Lexi.

White Shield looked slowly around him, from lodge to lodge, and saw no one but Blue Rain's people.

He sighed heavily and went on inside Blue Rain's lodge as the chief stepped aside and gestured toward the door of his longhouse.

White Shield felt strangely at ease as he sat down on a pallet of furs beside the fireplace, while Blue Rain sat down opposite him.

Although he wanted to get answers quickly to his questions about Lexi, he knew that he had to be patient.

Talk of Lexi would come in time.

But first the pipe must be shared between himself and Blue Rain. As far as White Shield knew, no peace pipes had ever been shared between Haida and Skokomish.

He was a little hesitant to do so, but Blue Rain was already holding before him a long-stemmed calumet pipe, and a tomahawk festooned with red and white feathers. He lit the pipe with a twig from the fireplace, and White Shield knew that to refuse it would be the worst of insults.

Perhaps today *was* the true beginning of an alliance between two enemy tribes.

He wondered if his grandfather would approve. He had not even told his grandfather that he was coming today to Haida country. He had been afraid that his grandfather would give him a command he could not obey.

The pleasant smell of the smoke from the pipe came to White Shield as Blue Rain ceremoniously drew from its stem. Raising it in the air, he then presented it to the four corners of the compass.

When Blue Rain handed White Shield the pipe, he took it and puffed on it, drawing the rich, pungent tobacco smoke into his mouth.

As White Shield slowly blew the smoke into the air, he returned the pipe to Blue Rain.

Blue Rain silently nodded, drew on the pipe once more himself, then laid it aside on the hearth of the fireplace.

Food was then brought into the lodge by an elderly woman. She set a wooden tray piled high with food on the floor close to Blue Rain.

She then left and returned shortly with two

smaller wooden platters, on which sat two cups. In her other hand was a jug filled with cool clam juice.

She stayed long enough to pour the clam juice into the cups, handing one each to White Shield and Blue Rain, then left.

"We will share food, drink, and then talk," Blue Rain said, handing a plate to White Shield.

He held the platter of food for White Shield. "Fish stuffed with seeds and pine nuts, then slowly roasted over a fire, is one of my people's favorites," he said. "That is why it is offered to you today, to please you as it pleases us."

"I have eaten it before," White Shield said. "The women of my village also prepare this for their families. My people find it one of their favorites, also."

White Shield saw Blue Rain's eyes light up and knew that what he had just said pleased him.

They ate and drank in silence, then pushed their empty dishes and cups aside.

"Now tell me what is in your heart," Blue Rain said, allowing the blanket to fall from his shoulders. "What is the true purpose of this special council?"

"I have come to inquire about a child," White Shield said, resting his hands on his knees where his bare legs were crossed comfortably before him. "This child belongs to a woman I rescued after a shipwreck in the waters of the Sound."

"I know of the shipwreck," Blue Rain said,

nodding. "Much debris floated to our shores. I sent warriors to see where it came from. They returned with the news of a capsized steamer."

"During that wreck many people were thrown into the water," White Shield said. "A woman was among the survivors. I found her unconscious along the shore. I took her to my home. When she awakened from her long sleep, she told me she had lost a brother named Seth and a daughter named Lexi. News came to my island that you have a child who was also rescued from the water. I have come to inquire about her. She is ten winters of age. She is Chinese."

"I do know of the child," Blue Rain said, nodding. "But she is no longer here. You said that this child's mother has a brother named Seth?"

"*Ah-hah,*" White Shield said, stunned to know that the child had been there, but that she was gone now. "Where *is* Lexi? You said that she is no longer here."

"A white man who goes by the name Seth came for the child," Blue Rain said matter-of-factly. "He said that he was her uncle. He took her away in a canoe."

"Seth was here?" White Shield said, his eyes wide. "He . . . took . . . Lexi? When?"

"He came during the night," Blue Rain said. "The child was still sleeping when he carried her to the canoe."

"By now then he should be in Tacoma," White Shield said, rising quickly to his feet. "He will have been reunited with his sister. I am anxious to see her happiness at being reunited with her brother and daughter."

"You seem to have feelings for the woman," Blue Rain said, now on his feet. He walked White Shield to the door.

White Shield wasn't ready to be *that* friendly with the Haida chief. He was not prepared to share his feelings with a man who only recently had been his enemy.

"I want to thank you for accepting my council today," White Shield said, reaching out to place a friendly hand on Blue Rain's bare shoulder.

"It should have happened long ago," Blue Rain said, placing his own hand on White Shield's shoulder.

"Peace is something earned," White Shield said solemnly. "I believe we have earned the right to share peace between us."

Blue Rain nodded, remaining outside the longhouse while Shield went back to his canoe.

As White Shield paddled his vessel away from the shore, he smiled at Blue Rain's wife. She gave him a gentle smile and a wave of good-bye.

He was touched by her friendliness. This, as well as the successful council, gave him hope that there could be a lasting peace between the Haida and the Skokomish, for women did have powers of persuasion where their husbands were concerned, even powerful chieftain husbands.

He drew his paddle more earnestly through the water when his thoughts returned to Janice and how happy she must be to have her loved ones with her again.

It made White Shield smile, for Janice's happiness was now his!

Chapter Twenty

Teasing, soft, silent
Winds of passion
I remember.
I miss you, my love,
I do remember.
—MARY ANN WHITAKER

Preparing the clams had not been as much of a challenge as Janice had thought it would be. She had never been given the opportunity to spend time in the kitchen in her mansion in San Francisco—having cooks to not only plan the meals, but also cook them—but Janice had watched Rebecca prepare the clams for cooking. Soon she had joined her, which helped ease the tension that had been brought on earlier by Janice's thoughtless question about the true father of her baby. She and Rebecca had even teased each other while preparing the meal.

Baked, the clams had been delicious and satisfying.

The women had stuffed themselves with so many, they had both retired to their respective beds for a nap.

Janice had not been able to fall asleep. She couldn't get White Shield off her mind and wondered what he might have found at the Haida village. *Was* the child Lexi? If so, would he be able to bring her home?

A shudder ran through Janice at the possibility that White Shield had not been welcomed at the Haida village. He had gone alone. He would not be able to defend himself against the whole band of Haida should they decide to take advantage of his vulnerability.

"But he must have thought it was safe enough," she whispered to herself, turning on her side to look out the window.

She forced herself to think of other things.

The sky.

Ah, yes, the sky.

It was a beautiful, serene blue, with only a few puffs of white clouds flitting across it.

And bird song was sweet in the forest.

She smiled when she heard a scampering on the roof just above her head and knew it was the patter of a squirrel's tiny feet.

Finally feeling drowsy, Janice fluffed a pillow beneath her head, but just as she closed her eyes, she opened them again abruptly. A sudden scream was coming from the room in which Rebecca was supposed to be resting.

When she heard Rebecca scream her name, panic filled her. She couldn't get off the bed quickly enough.

As her bare feet hit the oak flooring, she tossed the blanket aside and grabbed her dress from the foot of the bed.

Her fingers trembling, she yanked the buckskin dress over her head, then ran from the room, her heart pounding.

When she entered Rebecca's room, she stopped and stared, her lips parting when she saw the pool of water in which Rebecca lay.

In the water she saw a tinge of blood.

Janice's feet seemed glued to the floor, for she had never before been around anyone who was ready to have a baby.

And from the way Rebecca was clutching at her belly and sweating, her breaths coming in short pants, Janice knew that no matter when the child was supposed to arrive, there was no question that it had chosen today to make its grand entry into the world.

"My water broke," Rebecca cried, looking with panic-stricken eyes at Janice. "I'm afraid, Janice. Oh, Lord, Janice, I wish I'd never gotten pregnant. I . . . hurt . . . so badly! I'm . . . so . . . afraid!"

Seeing Rebecca's panic seemed to bring Janice to her senses. There was only the two of them. That meant that it was up to Janice to deliver the child. She did not have time to go for Doc Rose. She couldn't chance leaving Rebecca alone while she went for him.

And she only now remembered having left the horse and wagon at White Shield's friend's blacksmith shop. They had beached the canoe near enough to the cabin to walk.

"What am I supposed to do?" Janice asked as she went and knelt on the floor beside Rebecca.

She took Rebecca's hand and held it as she gave her a worried stare. "Tell me what to do," she said, her voice breaking. "Rebecca, what do you *want* me to do?"

Rebecca clutched Janice's hand more tightly while she closed her eyes and screamed as another sharp pain shot through her belly.

Janice's thoughts were scrambled. She tried to remember what people had told her about bringing children into the world.

Water.

Yes.

She needed to boil some water.

Then she needed to collect some white towels from the linen cabinet.

And scissors.

She had to have scissors to cut the umbilical cord.

"Please, oh, please help me," Rebecca cried. The pain was gone now, but she knew she would soon have another. "Janice, you don't have time to boil water. I feel the baby. It's almost here!"

Janice nodded. "Tell me what to do *now*," she said, already pulling the blankets down away from Rebecca, rolling them up and placing them at the foot of the bed.

"You won't have to do much," Rebecca said. "The baby is going to do it for you!"

Rebecca screamed again and bore down hard when the pains shot through her again. "Oh, Janice!" she cried, panic in her eyes. Janice was now busy shoving Rebecca's gown up past her waist. Her pulse was racing and she felt the heat of anxiety burning her cheeks as she watched Rebecca spread her legs widely apart, then grunt hard.

"It's . . . almost . . . there!" Rebecca cried through clenched teeth. "I feel it, Janice. Oh, Lord, catch it!"

Janice didn't have time to question Rebecca. The child's head was suddenly there, and as Rebecca bore down again and grunted hard, Janice reached down just in time to catch the baby as it slid completely out of Rebecca's body.

Janice was stunned speechless as she stared down at the baby.

She gasped when she saw that the baby's skin coloring was so blue. That didn't seem natural.

She looked with frightened eyes at Rebecca. "It's . . . not . . . breathing!" she cried. "Rebecca, the child's color is poor. What should I do?"

Rebecca moaned as she sat up, then held her

hands out for the child. Janice watched while Rebecca turned the baby upside down and gently slapped its bottom until it began to cry and turned a beautiful soft pink.

"He's so sweet," Rebecca said, a sob of joy lodging in the depths of her throat as she held him in her arms and gazed down at him. "A son. I've given my darling Seth a son."

Janice knelt down beside the bed and gave the baby a long, wondering gaze. "He is the exact image of his father," she said, tears filling her eyes. "And he's perfect in every way."

"Seth," Rebecca murmured. "In Seth's honor, I am naming our child after him. Seth Eugene, after my long-dead grandpa whose name was Eugene."

Janice knew at this moment that Rebecca's love for Seth was true and enduring. She would never doubt her loyalty to him again, or wonder if he was the child's true father.

"Cut the umbilical cord," Rebecca said, her eyes drifting closed. She trembled as she clung to the child. "Janice, there's another pain. It must be the afterbirth. I'm so weak. I . . . I . . . feel as though I might faint."

"No, please don't do that," Janice said, scurrying away to get a pair of scissors.

When she returned, she saw that the baby was lying beside Rebecca, and the placenta had been expelled. Rebecca seemed to have drifted into a deep sleep.

"Rebecca?" Janice said, placing a gentle hand

on Rebecca's cheek. "Can you hear me, Rebecca?"

When Rebecca didn't respond, and seemed to be in some sort of comatose state, Janice grew cold inside with fear.

She looked down at the child, whose eyes were open and seemed to be looking back at her. Then she gazed at Rebecca again.

"What am I to do now?" she whispered.

But knowing that the chore of cutting the umbilical cord still lay before her, she prayed that she was doing everything right when she snipped through it, then tied the end flush with the child's tummy.

When the baby started to sob and fuss, its tiny arms waving in the air, Janice laid the scissors aside and took him from the bed.

"Hello, there, little Seth Eugene," she whispered, a sob catching in her throat as she again glanced down at Rebecca. If she died . . .

No, she quickly corrected. "Rebecca can't die," she whispered.

She slowly rocked the child back and forth in her arms as she tried to decide what to do next. She needed to go for help, but she was afraid to leave Rebecca.

"Oh, White Shield, please hurry back," she whispered, carrying the baby into her bedroom and placing him on the bed.

She hurried into the kitchen and warmed some water over the wood-burning cook stove, then filled a basin with it and took it and a washcloth and towel back to her room.

As she cleansed the baby, she kept listening for Rebecca to cry out to her. But there was nary a sound.

And after she got the baby clean and wrapped in a soft blanket, she left him on her bed. Then she got fresh, clean water and went back to Rebecca.

As she bathed Rebecca and changed her bedding and clothes, Janice was growing more frightened by the minute. The longer Rebecca was unconscious, the greater the chances that she might not survive the birth of her precious child . . . her darling little Seth!

"She has to live," Janice whispered, now slipping a beautiful, lacy gown over Rebecca's head. "The poor thing has only recently found a decent life."

Sighing, she finished dressing Rebecca, drew a clean, soft blanket up beneath her armpits, then went to the window and stared into the dark depths of the forest. Never had Janice felt so helpless, nor so doubtful about the outcome of things.

Chapter Twenty-one

Misty shrouds,
Darkest night,
Driftwoods' whispered
Plight.
—MARY ANN WHITAKER

Seth was rolling and pitching in his bed. Sweat shone on his brow as he cried out in his sleep. In a dream he was seeing the likeness of his wife Rebecca. She was standing amid white clouds, reaching out for him. She was calling his name. And he heard a baby crying from somewhere in the distance.

Seth awakened with a start. A panic seizing him, he still saw Rebecca in his mind's eye. He could even hear her crying out his name. He could still hear a baby crying from some distant place, as though it was coming from a deep, dark tunnel.

"It must be an omen of some sort," Seth whispered, pale as he pushed himself up into a sitting position. "I must get to Tacoma! Rebecca needs me!"

Oh, surely she has had the child, he thought desperately to himself. Did something go wrong? Had she given birth? Had the child lived or died? Or were they both in Heaven now, trying to communicate with him?

He began shouting for a nurse.

When one arrived, he reached a desperate hand out for her.

"Help me get out of bed," he cried, his eyes wild. "I must return home. I am needed!"

"But, sir, you aren't strong enough," the nurse said. She rushed to his bedside and placed a gentle hand on his arm as he tried to shove the blankets away from him. "You know that you can't walk. Please settle down. You are only going to make things worse for yourself."

"Damn it, help me from this bed," Seth demanded, yanking his arm free of her grip. "I've got to get to Tacoma. My wife needs me. And my child . . ."

Wild-eyed, the nurse fled the room, then returned quickly with Dr. Adams.

Seth's eyes widened when he saw the doctor preparing a needle.

"I'm giving you a shot," Dr. Adams said, stepping to the bedside and reaching a hand out for Seth's arm. He flinched when Seth yanked it away. "Come on, Seth. You know you need to calm down. You are only going to wear yourself out by being so agitated."

"I don't need any damn shot, and to hell with being agitated," Seth exclaimed his face flushed with anxiety. "Doc, I need to get to Tacoma. I'm almost certain something has happened to my wife."

"Seth, you aren't a fortune teller," Dr. Adams said, again trying to grab Seth by an arm and failing.

He stepped away from Seth and slid the hand with the needle behind him, his jaw tight as he watched Seth glare at him.

"Doc, please give me my clothes," Seth said thickly. "I'm going home."

"Seth, you aren't going anywhere," Dr. Adams grumbled. "You can't even walk."

"Well, we'll see about that," Seth said, his teeth clenched.

In a nightshirt, and with sweat pouring from his brow, Seth threw back the covers and placed his hands solidly beneath each of his legs. He could still hear the despair in Rebecca's voice, and the baby crying.

"Seth, don't," Dr. Adams said. The nurse was nervously chewing on her lower lip beside him. "You've tried before. You know you can't."

"To hell with that," Seth growled. "That was

then. This is now. I'm not going to continue to let my damn legs stop me from going to my wife."

The room was perfectly quiet as Seth held his legs and swung them over the side of the bed.

He gritted his teeth and trembled as he placed his bare feet flat on the floor.

Then something mystical seemed to enfold him and hold him up as he stood steady beside the bed.

Tears of determination filled his eyes as he victoriously took that first step, and then another.

"Well, I'll be damned," Dr. Adams said, his eyes wide as he saw the miracle happening before his eyes.

"It's wonderful," the nurse breathed out. "He *can* walk."

"I don't know why you both are so surprised," Seth said, smiling from the doctor to the nurse. "You said that my problem was all psychological. Well, I've just proven you're right."

But soon realizing how weak he was from not being on his feet for several days, Seth reached out for the bed and eased himself back onto it slowly.

Breathing hard, he stretched out on his back and closed his eyes. "I guess I am too weak to do as I had planned," he said somberly.

He opened his eyes and gazed at the doctor. "But I will leave tomorrow," he said throatily. "Doc, can you get my clothes so that I can have them ready to wear early tomorrow? I vow to you that I won't do anything foolish like try to leave today."

"Get his clothes," Dr. Adams said looking at the nurse as he gave her the order. He laid the needle down on a table, went to Seth and checked his pulse, then smiled down at him. "Although you think you can leave tomorrow, you might decide that you need a few more days. Whatever you wish, Seth, I'll go along with it. I know how anxious you are to get back to your wife."

"Also my baby," Seth said, looking past the doctor as the nurse brought his clothes into the room and laid them on the bed beside him.

"You think your wife has had the baby?" Dr. Adams asked as he clasped his hands together behind him.

"Something tells me that she has," Seth said, nodding.

He gazed at his black wool suit, grimacing when he saw the water damage.

Not only had the wool fabric shrunk, but it was also ripped and torn.

"I can get you something else to wear, if you wish," Dr. Adams said after watching Seth's hands going over his ruined suit.

"I'd appreciate it," Seth mumbled. "But first, let me empty my pockets of my belongings."

As he sat up and spread the suit jacket across his lap, his fingers slid into the inside pocket.

His jaw dropped when he discovered that nothing was there.

Where was the huge wad of bills that he had fastened together in a tight ball before he left San Francisco?

He looked desperately up at the doctor.

"It's gone," he gasped out. "My money. It's gone."

Dr. Adams smiled and placed a gentle hand on Seth's shoulder. "You need not get so excited," he said softly. "I personally placed your money in a safe. I'll go now and get it."

Relieved to know that his money had not floated out of his pocket, Seth sighed. This money, along with his home in San Francisco, were all that remained of his wealth.

Only yesterday he had inquired about the name of the one bank in Tacoma that was still in business.

When he had been told the name, his heart sank. He had decided while he was in San Francisco that he was going to do business with the First International Bank when he returned to Tacoma. Accordingly, he had transferred his money there, with only his loans left now at the other bank, which he had not been satisfied with.

He had planned to pay off his loans and cut off all dealings with that bank.

It was ironic that this was the very bank that had survived the crash, whereas the other one, which he had had more faith in, had not.

When the doctor returned and handed Seth the rolled wad of bills, Seth took it and stared at it. Was this all that was left? Was he truly going to be forced to begin all over again?

Sighing, he slid back down onto the bed. Clutching the money to his chest he closed his eyes.

"We'll leave you now," Dr. Adams said thickly. "I'll be here tomorrow, early, to check you out of the hospital. But if you change your mind, I'll wait and do that another day."

"I'm leaving," Seth said, opening his eyes to give the doctor a determined stare. "I've lost too much already. I can't wait to see if Rebecca is all right." He swallowed hard. "And my baby . . . I have to see if my baby has been born."

Dr. Adams patted him on the shoulder, then walked out of the room with the nurse.

Seth closed his eyes. If he thought hard enough, he could envision himself in Tacoma with his wife, his child in Rebecca's arms, suckling from her breast.

"Yes, things are going to be just fine," he whispered, trying to encourage himself not to lose hope. At least, not yet. Where there was hope, there was a way, his father had always told him.

"I pray that is so," he whispered. Yet he felt strangely empty and alone.

Chapter Twenty-two

Dance moonbeams on the water,
Dance moonbeams, chase
evil spirits away.
                    —MARY ANN WHITAKER

Her eyes troubled, Janice gazed down at
Rebecca. Although she was still in some sort of
deep sleep, her breathing was regular, her pulse
was normal, and her color was good. Janice
surmised that Rebecca wasn't unconscious
because of some health problem. She hadn't
even lost that much blood during childbirth.
She seemed more exhausted than anything else.

Wanting a breath of fresh air while the baby

was still sleeping, Janice took one last look at
Rebecca, then turned and went outside and sat
down on the porch swing.

As she swung slowly back and forth, she
watched the path that led to the cabin. It
seemed an eternity since White Shield had left
to go to the Haida village to inquire about Lexi.

"Why haven't you returned?" she whispered,
reaching up to smooth sweat-dampened locks
of hair back from her face.

She gazed down at herself. Still somewhat
shaken from helping Rebecca during the delivery, she saw now what a mess she was in. There
were spots of blood on the skirt of her dress; her
entire body was still damp from nervous perspi-
ration; and she still had nothing on her feet.

"Lordy, lordy, I hope I don't have to go
through that again," she said, laughing softly to
herself.

There was one exception, of course. She
could hardly wait for one delivery in particular.
When she would give birth to White Shield's
first child. After all of this confusion, after her
brother and Lexi were with her again, she
hoped to be able to go with a free mind and
wondrous heart to White Shield. Living with
him as his wife would be like living a fantasy
come true.

She smiled. Yes, it would be wonderful to
wake up in his arms each morning and make
love each evening when they went to bed, but

she knew that it would not all be a bed of roses. The life of an Indian had to be hard, for the Shokomish had to not only provide their own food, but also make their own clothes.

And their homes, such as White Shield's long-house, had none of the comforts that she was accustomed to. In her mansion she never wanted for a thing and did not have chores beyond giving herself her own bath.

Otherwise, everything had been done for her by maids, servants, butlers, and cooks.

"Can I truly live so differently?" she whispered, not wanting to doubt that she could. She could do anything if it meant that she would be with the man she loved.

She stayed near the open door in case Rebecca awakened and cried out to her, or the tiny newborn began crying. She prayed to herself that Rebecca would be awake by the time the baby's tummy began aching from hunger.

Otherwise, how could Janice see that his hunger was fed?

She knew that Rebecca had milk-filled breasts.

But Janice didn't want to think of having to find a way to place the baby to the breast while Rebecca was still in her deep sleep!

Sighing heavily, Janice looked up at the sky and saw that the sun was now descending toward the horizon. It seemed that suddenly it was sinking faster in the sky. She did not want to think about spending another night without knowing Seth's whereabouts, or Lexi's.

"Please, oh, please, God, let White Shield find Lexi," she prayed as she peered into the blue heavens. "Let her be in my arms soon!"

She turned quickly when she heard a noise at her right side.

Her mouth went dry when she saw White Shield riding toward her in her wagon, the old mare pulling it slowly along. She gasped as she realized that Lexi wasn't with him.

She was filled with a despair that made her whole insides ache. Her hopes had just been shattered; her heart seemed to have broken into a million pieces.

She slid from the swing and waited for White Shield to approach.

When he left the wagon, she fell into his arms, clinging, sobbing.

"There is no need to cry," White Shield said, gently placing his hands on her arms and holding her away from him. "Just because you do not see the child with me does not mean that you will not be seeing her *soon*."

Janice scarcely breathed. "What do you mean?" she asked, searching his eyes.

When he looked past her, and appeared to be peering questioningly toward the door, Janice was puzzled. Who was he looking for?

"I would have thought Seth would have been here before me," White Shield said dryly. "He was at the Haida village. He took Lexi. It puzzles me that they aren't here now."

Janice's eyes widened. Her heart began to race. "Seth? Seth was there?" she cried, filled with wondrous joy that her brother was alive and well. "And . . . he . . . came for Lexi? She was truly there? She was all right, also?"

She broke free of his gentle grasp and grabbed hold of one of his arms. "Did you see them?" she asked excitedly. "Did you? Did you see with your own eyes that they are all right?"

When she saw a sudden look of apprehension enter White Shield's eyes, Janice grew fearful again. His ensuing silence truly alarmed her.

"You *did* see them, didn't you?" she repeated.

"No, I saw neither of them," White Shield said. "But I was told by Chief Blue Rain that Seth had been there. He took Lexi. I truly believed they would be here by now."

"I haven't seen anyone except for . . ." Janice stopped short before speaking Rebecca's name, for it was at this instant she remembered that White Shield didn't know about the baby.

And she realized where Seth must have gone. Certainly he wouldn't come immediately to the cabin. He would expect Janice to be at his mansion with Rebecca. He would go there first, and when he realized that the mansion no longer belonged to him, he would then assume that Rebecca and Janice had gone to Mema's cabin.

Surely Seth would come soon, and Lexi would be reunited with her mother!

"Come inside," Janice said, taking White Shield by the hand and half dragging him through the open door. "I have something to show you."

She first took White Shield to her room and watched his expression as he gazed down at the baby.

When she saw his eyes light up, and the way he gently scooped the tiny bundle up into his arms, she knew just how good a father he would be.

"Janice . . . ?"

Rebecca's voice calling Janice's name caused a surge of relief to rush through Janice.

Finally!

Rebecca had awakened!

Not waiting to explain everything to White Shield, Janice hurried from the room and went to Rebecca's bed.

"How are you feeling?" she asked, so glad when she saw Rebecca's lips quiver into a soft smile.

"Heavenly," she murmured as she reached down and ran a hand over her belly, smiling even more broadly when she discovered just how flat it was. "I *did* have the baby, didn't I? It wasn't just a dream."

"You had a *son*," Janice murmured, reaching for Rebecca's hand and holding it. "Little Seth. Little Seth Eugene."

"Ah, yes, now I remember naming him," Rebecca said, sighing contentedly. She looked past Janice, toward the door. "Is he asleep?"

"No, he isn't asleep," White Shield said as he entered the room carrying the baby, a corner of the blanket folded open to reveal the tiny child's sweet face. "He is very much awake."

"And so there is my baby," Rebecca said, smiling. "White Shield, will you bring him to me?"

White Shield took the baby and gently laid him in her arms.

"Surely he is hungry," Rebecca said, gazing with wondrous pride down at her baby's tiny, pink face.

"We can take a hint," Janice said, taking White Shield by the hand. "We'll leave so you can feed him."

After they left the room and went and stood at the front door, peering down the long path, White Shield turned her to face him. "You did not tell her about her husband," he said thickly.

"I know," Janice said, swallowing hard. "I don't want to get her hopes up. At least not until we know for certain that Seth is safe and sound, and here in person as proof."

She moved into White Shield's arms as he held them out for her. "For now, the baby will bring a gentle peace into Rebecca's heart," White Shield said thickly, slowly stroking a hand up and down Janice's back.

"I doubt that she will truly feel such peace until Seth arrives and she knows that he is all right," Janice said.

She stepped away from White Shield and looked toward the empty path again. She clasped her hands behind her. Still there was no sign of anyone arriving.

She glanced up at the sky. There was a rosy hue now spreading along the horizon like a woman's blush as the sun sank slowly out of sight.

"I'm truly worried," she said, turning quickly to look up into White Shield's eyes. "They should have been here by now."

White Shield stepped up next to her. His eyes narrowed as he, too, gazed down the empty path and saw only vague, muted shadows.

"Surely when he found his house deserted this would be the next place he would go," Janice said, sighing heavily.

She turned on a quick heel. "Rebecca seems to be all right now," she blurted out. "Will you go with me to Tacoma?"

White Shield saw the anxiousness in Janice's eyes and heard it in her voice. He, too, felt the same anxiety, for he could not understand what was delaying Seth. He nodded.

"I'll go tell Rebecca," Janice said, hurrying inside.

She stopped as her eyes caught the shine of the glass in the gun case as the fire's glow illuminated it.

Then she turned and saw the rifle that was

still resting against the wall just inside the door. She grabbed the rifle, then went to Rebecca's room.

When Rebecca saw Janice holding the rifle out to her, she groaned.

"No, please don't tell me that you are going to leave me alone," she said, her voice breaking. "Why would you?"

Janice rested the rifle against the bed, then sat down beside Rebecca.

She melted inside when she saw how contentedly the baby was suckling milk from Rebecca's breast, his tiny fingers kneading the soft, pink flesh.

"He is so adorable," she said softly, but when she felt Rebecca's eyes on her, silently questioning her, Janice knew that she must explain.

"I'm almost certain that Seth is alive and well," she blurted out, smiling when she saw the joy that news brought to Rebecca's eyes. "White Shield was told that he was at the Haida village. He went there to get Lexi. He must have gone to Tacoma next, to your mansion. But perhaps after seeing that he lost his home to the creditors, he might not be thinking clearly enough to know that he would find us here at Mema's cabin."

"He doesn't even know yet about Hannah's death," Rebecca said, her voice breaking.

"Yes, he has much to accept now, and perhaps he is uncertain what to do next," Janice said. She rose from the bed. "White Shield and I are going into Tacoma. We'll find Seth. He'll be here soon, Rebecca. His unhappiness over his losses will be not so overwhelming when he sees that he has gained something even more valuable . . . a son."

"I hate to be left alone, though," Rebecca said.

"I don't think that I should travel through the forest alone since darkness is upon us," Janice murmured. "White Shield is going to go with me." She nodded toward the rifle. "Use it, Rebecca, should anyone come in and threaten you and the child."

"I don't even know how to fire it," Rebecca softly confessed.

"Do you want to know something?" Janice said, laughing softly. "I don't either."

Rebecca's eyes widened. "You . . . don't . . . know how to use a rifle, yet you . . ." she stammered.

"No, not one tiny bit," Janice said, then laughed. "But if I was ever threatened by the likes of Stumpy Jackson again, I'd sure learn fast how to shoot that damn rifle."

Rebecca giggled. "Me too," she murmured. She nodded toward the door. "Go on, Janice. Me and little Seth Eugene will be all right."

"Are you sure?"

"Just go and find my Seth."

Janice bent over and placed a soft kiss on Rebecca's brow, took the time to light the wicks on the lamps throughout the house to make it look fully occupied, then rushed from the cabin and boarded the wagon with White Shield.

The mare lurched forward when White Shield gave it a slap with the reins. A loon sent its lonely, eerie call through the darkening forest. Janice gave the cabin one last look. She was trying to believe that everything would be all right, and that she would soon be in her brother's arms!

But a part of her doubted that was possible. If he was all right, he would have found a way to get to his wife before now.

Also, he knew just how anxious Janice was to be reunited with her child.

No, things didn't look all that promising. She would just have to wait and see.

But, Lord, she was sorely tired of waiting. Of hoping in vain.

Chapter Twenty-three

To know his love,
On thick, soft furs,
Ah, passionate ecstasy.
—MARY ANN WHITAKER

Feeling utterly confused after arriving at Seth's house and discovering that he wasn't there, Janice sat forlornly in the wagon, staring at the empty house.

"I just don't understand," she said, giving White Shield a wistful look. "If he went and got Lexi, surely we'd have seen him by now. Yet he's not here, nor did we pass him on the path that leads to and from the cabin."

"Perhaps he did not think to check your

grandmother's cabin when he found the house locked up," White Shield said, slapping the reins, so the mare moved away from the mansion. "Or perhaps he is so distraught over finding the house no longer in his possession, he is trying to find someone to question about it."

"I truly believe that he would be more concerned about Rebecca than his house," Janice said, sighing heavily. "And he would know how anxious I am to see that he and Lexi are all right. He would do everything in his power to find me."

"Or he might need rest before going farther with his search," White Shield said, giving Janice a quick look. "He must have been injured somehow to have been missing all this time. Surely he has been somewhere recuperating and only today felt well enough to travel."

"If that is the way it is, he *would* need a place to rest," Janice said, again feeling hopeful of finding Seth. She glanced at the one hotel that was still open for business as they moved past it. It was the Hotel Blackwell, the finest hostelry on Puget Sound.

She grabbed his arm. "Stop," she said quickly. "Maybe Seth is at the hotel."

White Shield drew the horse and wagon to a quick halt, then watched Janice as she climbed from the seat and ran inside.

Doubts were beginning to form in his mind. Had the Haida lied? But surely not. Chief Blue Rain had known not only Lexi's name, but also Seth's.

There had to be truth in their tale of an uncle coming for his niece. There was no way they could make it up. And why would they? No, none of it made any sense.

He looked slowly around him, up and down the streets, and then gazed at the long row of tents where people were milling about.

Now and then he heard an outburst of crying, but for the most part, everything was calm.

There were fewer tents than before, which meant that there were fewer injured people.

He looked up at the hospital and caught sight of Doc Rose as he lumbered down the steep steps.

White Shield was tempted to go to him and ask him if, by chance, Seth had shown up there.

His thoughts were interrupted when he saw Janice walk slowly from the hotel.

By the way her head hung, and her dispirited walk, he knew that she had found no answers at the hotel.

Seth and Lexi's whereabouts were a total mystery.

It was as though they had materialized only long enough to get Janice's hopes up, and then disappeared into thin air.

"White Shield, they aren't there, nor have they been," Janice said, swallowing hard.

When he reached a hand out to help her into the wagon, she gladly accepted. Suddenly she felt so empty and tired . . . so drained and broken-hearted. She wasn't sure if she had the courage or strength to continue.

She sat down on the seat and stared at the hotel. "It just makes no sense," she murmured. She then gazed at White Shield. "None of it. The Haida's story about Seth and Lexi . . . surely it was false." She choked back a sob. "But, why? Why would they play with my heart like this?"

A quick anger filled White Shield. "I will take you home and then I will return to the Haida village and demand answers," he said, his voice tight.

He slapped the reins and made a wide turn in the street so they could go back to the cabin.

"I will return you home so that you can be with Rebecca," he said. "Then I will go to have council with Chief Blue Rain again."

His eyes narrowed. "But this time I will not go alone," he said solemnly. "I will take many warriors with me in many canoes. The Haida will know that I am there for serious business, the business of proving that no Haida chief makes a fool of a Skokomish sub-chief."

Panic rushed through Janice.

She grabbed White Shield by the arm.

"No," she said, her voice anxious. "Please don't do that. I don't want to be the cause of warfare between two rival tribes. We must give Seth more time. Surely he will come home soon."

"If that is what you want, that is the way it

will be," White Shield said. He slapped the reins and sent the mare down the narrow lane that led to the cabin.

Janice became quiet as her troubled thoughts battled within her mind.

She was so weary, so bone-tired, her exhaustion brought on by the loss of hope.

She had been so happy when she'd heard that Seth had gone for Lexi.

And now to think that it had never happened . . . that he might not even be alive . . . She was so filled with grief, she could hardly stand it.

When she saw the cabin a short distance away, she grabbed hold of the seat and leaned forward, her eyes scanning the yard for signs of a wagon or horse.

"We are at your cabin and there are no signs of Seth having been here," White Shield said. He drew a tight rein and brought the horse and wagon to a halt before the steps of the cabin.

"Yes, I have already noticed that," Janice said, sniffing back tears of disappointment.

She forced a smile as she gazed over at White Shield. "I am so anxious to see little Seth again," she said, trying to find some hope in her heart by thinking of the sweet, darling bundle of joy. "Come on, White Shield. Let's see if he's grown any."

White Shield laughed, for he knew that Janice was trying to lighten her sorrow by being facetious.

"Ah-hah, I am certain he has outgrown his blankets," he teased back.

Before Janice could step from the wagon, he reached over and slid his arms around her waist. He drew her next to him.

He eased his arms from around her and framed her face between his hands as he brought her eyes up to meet his. "My sweet Soft Sky, there is still so much to smile about," he said thickly. "There is the newborn child. There is our newborn love. I will help you get past your disappointment if you will let me. After Rebecca and the child are sleeping comfortably, come to bed with me. I will take your mind where there is only happiness and pleasure."

"I would like that so much," Janice said, tears filling her eyes.

She felt wonderfully warm inside when he brought her lips to his and gave her a long, deep kiss. She knew that only he had the power to erase the sadness from her heart.

She twined her arms around his neck and returned the kiss, then laughed softly when he swept her fully into his arms and managed to get down from the wagon, holding her close to his heart.

White Shield gave her another kiss, then released her and walked beside her up the steps and into the cabin.

Everything was quiet and serene. There were

271

no signs of anyone having been there besides the child and his mother.

And Janice accepted that. She had even accepted that she might never see Seth again.

She tried to forget the way the Haida had played games with her mind, as well as White Shield's. All she could imagine was that the Haida had somehow heard of White Shield's involvement with her. They had searched further and discovered her anxieties about her brother and daughter. They had schemed and had used their knowledge to draw White Shield to their village for a mock council.

If that was how it truly was, Janice knew that White Shield would not wait long before he took revenge.

She hoped a war would not erupt between them, for something told Janice that was exactly why the Haida chief had played such a game with White Shield.

"I will place wood on the lodge fire while you go and check on Rebecca and the child's welfare," White Shield said.

He went to the fireplace and knelt down before it on one knee. As he placed a large log on the grate, Janice went to Rebecca's room.

When she found both Rebecca and her son contentedly asleep, the baby nestled in his mother's arms, she smiled and stepped slowly out of the room again, quietly closing the door.

Just as she did that, arms swept around her waist.

She trembled with pleasure as White Shield turned her to face him.

"They are asleep," she whispered, her pulse racing. He was already sliding her dress up past her waist.

He yanked it completely off her, but she grabbed it before he could drop it to the floor.

"I must have it ready should Rebecca call for me," she whispered.

She sucked in a wild breath of rapture when White Shield leaned down and swept his tongue over one of her taut-tipped nipples.

"Oh, what you do to me," Janice whispered, closing her eyes as a sensual thrill rode her spine.

Feeling as though she were floating, she twined her arms around his neck as he swept her up into his arms and carried her to her room.

With a foot he closed the door, then carried her on to the bed and gently laid her atop it.

As she watched, her eyes taking in every inch of his muscled body, he disrobed.

And now nude, he crept onto the bed and lay beside her, his hands and tongue moving over her body, arousing her to the point that she wanted to cry out with pleasure.

But reminding herself that she was not alone with White Shield, she bit her tongue and closed her eyes and allowed the pleasure to sweep over her without making a sound.

For the moment the world and its problems were forgotten.

She needed this, or else she might explode from her anguish at losing Lexi and Seth.

"I do love you so," she whispered, trembling beneath his caresses. His lips and tongue were now on her breast, flicking, licking, sucking.

Soaring with rapture, she ran a hand down his body in a slow caress, then rediscovered that awesome part of him that could give her such wondrous pleasure.

As she wrapped her fingers around his thick shaft, she felt its heat against her flesh. She felt it throb as she began moving her hand on him.

She gazed at White Shield as he threw his head back, his eyes closed in mindless ecstasy.

Almost to the point of bursting, White Shield reached down and moved her hand away from him.

Then he took her mouth by storm with a deep, long kiss. His hands molded her breasts, her response turning him wild and weak as she pressed her body against his in a silent invitation to fill her with his heat.

He swept his hands beneath her and his fingers pressed urgently into her flesh. As he moved over her, he lifted her toward him.

In one shove he was inside her, her legs parting to enable him to thrust more deeply.

He gathered her into his arms. With a savage fierceness he held her close. He kissed the softness of her neck, his sexual excitement building with each of his thrusts inside her warm tunnel of love.

His mouth sought hers and covered hers with a kiss frenzied and wild.

With a moan of bliss, she gave him back his kiss, clinging, floating, and then sucked in a wild breath of wonder when he yanked himself free of her and with his hands guided her into a position that seemed strange, even frightening to her.

Yet trusting him, she did as he bid her.

As she knelt on her knees, he positioned himself behind her, and again thrust himself into her warm, wet place. She closed her eyes and let him ride her, his hands now reaching around to caress her breasts.

As the pleasure mounted, each thrust inside her like a burning flame of desire being awakened anew, Janice was lost in ecstasy.

With quicker, even more eager thrusts, White Shield clung to her, his passion mounting, cresting, and then exploding.

He placed his hands at her waist as he drove into her in deep, full thrusts, smiling when she moaned and pushed back against him in the throes of her own ecstasy.

And when they both floated down from the clouds of bliss and were lying side by side, their bodies still throbbing from the aftermath of pleasure, White Shield cupped her chin in his hand. Their eyes met and held.

"Soft Sky, I want to be your protector, forever," he said thickly. "We have spoken of marriage between us. It should be *soon.*"

"Oh, how I want to be your wife," Janice mur-mured, sighing contentedly. "I want nothing more than to marry you, but don't you see? Now is not the time. I can't even consider get-ting married until . . . until . . . I know that Seth and Lexi are all right."

"But now is when you need the happiness of marriage in your life," White Shield softly argued.

"White Shield, I know what you are saying, and I understand," Janice murmured. "But please understand how I feel. This just isn't the time for us to get married. I want my wedding day to be a happy, carefree day, not overshad-owed by concern over my brother and daughter. Only after I know that Seth and Lexi are all right can I be truly happy again."

He drew her into his arms and held her. He didn't say what he was thinking . . . that in time she might have to accept that she might *never* be reunited with Lexi and Seth. Would she wait for-ever and never give herself a chance at happiness?

If she didn't marry him, he would have to move on in his life without her. He wanted a wife. He wanted children. And he wanted them before his grandfather passed on to the other side! But despite all that, he believed his life would be empty without her.

Janice felt something different about the way White Shield was holding her now. It didn't seem as tender, as true.

Panic seized her at the realization that what she had said was causing him to distance himself from her.

Yet . . . what she had said was true. She could not go on with the rest of her life until she found Seth and Lexi! If that meant losing White Shield, oh, Lord, she just didn't know. . . .

As White Shield left the bed and dressed, Janice watched him.

When he turned to her, his breechcloth in place, his moccasins on his feet, she saw a look in his eyes she had never seen before. A shiver ran across her flesh.

"I will go now," he said, sounding sad. "My heart is with you. Know that."

She nodded; then tears filled her eyes when he left, and everything seemed so strangely quiet.

"What have I done?" she whispered, placing a hand over her mouth, for she sensed that she had just caused their relationship to take a different direction. Even though he had said that his heart was with her, was . . . it . . . truly? She felt, instead, that he had turned away from her!

She pulled a blanket over her and then turned onto her stomach and cried and beat at the mattress with her fists.

Chapter Twenty-four

This is the secret of despair,
Long in its cloudy bosom hoarded,
Now whispered and revealed,
To wood and field.
—HENRY WADSWORTH LONGFELLOW

Janice awakened with a start. She had heard something.

She slowly sat up on the bed and listened again as she peered toward the door.

Yes, she thought, her throat growing dry at the sound.

A horse and buggy!

She was hearing the approach of a horse and buggy outside the cabin!

She glanced quickly toward the clock that sat on a table against the far wall, its hands visible to her in the moonlight.

"Midnight," she whispered, hurrying out of bed and pulling on a robe. "Who could be arriving at such a late hour in a horse and buggy?"

She sorted through the people she knew here.

It wouldn't be White Shield. When he had left, he had left on foot. He would come again in the same way. And knowing that it would frighten Janice, White Shield would not come at such an ungodly hour.

Stumpy Jackson? she wondered as she tied the belt of the robe around her waist. No, he wouldn't come in such a way, making such a racket. He was the sort who would sneak up on the cabin, his reason for being there anything but good.

"Then, who . . . ?" Janice whispered, sliding her feet into soft slippers.

Just as she left the room, she heard Rebecca calling her name.

"Janice, who's out there?" Rebecca asked as Janice opened Rebecca's bedroom door and peered inside.

"I don't know, but I'm going to find out," Janice whispered, hoping that all of the commotion wasn't going to awaken the baby. He had just gotten to sleep a while ago after crying for almost two solid hours. It seemed that he was having as much trouble adjusting to his new life as Rebecca, because Rebecca had become tearfully upset over the child's crying.

Janice reached inside the room where she had left the rifle resting against the wall when she had left to go into Tacoma with White Shield. She grabbed it and rushed away from the bedroom.

Her pulse raced as she went to a front window and gazed outside. Her heart lurched when she saw the horse and buggy, but whoever had arrived in it must be already on the porch, ready to knock. . . .

She jumped with fright when someone *did* knock on the front door.

Her heart pounding, Janice turned and stared at the closed door. She saw the doorknob being tried. She was thanking her lucky stars that she had a good bolt lock on the door and that it was in place. No matter how much someone tried to turn the doorknob back and forth, he would not be able to enter the cabin.

When she heard her name being spoken through the closed door and recognized the voice, she dropped the rifle to the floor with a crash. Tears of joy filled her eyes as she yanked the bolt free.

Sobbing, she jerked the door open and fell into her brother's arms.

"Oh, Seth!" she cried, clinging to him. "Oh, Lord, Seth, I've been so worried . . . so afraid for you."

"I know," Seth said, caressing her back. "I just couldn't get here before now."

"Seth, so much has happened," Janice said, hating to have to step away from him. His arms felt so wonderful as he held her. The fact that Seth was there meant that the Haida had been telling the truth. That also meant that Lexi was safe, and White Shield would not have to go to war with the Haida.

"I found my house locked up, so I knew the next place to look for you and Rebecca was here," Seth said, anxiously looking past Janice as he stared into the cabin. "Is she here, Janice? Is Rebecca here?"

"Yes, she's here," Janice said, wiping tears from her eyes with the backs of her hands as she turned and gazed into the cabin, smiling as Rebecca lit a lamp and appeared.

"My darling!" Seth cried as he forced his weak legs to take him into the house. He grabbed Rebecca and clung to her.

"My dearest darling," he said, holding Rebecca, his eyes feasting on her beautiful, loving face. "I'm sorry if I've frightened you."

Then he stepped away from her and gazed with wide eyes at her belly. "Your . . . belly," he gasped. "It's . . . it's . . . flat."

"Yes, Seth, it's flat," Rebecca said, giggling with euphoria at his return.

But Rebecca stopped giggling when she saw her sister-in-law go pale as she stared hard at the buggy and realized no one was there. Janice hurried to Seth and grabbed him by an arm.

Cassie Edwards

"Where is Lexi?" she said in a rush of words. She swallowed hard. "Seth, she is supposed to be with you. Chief Blue Rain said that you went to his camp and got her."

"Who is Chief Blue Rain?" Seth asked, scratching his brow.

"You don't know him?" Janice gasped out.

"I don't know what you're trying to say," Seth said, not even aware that Rebecca had left the room. He was totally absorbed in the realization that something was very wrong here . . . that Lexi wasn't with Janice . . . that no one knew where Lexi was!

"He *did* lie!" Janice cried, covering a gasp of horror with her hands. "Oh, lord, the Haida chief lied."

And then she went even more pale and her knees almost buckled beneath her when she thought of Stumpy Jackson and his possible role in this confusion over Lexi's whereabouts. Just perhaps the Haida chief *hadn't* lied. Stumpy Jackson could have gone for the child and used Seth's name falsely to get the child in his possession. The thought made her feel sick to her stomach.

Seth grabbed Janice by the arms and gave her a slight shake. "Get control of yourself and explain what's happening here," he said, his voice tense.

Janice blurted it all out, and then Seth quickly explained what had happened to him,

282

where he had been, and his close call with being paralyzed.

"But I haven't seen Lexi since . . . since everything went black in the water," he said, swallowing hard. "I blacked out. I don't know what happened to Lexi then."

He lowered his eyes and ran his fingers through his hair as a sob caught in his throat. "I thought she was with you," he said thickly. "All along I thought that somehow you had managed to find her. Damn it, all this time I thought she was with you . . . and . . . she wasn't."

"I had hoped she would be with *you*, but we were both wrong," Janice said. She brushed past him and hurried toward her bedroom. "I've got to change clothes and go to White Shield. He can help me. He'll go with me to the Haida village."

"Who is this White Shield?" Seth asked. Limping, he grabbed at the wall along the way to support himself when he felt that his weak knees might buckle as he followed Janice to her room.

Forgetting he was standing there, in her rush to be on her way, Janice let the robe drop from her shoulders and hurriedly pulled on travel skirt and blouse that she had taken from her grandmother's closet.

She slid into boots that she had also found there, thankful that her feet and her grandmother's were the same size.

Cassie Edwards

"Who is White Shield?" Seth prodded.

"I don't have time to explain," Janice said. She stopped and gazed into Seth's eyes. "I'm so glad you are all right. I prayed and prayed, Seth."

She gave him a hug, then left the room.

She stopped and waited for him to come into the parlor, where Rebecca was now waiting with her son. When he did, she saw how his eyes lit up as he saw Rebecca standing with the baby in the soft lamplight.

"A baby?" Seth gasped out. "You have had our baby?"

Rebecca smiled softly. "His name is Seth," she murmured, slowly unfolding the blanket from around their son so that Seth could get a full look at him. "Seth Eugene."

Seth held his arms out for the child.

When he took the baby and gazed down at him, he laughed huskily. "I'm a father," he said. "I'm a father!"

"I've got to go," Janice said, hating to break into the wondrous scene of her brother holding his son for the first time.

Seth turned his head toward Janice. "Janice, I can't let you go," he said, his voice flat. "It's too dangerous. Wait until morning."

"Seth, you know that I'm doing this for Lexi," Janice said, her voice breaking. She grabbed the rifle up from the floor. "I should've known that you hadn't gone for her, for you would have

284

arrived here hours ago. I . . . I . . . just didn't want to think the worst."

"I still don't understand anything about what you plan to do," Seth said, gently placing the baby back in Rebecca's arms. He went to Janice and tried to take the rifle.

She yanked it behind her back.

"I must do what I must do," Janice said, turning and rushing from the cabin.

Seth limped outside and stood on the porch, and for the first time Janice noticed his limp and his unsteadiness.

She gave him a questioning look.

"I'm going to be just fine, sis," he said, leaning his full weight on the porch banister.

"I will, too," she said, swallowing hard. She turned and gazed at the horse and buggy. She knew that they couldn't be had without money.

She turned and gazed at Seth again. "How did you afford these?" she asked, gesturing toward the horse and buggy.

"I know that for the most part we are both busted, but I had a wad of money in my pocket when I left San Francisco. Thank God, I still have it," Seth said softly.

"How long have you known about what's happened in Tacoma?" Janice asked softly.

"I read it in the newspaper only a day or so ago," he said thickly.

"Then you know that you lost the house and . . . and . . ."

"And my dreams for the opera house are shattered, but only temporarily," Seth reassured her. "I have enough money to get my house back, but I must find a way to rebuild my wealth before opening the opera house."

"I'm proud of your courage," Janice said, then nodded toward the horse and buggy. "May I borrow these? I don't want to take the time to hitch my mare to my wagon."

"What is mine is yours," Seth said, smiling down at Rebecca as she came out on the porch and stood beside him, the baby still asleep and snuggled in her arms.

"Please don't worry about me," Janice murmured as she climbed into the buggy.

She placed the rifle on the seat next to her, then grabbed up the reins. She didn't want to tell him that it scared her to death to think of being out alone at this ungodly hour of night, and especially how she hated to cross Puget Sound to get to the Skokomish Island.

"Sis, by God, I wish you'd listen to reason," Seth said, doubling a fist at his side. "I'd go with you, but I think I'd better stay with Rebecca and the baby."

"I'll be all right," Janice said, then slapped the reins and rode away from them.

"She will be all right," Rebecca reassured Seth. "You wouldn't believe the courage your sister has displayed since her arrival in Tacoma."

"Lord, I clean forgot to ask where Mema is," Seth said, brushing past Rebecca as he rushed back inside.

Then he stopped and turned and gave her a questioning look. "I don't know what's going on here," he said, his voice breaking. "Janice was using Mema's room. Where is Mema?"

The color drained from Rebecca's face when she realized that Seth didn't know that his grandmother had died.

She dreaded having to tell him.

She reached a hand out toward him. "Come and let's sit before the fire," she said, closing the cabin door behind her.

Seth's brow furrowed as he went and sat down on the sofa beside his wife. He gazed at her intently, then winced when she began telling him what he could hardly bear to her.

When he knew it all, he hung his head. "Mema," he choked out. "Mema."

When the baby began crying, Rebecca touched Seth gently on the arm. "Darling, sometimes during the worst of times, God gives us something to help guide us through our sorrow," she murmured. "Seth, he gave us little Seth. Hold him. He will help take away your pain."

A smile quivering on his lips, Seth nodded and took his baby. Slowly he rocked him back and forth in his arms. "Yes, God has blessed us," he said. "As He will bless us by bringing our Lexi back to us."

"Yes, in time, I am sure she will be with us again," Rebecca said softly. "In time. We must learn to be patient."

"Yes, patient . . ." Seth said, sighing heavily.

Chapter Twenty-five

Bottomless vales and boundless floods,
And chasms, and caves, and titan woods,
With forms that no man can discover,
For the tears that drip all over.
                                        —*EDGAR ALLAN POE*

Almost the very moment Janice got the canoe beached on the Skokomish Island, and had grabbed the rifle and turned to run to White Shield's longhouse, she was surrounded by warriors. She went pale with fear.

The moon was hidden beneath dark clouds, giving the warriors no chance to get a good look at Janice, or to recognize her as White Shield's special woman friend.

And since she was dressed in her grand-mother's clothes, the attire of a white woman, instead of the Indian dress that they were used to seeing her wear, she looked like any other white woman.

She most certainly didn't look like a friend with the rifle clutched in her right hand.

The rifle was grabbed away from her.

Two warriors quickly stepped on each side of her and sank their fingers hurtfully into her arms.

Struggling to speak despite her fear, Janice blurted out who she was.

And just as she spoke her name, the clouds slid away from the moon and gave the warriors enough light to see that what she said was true.

"Janice Edwards," one warrior said, stepping up to her. He gazed intently down at her from his six-foot height. "Why have you come at such a late hour to our island?"

"I must see White Shield," she explained, her eyes anxious as she peered up at him. "Please let me pass. I need his help." She inhaled a nervous breath as she looked from warrior to warrior. "I might need all of you to . . . to . . . help me get answers about my daughter."

"You are speaking of the child called Lexi?" the warrior said, lifting an eyebrow.

"How did you know?" Janice asked, surprised.

"White Shield called a council late tonight," he said. He nodded to the two warriors who still held her hostage. At his silent command, they quickly dropped their hands away from her arms.

"Why?" Janice asked warily, recalling those last moments with White Shield, how his attitude toward her seemed to have changed after they had disagreed about when they should be married.

She had regretted having caused tension between them the very moment he left the cabin, yet she had not gone after him to apologize.

She *did* have to place her brother and daughter first, especially before making plans of marriage.

And now that Seth was home, all her waking moments must be focused on finding Lexi, for without her, Janice could not think of ever being truly happy.

"In council, plans were made for us Skokomish to pay a visit to the Haida village at first light," the warrior said tightly. "After we arrive there, we will request council with Chief Blue Rain. The reason for the council is to find answers about your daughter. White Shield is adamant about getting them for you."

"I don't know what to say," Janice said, her voice breaking.

"You do not have to say anything," White Shield said, walking out of the shadows so that Janice could see him. "What I do is something I do because of my love for you, and yours for your child."

Janice was stunned to discover just how deeply devoted he was to her.

She broke away from the warriors and went to White Shield. Not even caring that his men were watching, she flew into his arms and desperately hugged him.

"You are so special," she whispered. She gazed up into his eyes and felt warm all over at the love she saw in them. "You are perhaps the kindest, most wonderful man in the world."

White Shield chuckled and put his hands around her face, framing it. "Let us go to my lodge," he said, his fingers moving farther back, to twine through her thick locks of red hair. "There you can rest until morning."

"I want to go with you to the Haida village," Janice said, searching his eyes. "Please allow it?"

"I would not want to go without you," White Shield said thickly. "I had planned to come for you before I left for the Haida village in the morning. I was planning to ask you to accompany me there. It is only fair that you do. The child is yours. You should be the one to question the Haida about her."

"Oh, White Shield, I have so much to tell you," Janice said. She looked over her shoulder at the warriors who were still standing there, watching, listening.

She looked up into White Shield's eyes again. "I want to speak in private," she murmured. "Can we go to your lodge now?"

White Shield nodded. "Warriors, return to

your families," he said. "You must be rested for our journey to the Haida village tomorrow."

They nodded and walked away in a group.

"Why were they stationed at the beach?" Janice asked as White Shield swept an arm around her waist and walked her toward his lodge.

"I want to believe that there is peace between the Haida and Skokomish, yet one cannot be certain, especially now, when it looks as though Chief Blue Rain might be playing some sort of game with White Shield," he said in a low growl. "If it was a ploy to distract this sub-chief in order to find a way to attack my village, I had to be prepared for trickery."

Janice went quiet as she remembered that Seth had said he had not been to the Haida village and knew nothing about Lexi's whereabouts.

She wanted to blurt it all out to White Shield, to get his reaction, but she held her tongue until they reached the privacy of his lodge. She shivered and welcomed the warmth of the fire as she stepped inside and the door closed behind them.

Standing with her back to the fire, feeling its delicious warmth on her shoulders and legs, she explained everything to White Shield.

"Isn't it wonderful that Seth is alive and well?" she said, her voice breaking. "Aside from some weakness in his legs, and a slight limp, he came through the terrible ordeal quite well."

White Shield went to Janice. He took her hands and held them as he gazed down into her eyes. "And Seth has not been at the Haida village?" he asked thickly. "He has not seen Lexi?"

"No," Janice said, swallowing hard. "What do you make of it? Do you think the Haida made it all up?"

White Shield urged her down onto a pallet of furs beside the fire. He drew her next to him, yet his eyes were on the fire. "After having council with my men, I believe it is unlikely the Haida chief would lie so blatantly. He has nothing to gain from a strained relationship between the two tribes," he said. "We both are enjoying peace. And it *was* Chief Blue Rain who made the first gestures toward a peaceful relationship between the Haida and Skokomish."

"Yet you posted sentries at the waterfront tonight in case the Haida came to raid?" Janice said, searching his eyes.

"One cannot ever be certain about anything, especially a people who seem to have been put on this earth to be enemies to the Skokomish," White Shield said. "Although I placed sentries tonight, I did not truly believe it was necessary."

"Yet you still did it," Janice said softly.

"*Ah-hah*, but did you notice how I sent them all to their lodges after your arrival?" White Shield said. "After thinking more about it, I decided that it was wrong to anticipate a raid from a man who has never been responsible for taking any of my people's lives. He wants peace between us so that our two tribes can work together against the ever-growing threats from whites."

"Then you do believe Lexi *was* at the Haida village?" she asked softly.

"I do believe that she was there," White Shield said, his voice drawn. "And if she is not there now, someone tricked Chief Blue Rain and took the child under false pretenses . . . using a false name."

"Some man knew to say he was Seth in order to get my daughter," Janice said, nodding. "I, too, believe that is how it happened."

"We will go to the Haida village tomorrow and get a description from Blue Rain," White Shield said flatly. "We will then look for a man of that description and when we find him, we will also find your Lexi."

"I am almost certain that the man's description will fit Stumpy Jackson's," Janice said, visibly shuddering at the very thought of her beloved, tiny, vulnerable daughter being at the mercy of such a man as Stumpy.

She grabbed White Shield desperately by the arm, her eyes wide. "If it is Stumpy, why would he do this?" she asked. "Where could he have taken Lexi?"

"I have had some of my warriors looking far and wide for that man since the day you told me about Stumpy accosting you on my island," White Shield growled out. "He is skilled at eluding those who search for him. No signs of him have been found." His eyes wavered. "How could he have gotten so close to my village without being seen by my people?"

"I don't know, but I do believe that he now probably has Lexi," Janice said, tears filling her eyes. "If no one was able to find him before, surely they can't now."

"Perhaps a reward will bring him out of hiding," White Shield said, his eyes narrowing. "He might want money in exchange for the child."

"He knows we have no money to pay him for anything," Janice said, flickering tears from her eyes.

"He might not have done it for money then, but for revenge," White Shield said, regretting his words when he saw the alarm they caused in her eyes.

"You mean because he knows about our relationship?" Janice asked, her voice breaking.

"He even knows Seth and his relationship to you," White Shield said. "So he would know to use Seth's name in order to get the child."

"Do you think he is acting out of hatred for you?" Janice said, shivering again. "To be honest, I believe that is how it is."

"Perhaps we are completely wrong about what has happened," White Shield said, again taking Janice in his arms and holding her close. "Let us not think anymore of who, or why, until tomorrow, when we can go and question Blue Rain about the man's identity."

"Will you do me another favor?" Janice asked as she leaned back and gazed into his eyes.

"Anything," he said, brushing a soft kiss across her brow.

"My brother will be so worried about me," she said, swallowing hard. "Could you send a warrior to the cabin and tell him that I am all right, and also tell him what our plans are?"

"It will be done," White Shield said, nodding. "The moment we push out into the Sound, a warrior will be at your cabin explaining things to your brother."

Then he gently laid her back onto the pelts. "But for now, my woman, close your eyes," he said, lying down beside her. "Come next to me. Sleep in my arms. I will hold you close until morning's new light."

With tears spilling from her eyes, Janice nodded and snuggled next to him.

She would not allow herself to think ahead to tomorrow.

Chapter Twenty-six

Blend our dreams, souls, and spirits,
As one, we'll soar the lofty skies.
Born of freedom, gliding across time,
The majestic eagle flies.
—MARY ANN WHITAKER

Again dressed in the clothes of White Shield's people, feeling more comfortable in a buckskin dress now than in the prim and proper clothes of the rich, Janice sat in the middle of White Shield's canoe as it slipped silently through the waters of the Sound.

Janice was touched deeply by the gifts of dresses from Snow Flower. It was a positive

298

sign of her acceptance by the Skokomish people, especially the women. She knew the importance of this. When she married White Shield, she would be faced every day with the challenge of being among the other women of the village. Her acceptance would make it much easier for her to learn their ways.

And she hungered to know all of the Skokomish customs. Snow Flower had already taught her some; for example, how great faith was put in the potency of the elk-hoof as a good-luck charm. Snow Flower had said that after an elk was slain, its hoofs were saved. The women would then scrape them, bore a hole in them, and string them together to be worn on special occasions.

Snow Flower had also told Janice that she adored decorating clothes with colored glass beads and little shells.

Yes, Janice wanted to be the best wife possible for White Shield.

And one day, when Night Fighter died and White Shield was chief, Janice would be a chief's wife!

Touched by White Shield's warriors' acceptance of her, Janice looked over her shoulder at the canoes that followed White Shield's in single file. There were four men in each canoe, their paddles moving rhythmically and without pause through the water.

They were all there to help Janice in her

search for her daughter. Not one warrior had frowned at her or seemed to begrudge her the efforts they made today.

She had even felt their warmth and camaraderie as they assembled on the waterfront and boarded their canoes. Even now she felt this same goodwill as her eyes met and held the gaze of each man. She felt the friendliness in their eyes.

She smiled and turned back to face front as the lead canoe continued onward.

They were some distance from the Skokomish Island, and Janice studied the new terrain. As White Shield and the men in his canoe were forced closer to the edge of the shoreline to avoid an upcropping of rock in the center of the Sound, they all had to duck under ancient deadfalls of red cedar cushioned with jade covers of moss. Ravens croaked and a belted kingfisher squawked a loud complaint.

Then, as the canoe went back to the center of the black tongue of water, the paddles moving quietly through it, Janice gasped in awe as she watched an immature bald eagle rise off a towering snag of Sitka spruces.

Suddenly a single tail feather separated from the bird and fell away.

Eyes wide, Janice watched it sway as it descended, scattering golden light in the dappled sunshine that filtered through the muted green of western hemlocks, cedar, and spruces.

She wished that she could reach out and grab up the feather, for it seemed to represent something—perhaps a good omen?

As the canoe slid past it, Janice watched the feather. A tiny whirlpool of water caught it in its swirl, soon gulping it down below the surface.

A shiver ran up and down Janice's spine, for now she felt as though what she had just witnessed might be a bad omen.

She tried to brush such thoughts from her mind and continued looking straight ahead for the first signs of totem poles. White Shield had explained to her that there were four giant totems placed along the shoreline of Haida land. They were placed there to protect the Haida from evil spirits and intruders who might come in the darkness of night to attack them.

Thus far she had not seen anything akin to a totem. White Shield had said that the tall, thick poles were carved in the likenesses of birds and animals. They sounded grotesque to her and she did not look forward to standing in their shadows.

But for Lexi? She would do anything to find her!

Free and clear now of all overhanging trees, the canoes pressed onward, sweeping along in the water at a more rapid speed.

Janice was getting restless.

The longer she sat there, the worse her apprehension grew.

She hated to think that she wouldn't be reunited with Lexi anytime soon, but just getting a lead on her whereabouts would be something.

That was all that was important now.

If it was proved that Stumpy Jackson did have Lexi, Janice would die a slow death inside, for she would always regret not going with him to the Haida village when she had the chance.

But at the time she just couldn't believe him. Or. . . .

She gasped when schools of salmon exploded in the water on each side of the canoe, leaping, then diving again to the depths of the sound. It was as though the salmon were enjoying a free ride in the waves that were created by the movement of the canoes.

She glanced at White Shield and saw his eyes darting quickly at the sight of the fish. She could almost read his mind, how he would love catching some of the salmon.

He had only recently explained to her that salmon was one of the Skokomish's favorite dishes, that they took several days a year to participate in the salmon run. She hoped to one day be a part of that exciting moment in his people's lives.

Then Janice noticed that White Shield's eyes moved swiftly away.

Hers followed, and everything within her went cold with fear when she saw two long rows of large carved canoes. They suddenly appeared from around a bend in the Sound, moving in single file toward the Skokomish canoes.

Janice was keenly aware of how quickly all of the Skokomish warriors' paddles had grown quiet, now resting inside their canoes. Everyone's eyes were on the approaching Indians.

Her pulse racing, Janice glanced at White Shield, who was staring, tight-jawed, at the canoes as they continued to approach at an even more rapid pace.

Janice clutched the sides of the canoe. She swallowed hard as she stared at the many Indians coming toward her. She shuddered when she saw how hideously tattooed they were, not only on their bodies, which were fully exposed up past the waist of their breechclouts, but also on their faces. As the sun poured down upon them from the brilliant blue sky, it accentuated their slick, oiled bodies.

She also noticed that most warriors had eagle feathers tied in a lock of hair, some painted red, some black.

Just as the approaching canoes began separating, as though to surround the Skokomish vessels, another lone canoe came in view from around the bend. In it were five warriors, but one had no paddle. He sat at the bow of the canoe, his muscled shoulders squared, his back straight, his arms folded across his bare chest.

Janice noticed quickly that if it were not for the hideous tattoos on his face, she would think him almost as handsome as White Shield.

Cassie Edwards

Full of questions, Janice left her seat and scooted forward behind White Shield.

"Who are they?" she asked.

"Chief Blue Rain approaches," White Shield said, not taking his eyes off the young chief. "These warriors are Haida, the tribe who for so long have been my people's enemy."

"But you . . . aren't . . . now . . . ?"

"I hope not. We shall soon see what Blue Rain's true role is in the scheme of things."

"Can he be trusted?"

"A week ago I would have said no. Today? Well, we shall soon see."

As the Haida's heavily carved canoe came side by side with White Shield's, Blue Rain and White Shield momentarily gazed at one another.

Then Blue Rain broke the silence. "Why have you brought so many of your warriors so close to Haida land?" he asked gruffly.

"Do you see weapons?" was White Shield's response.

"I am certain they are there," Blue Rain said, slowly smiling. He turned to look at Janice. "And a white woman? Why is she in your canoe, White Shield?"

"Today I come with warriors and the white woman for council with Blue Rain and *his* warriors," White Shield said tightly. "We have come in peace."

"The council is for what purpose?" Blue Rain asked, his voice filled with wariness.

304

"The same as yesterday's," White Shield returned just as warily.

Blue Rain looked surprised as he slid his eyes back to White Shield. "The child?" he asked dryly.

White Shield nodded. "*Ah-hah*," he said. "This woman is the child's mother."

"You were told yesterday that the child was taken by Seth Edwards and *you* said that Seth is this woman's brother, so why do you still inquire about the child? Did not the brother return home with the child?"

"Her brother returned home, but without the child," White Shield said, his jaw tight.

"Why is that?" Blue Rain asked, slowly unfolding his arms from across his chest as he looked at Janice, and then White Shield.

"It was not Seth who took her from your village," White Shield said, his voice drawn. "It was an imposter."

"Imposter?" Blue Rain said, his eyes widening.

"We came to get a description of the man who took Lexi from your village," White Shield said.

"That is simple enough," Blue Rain said, relaxing.

"What did he look like?" Janice blurted out, finding it impossible to stay quiet any longer.

Blue Rain turned his gaze her way. "This man's face was hideously covered with red whiskers and his walk was not a natural one," he said tightly.

"He limped?" Janice asked.

"Yes, he limped," Blue Rain confirmed, nodding.

Janice inhaled a deep breath and lowered her eyes. The realization that Lexi *was* with Stumpy Jackson was so unbearable, she felt as though her heart might break.

"The man with the red whiskers and limp is not called Seth Edwards. His name is Stumpy Jackson," White Shield said thickly, his eyes narrowing angrily. He gave Janice a look over his shoulder. His heart went out to her when he saw her head drooping in sorrowful disappointment.

"Come now," Blue Rain said. "Come on now to my village for council. For food. For drink."

"No, no council is needed now," White Shield said, sighing as he looked at Blue Rain. "We have gotten from you what we came for. You have confirmed what we hoped was not true. This woman's child is with a man no one can trust."

"What I did by giving up the child to this man was done innocently enough," Blue Rain said solemnly. "Had I known . . ."

Janice heard the regret in Blue Rain's voice. She looked slowly up at him. "No one holds you to blame," she murmured. "I do want to thank you, though, for having cared for my daughter after rescuing her. I hope someday I can find a way to repay you for your kindness."

"Come again with White Shield and have food and drink with this chief and his wife," Blue Rain said, smiling broadly at Janice.

Savage Devotion

Blue Rain turned his smile on White Shield. "I do still wish to have a lasting peace with you," he said kindly. "Come for a smoke. Bring this woman. And when you find her daughter, bring her also. The children of my village have grown quite fond of her. She was the sort of child that lit up a longhouse."

Tears filled Janice's eyes. "Yes, that is my Lexi," she said, her voice breaking.

"Then you will bring her again to play with our children?" Blue Rain asked anxiously.

Seeing this new side of Blue Rain, White Shield truly believed that there could be a lasting peace between the Skokomish and the Haida.

He glanced at Janice and smiled, for he knew that, in part, she was responsible for this turn of events.

"I would be glad to accept your invitation," Janice said, now finding it easy to look past his tattoos and like the man.

"I will pray to the Great Spirit that you will find your daughter," Blue Rain said, then nodded to the warriors in his canoe. Soon they were all heading away from the Skokomish canoes.

Janice reached a hand to White Shield's shoulder. "At least something may have been accomplished today," she murmured. "It seems that the Haida chief was moved by the sweetness of my Lexi."

"Not only Lexi, but also you," White Shield said, turning to face her. He wrapped his arms

307

around her and held her for a moment, then eased her away from him.

"Now what?" she asked, searching his eyes. "What can we do now to find Lexi?"

"Although it has been done already, I will once again send my warriors out to search far and wide for Stumpy Jackson," White Shield said, picking up his paddle. "I will return you home. A more extensive search can be done without you."

"I hate to tell Seth the news," Janice said, settling down on the seat as the canoe was turned slowly around back toward the Skokomish island. "But I am so glad, so thankful, that Seth is alive and well. If he was also gone . . ."

"But he isn't," White Shield said as he gave her a quick look over his shoulder. "Now relax. Take in the beauty of the land. Let it be an elixir for your weary soul."

"I do feel so very, very weary," Janice said, sighing.

When he looked away from her again and rhythmically drew the paddle through the water, Janice tried not to envision that horrible, red-whiskered man in her mind's eye, but nothing would drive his image away. She didn't want to believe that he was there to haunt her forever and ever, but he would, if Janice wasn't able to save her precious Lexi from this man's evil clutches!

Chapter Twenty-seven

Dance moonbeams with strength,
power and spirit.
Dance moonbeams always and forever,
on my love.
—MARY ANN WHITAKER

Using every man possible, leaving only enough home to protect his village, White Shield was conducting an extensive search. He and his warriors had left the island in their canoes, but now they were on the other side and traveling on foot. He had sent his warriors in many different directions in the forest. Today he was not going to leave one stone unturned until he found something that might eventually lead him to Stumpy Jackson. The child was in terrible danger, for who was to say what the madman's plans were for her?

Thus far he had not tried to contact Janice with any demand for money.

White Shield hated to think of the innocent child even being touched by the man, much less being at his mercy.

The sun was high in the sky now, sending rays of gold through the autumn leaves of the trees overhead. Birdsongs were sweet all around him. Squirrels scampered playfully over the dried vegetation beneath the trees. Chipmunks occasionally ran along the ground, looking like brown-and-white-striped mice.

Deer were plentiful in this section of the forest, for it was not much traveled.

Even now White Shield could see the reddish gleam of a deer's eyes in the shadows up ahead, and then he heard the rustle of leaves and the eyes were suddenly gone, as was the deer.

White Shield glanced from side to side, watching his men search every nook and cranny. But no one had found anything yet. If his warriors found something, gunfire would ring out through the forest.

That was their plan. White Shield held a rifle tightly in his right hand, ready to fire it, either to warn the other warriors that Stumpy Jackson had been captured, or to let them know that he had downed the man.

White Shield had hoped to hear the gunfire by now, for he didn't see how any man could hide this skillfully.

Yet he had to remind himself that Stumpy Jackson was not like any other man. He had worked these forests with the lumber companies. He knew each tree, even the caves hidden beneath them.

White Shield had already checked all of the caves that he, personally, was aware of.

He was now searching to see if there might be a cabin hidden deep within the darkest shadows of the forest. Unless Stumpy had boarded a ship and left the area entirely, he must be hiding where he could feed the child and give her a place to rest.

Suddenly the birdsong had gone quiet.

The squirrels were now hiding.

Even the tiny, scampering chipmunks were nowhere to be seen.

It was as though a wand had been waved over the forest, commanding that everything be silenced.

A warrior ran over to White Shield. "We might have found him," he whispered, his right hand clasping a rifle.

"Or he might have found us," White Shield whispered back, afraid that if Stumpy had heard their approach, he might already be seeking a new hiding place.

White Shield moved forward quickly, this time at a hard run. If the white man had the child in his arms and was trying to run deeper into the forest, he would have no chance against White Shield's muscled legs. Especially since Stumpy had a limp that slowed his movements.

The warrior panted hard as he ran beside White Shield. Other warriors closed in behind them. Their eyes searched everywhere, leaving nothing unseen.

White Shield stopped short when he saw the true cause of the sudden silence of the forest birds and animals. Standing stiffly in his path were many Haida warriors, with Blue Rain at the lead. Their eyes were as wide in wonder as the Skokomish warriors'. White Shield and Blue Rain approached each other warily.

"Why are you here?" White Shield asked, his dark eyes narrowing suspiciously as he glared at the Haida chief, in whose hand was a tall, sharp lance.

"You do not own the forest," Blue Rain retorted.

"Nor do you," White Shield replied.

"Why are you here on land that does not belong to the Haida?" he continued softly.

"Why are *you* on land that no longer belongs to the Skokomish?" Blue Rain asked, his eyes going past White Shield to the many Skokomish warriors standing behind their sub-chief.

"The child," White Shield said, his voice drawn. "We are here searching for the child and the evil man who took her."

Blue Rain's eyes moved back to White Shield.

"The child?" he said, leaning his face closer to White Shield's. "That is why the Haida are here. We are searching for the man who came and falsely took the child from us. We do not take to being tricked by anyone, especially a foul-smelling white man." He paused, then added more softly, "We also hoped to find the child, unharmed."

White Shield was taken aback by these words. He was touched to learn that the Haida chief was actually taking time to look for Lexi. White Shield felt guilty for having doubted Blue Rain again. He should not have had so little faith in the other man's gesture of friendship. But in the past, the Haida had been anything but trustworthy. They raided, they murdered, they schemed.

But today, here was a great Haida leader who was thinking of something other than his own interests. He had summoned his warriors to search for a child whose mother was white.

White Shield could not help being touched by this gesture of kindness.

"I have brought my warriors to search for the child because I feel responsible for what has happened to her," Blue Rain blurted out. "I should have seen right through Stumpy's lies. I should have awakened the child and asked her if the man was her uncle."

"It is a mistake anyone could make," White Shield said, finding himself sympathizing with a Haida, whereas only a short while ago he would have laughed at the man for having been duped.

"I would like to join forces with you today to search for the small child," Blue Rain said. "If we work together, surely the child will be found. We can even work together on a plan as to what to do with the man who wrongly took her."

Almost rendered speechless by Blue Rain's conciliatory words, White Shield said nothing, only gazed in wonder at the man who had been his ardent enemy just a short time before.

"I know it comes as a surprise to you that Blue Rain would want to join forces with you, my long-time enemy, but, White Shield, I was speaking the truth when we talked of peace between us while you were at my village," he said, his voice drawn. "Do you not see? This is a prime example of how two forces joined together can do more than just one. Together we can achieve so much more than if we remain enemies trying to outdo each other. The white man has crowded us both off land that we revered. Together we can make sure they do no more pushing or shoving. We can stand together like a wall of steel against the whites."

"You speak so adamantly against whites, yet you are taking time today to search for a child who belongs to that world," White Shield said, his eyes narrowing.

"Because the child means something to you, because the child's mother seems important to you," Blue Rain said. He dared to reach over and place a hand of friendship on White Shield's bare shoulder. "What is the woman to you?"

Feeling the heat of the Haida's hand on his shoulder, and understanding the gesture of friendship behind it, White Shield found himself saying things to Blue Rain that were only said between true friends.

"She is my woman and she is soon to be my wife," he revealed.

Blue Rain's eyes widened, and then his lips curved into a smile as he slowly lowered his hand from White Shield's shoulder. "You are a clever man," he said, his eyes gleaming. "By marrying a white woman you will be able to persuade all whites to pay more heed to what you say in the future."

"That is not at all why I am marrying her," White Shield replied, his jaw tight. "The reason for marriage between us is a mutual love."

"I see," Blue Rain said, slowly kneading his chin.

And then he smiled widely. "Someday soon bring this woman so that she and my wife can know each other better," he suggested.

"All she thinks about now is the child," White Shield said tightly. "But sometime in the future, once things are right in my woman's life again, I will ask her if she wishes to join me as I come to your village again as your friend."

"That is understandable. And so let us join forces now and find the child," Blue Rain said, reaching his free hand out for a handclasp of friendship with White Shield.

"*Ah-hah*, that is good," White Shield said, smiling as he gripped Blue Rain's hand. "You know that this will be a first in the history of both our tribe's, do you not?"

Chuckling, Blue Rain nodded. "Yes, the first of many friendships between our tribes," he said.

Together, side by side, they made a sharp turn left and traveled land neither had yet searched.

Chapter Twenty-eight

Family albums filled with pictures,
All our cousins, brothers and sisters,
Happiness on the face of generations,
Love for building solid foundation.
　　　　　—MARY ANN WHITAKER

Seth had left to try to buy back his house, this time paying cash for it in its entirety so that no one could ever take it away again, no matter how the economy fared in Tacoma, or elsewhere.

Still somewhat weak from childbirth, Rebecca had stayed behind. She sat now in her bed, proudly feeding her baby, as Janice paced in the parlor.

Feeling so fidgety she thought she might

scream, Janice knew that she had to do something to busy herself while she waited to hear
the outcome of the search for Lexi.

As a fire sent its golden fingers around the
logs in the fireplace, giving a soft glow to the
parlor, Janice sat down before the fire and tried
to will herself to relax.

But she just couldn't. She now wished that
she had gone with White Shield.

She glanced at the steep staircase that led up
the stairs to the second floor. She hadn't yet
taken the time to go through that part of the
house. She wasn't even sure what was up there.

Thinking this would be a good time to
explore, she rose from the couch and went to
the steps.

Lifting the hem of her buckskin dress up past
her ankles, she started up the steps, her eyes
eager. When she got to the second floor, she
stopped as she noticed that it was all one huge
room. The walls were made of rough cedar, and
the fragrance of cedar was strong, yet sweet.

She looked slowly around her. It was obvious
her grandmother had spent much of her time
up here. She saw her grandmother's sewing
machine, her embroidery paraphernalia, books,
magazines, and huge stacks of newspapers
lined up against a far wall.

As she walked across a rag rug made by her
grandmother's own deft fingers, she continued
to take in everything, realizing that most of

these things had not been in her grandmother's San Francisco home.

She noticed many boxes and chests and guessed that her grandmother had stored things in them that she did not feel fit the design of her large San Francisco mansion.

One old chest, in particular, caught Janice's eyes.

Light poured in from a side window, seeming to single out this same chest. Janice went and knelt down before the old chest made of aged cedar.

"It is so old, but I don't remember seeing this in Mema's San Francisco home," she whispered, slowly running a hand over the dark, discolored cedar.

Then it came to her. She knew that her grandmother had stored many things in her attic in San Francisco. When anyone mentioned going to the attic for any reason, her grandmother had downright forbidden it.

"Why?" Janice whispered, more curious than ever to know why her grandmother had been so secretive about some things, even though she had been an open, happy, loving person.

Janice drew her hand quickly away, as though a bee were there, stinging her. She felt a little guilty at wanting to look inside this particular chest. Her grandmother had kept it secret during her life; wouldn't it be wrong now to pry into it? Wasn't it invading her grandmother's private life?

Cassie Edwards

Janice started to rise, to go back downstairs, but her curiosity would not allow her to forget what she had found among her grandmother's belongings. A chest as mysterious as this could hold many fascinating things inside it.

And Janice was not the sort of person who could let something like this go.

She smiled as she recalled how curious Lexi had always been about everything, how she had questions about anything new that she discovered. Janice was responsible for her daughter's curiosity, for Janice was as curious as the proverbial cat. Ever since she was a child she had always asked questions about everything that intrigued her.

She had never been as intrigued as she was with this chest.

"Surely if Mema hadn't wanted anyone to see inside the chest she would have gotten rid of it," she whispered, then placed her fingers at the lock, hoping that she would not need a key to open it.

When she found the lock secure, her heart sank. She now knew for certain that she wasn't supposed to know what was inside the chest.

She rose quickly to her feet and started to go back downstairs. But just as she started to take the first step downward, something caught her attention. A picture on the wall had slid aside and now hung somewhat crooked, and behind it something shone brightly.

She scarcely breathed as she tried to make out what could be reflecting the sun filtering through the windowpane.

"A . . . key . . . ?" she whispered, her heart skipping a beat.

She glanced over her shoulder at the chest, and then at the key. She smiled broadly and lifted the painting from the nail.

She laughed out loud with excitement when she saw the key pasted to the wall with a sort of paste her grandmother had taught her how to make, oh, so many years ago when Janice was a child.

"A mixture of flour and water," she whispered as she set the painting on the floor, resting its back against the wall. "Mema taught me how to make paste out of flour and water. And that's how she secured this key on the wall."

She knew that with one flick of a finger the key would be free.

And as she watched it fall into the palm of her hand, she tried not to think that she was wrong to pry into her grandmother's private world.

" 'Naughty' she would call me," Janice whispered. The key felt like a hot coal against the flesh of her hand as she knelt on the floor directly before the chest.

Well, naughty might be how her grandmother would describe what Janice was about to do, but nothing would stop her now.

Her heart thumped wildly in her chest and her fingers trembled as she fitted the tiny key into the lock.

She slowly turned it, then heard the click, and opened the lid of the trunk.

She gasped with delight when she found one of her grandmother's velvet dresses, which had not joined the others when Mema had made that beautiful patchwork quilt.

It was maroon, with lace trimming the neckline and sleeves. It brought back memories of Janice's grandmother that made tears fill her eyes.

The day she had seen her grandmother in this dress, she had floated down the spiral staircase of her San Francisco mansion, looking petite and oh, so beautiful.

Her grandmother had been going to the governor's ball that night, accompanied by her husband, dressed in a black tuxedo. They had looked as if they'd stepped directly from a storybook.

"Oh, Mema, if only you were here now," Janice whispered.

As she ran her fingers slowly over the softness of the fabric, the scent of perfume rose into the air.

Her grandmother's.

"Lily of the valley," Janice whispered to herself, inhaling deeply.

Oh, how she treasured this moment, when at least for a second or two she felt as though she was with her grandmother again.

Then something else caught her eye that reminded her of reality, that she was alone there, with only memories.

She wiped her eyes free of tears and, gently moving aside the dress, found a diary, its leather worn thin from handling.

"Oh, Lord, I knew this trunk might hold many secrets of my grandmother's life, but I never anticipated this," Janice whispered. She swallowed hard as she carefully picked up the diary and held it before her eyes. "Oh, Mema, you actually kept a diary."

Dying to read it, yet knowing that she shouldn't, Janice quickly laid the diary on the floor beside her.

She tried hard to force herself not to look at the diary again, for if she did, she knew she would open it and read its entries.

She was absolutely certain that what her grandmother had written was much too private for a granddaughter's eyes.

Still fighting the urge to read the diary, she lifted several other dresses from the chest to get to whatever lay beneath them.

She felt close to her grandmother again as she looked at these things which she knew were dear to her Mema.

One by one she admired lacy handkerchiefs with her grandmother's initials embroidered on them.

Then she came to another dress, this time a silk one.

She gingerly lifted it into her arms, and as gently laid it aside with the velvet ones.

Then suddenly her heart lurched with surprise and wonder as she saw beneath a thin layer of lacy underthings something that looked like . . .

She hurriedly lifted the silken finery from the chest and her eyes widened.

"Buckskin dresses?" she whispered, running her hand over the softness of one of the dresses, its bodice decorated with fancy beadwork.

Filled with wonder, she slowly lifted the dresses from the chest, her thoughts scrambled as she tried to figure out why her grandmother would have such clothes as these in her chest.

And then she saw an expensive bear pelt at the very bottom of the chest. She could tell that something was wrapped inside it.

Anxious, her heart pounding, Janice quickly lifted aside one corner of the pelt, and then the other, until the pelt was totally open.

What Janice now saw made her gasp.

She could almost feel the color draining from her face as she stared at a stunningly beautiful doeskin dress with pink shells sewn thickly across its bosom.

As she took in what else lay there, it was evident that her grandmother had to have had a connection with Indians sometime in her life, for there before her eyes were moccasins the size of her grandmother's delicate, size-four feet.

There was even a lovely sterling-silver Indian

necklace in the trunk, adorned with at least two dozen dazzling turquoise stones. Unclasped it must be fifteen inches long. What made it even more special and beautiful was the separate teardrop-shaped cluster dangling from the main part of the necklace.

And then Janice's heart skipped a beat when she saw peeking from beneath the corner of the doeskin dress a lone, beautiful white eagle feather, exactly like the feather that Janice had seen yesterday, falling as though in slow motion from the eagle into the water.

"What does all this mean?" Janice whispered, her fingers trembling as she reached down and pulled the feather out.

She stroked it with her left hand, even as her eyes were drawn back to the diary.

Slowly she sat down, laid the feather on her lap, and picked up the diary.

She started to open it, but discovered that it was locked.

Eager to read what her grandmother had written, determined now to find the key, Janice put the feather and diary aside and started running her fingers over the inside lid of the chest.

Her heart skipped a beat when she found a loose corner of the fabric that had been tacked onto the inside of the lid.

As she slowly drew back the fabric, she gasped when a leather thong, on which hung a key, fell into her hand.

Her pulse racing, Janice again picked up the

diary. With trembling fingers, she placed the key into the lock and slowly turned it.

When she heard the snap and knew she had just been given access to her grandmother's secrets, she hesitated for only a moment, then opened the diary to its first page.

She dropped the key on the floor, then began reading her grandmother's handwritten passages.

She gasped and could hardly believe her eyes. She could not even imagine how her grandmother could have kept such a secret for so long, especially from Janice, with whom she had shared so many special things.

Her grandmother had always seemed so open with Janice. She had told Janice things only best friends told one another.

But here it was, in black and white, a secret that her grandmother had kept to herself, had even taken to the grave without breathing a word of it to anyone: She had been captured by the Skokomish Indians when she was a young girl of fifteen!

She had traveled to the Northwest with her parents, who came to seek a new life away from the squalor they had known in Missouri.

When her grandmother had arrived in the Northwest wilderness, she soon discovered that they had come to a place where Indians and whites were in frequent conflict over land.

" 'I was abducted,' " Janice read aloud, gasping.

Swallowing hard, she read onward, but this time to herself. Her grandmother had been captured to be used as a bargaining tool with whites.

But the unforeseen happened.

The young Skokomish chief and Janice's grandmother fell in love!

After the people realized this, they went into council to discuss this white woman to whom their chief had foolishly lost his heart.

And although the chief *did* love her, with all his heart and soul, he had no choice but to allow the council to have its way, or his title of chief would be taken from him. He might even be banished, with shame, from their tribe and land.

The council, as a whole, decided that hatred for the whites was too strong to accept a white woman among them.

The Skokomish people had ignored their chief's deep feelings for the white woman named Hannah, and decided to make her leave.

Janice sucked in a nervous breath. She looked away from the diary for a moment as what she had read soaked into her consciousness.

How could it be that so many years ago, her grandmother had also loved a Skokomish warrior?

And not only a warrior, but a powerful chief like White Shield.

Janice understood oh, so well, how it could happen, for she had fallen in love with White Shield almost the moment she had seen him and knew that he was a man of good heart!

"Mema, Mema . . ." she whispered. Compelled to learn what had happened next, Janice continued reading.

Strange how she felt so close to her grandmother at this moment. She didn't feel she was intruding on her grandmother's private moments anymore. It was as though this was meant to be . . . these precious moments when she was truly understanding her grandmother, perhaps for the very first time. . . .

" 'It was decided that I must leave," Janice read aloud. "Even though it would break my heart to leave my beloved, I knew I had no choice but to do as I was told. But I knew then I had to tell these people something that might change their minds, even though I took a chance they might kill me over the news. I had to take that chance, for if they were to understand and sympathize with me and my beloved, I might be able to stay among them, after all.' "

Anxious now to see what it was that her grandmother was referring to, Janice skimmed down the page, again reading the entries to herself.

She gasped when she read that her grandmother had been pregnant with the chief's baby.

And since it was the chief's child, she had been allowed to stay with the Skokomish, but . . . only until the child was born.

If it was a boy, a son, the child would stay with his Skokomish father.

But its mother would still have to leave.

If the child was a daughter, Hannah and the child would both leave.

Janice read in a whisper words that had surely broken her grandmother's heart . . . "I gave birth to a son . . . a child I could not keep as mine."

Janice went cold inside when she read the name of the man, the chief who had loved her grandmother, yet still sent her away, her arms empty as she left behind her child in his father's arms.

This chief's name was . . .

"Chief Night Fighter!" Janice exclaimed.

The man her grandmother had loved, and who forced her to leave without her child, was none other than . . .

"White Shield's grandfather," she gasped out.

"Oh, no," she softly cried. "Please don't let it be so."

But this man who was her grandmother's son *could* be White Shield's father.

Was White Shield's father the son Hannah had been forced to give up?

Did that mean Janice was in love with one of her own blood kin . . . her very own cousin?

Frantic at the thought, and feeling as though her heart was being torn apart, she read onward, but still didn't discover the identity of her grandmother's son.

The name that Hannah had given him, Aaron, had never been used.

She, herself, never knew the Indian name assigned her son.

But now Janice understood Chief Night Fighter's strange attitude toward her. Lithographs of her grandmother's likeness showed that Janice bore a remarkable resemblance to her.

That meant that when Chief Night Fighter looked at Janice, he saw the woman he had loved so many years ago.

And he must have guessed that Janice was the granddaughter of the woman he loved.

But *was* White Shield Janice's cousin?

So many things made sense now . . . the chief's attitude toward her, the reason her grandmother kept this part of her past locked away.

Janice now even understood the initials her grandmother had recently embroidered on some of her things . . . *N.F.* for Night Fighter.

Surely all her life she had clung to the love she had felt for that man, a love that might also have been mixed with hate. For she must have resented him and his people for forcing her to abandon her firstborn child.

Today's discovery made Janice feel so deeply for her grandmother. Mema had kept so many painful things to herself.

Now Janice was also in pain, because she was not sure what White Shield was to her grandmother. Hoping to learn more about her grandmother's son, Janice continued reading.

She soon discovered the mystery of the white feather in the chest, and why her grandmother had kept it. In the diary, her grandmother wrote of having been in a canoe with her Indian lover when a bald eagle suddenly appeared overhead.

Janice's heart began to race and her eyes widened as she read how her grandmother had described the mystical moment.

Goose bumps rose on her flesh as she read this passage out loud in a soft whisper, knowing that somehow, mystically, she had only yesterday had the same experience.

"A single tail feather fell from the beautiful eagle. It swayed as it descended, landing in the water in the dappled sunshine. Night Fighter saw the feather as well, and stroked his canoe into an eddy and then scooped up the snow-white feather and gave it to me, saying that it was a good omen, that it would forever be a sign of our shared love, even when we were apart. It was then that my beloved gave me an Indian name . . . Day Star!"

Tears spilled from Janice's eyes to know that her grandmother's first love was as genuine and true as her own.

She felt a soft warmth inside. She believed somehow that the feather yesterday had been sent to her by the will of her grandmother from above so that she would somehow become as one with her grandmother. It was as if her grandmother had wanted Janice to know the secret that she had kept to herself for too long.

Janice wondered if her grandmother had perhaps reached out from the heavens to alert her, to let Janice know that she and White Shield were wrong for one another.

"No, it just can't be," Janice whispered harshly.

She brushed tears from her eyes and continued reading her grandmother's final entries in the diary.

Her grandmother revealed that she had returned to live in the area where she had found that special love so long ago, in hope of seeing not only Chief Night Fighter from time to time, but also her son.

But she had never disclosed to Night Fighter that she was in the area, for she knew that he had a wife at the time of her arrival in the area.

Also, she had hoped to get a glimpse of her son, but had only seen her son's offspring, White Shield, and even then, only from a distance.

Those words almost tore Janice's heart from inside her chest.

She closed the diary and hung her head as tears splashed onto the leather of the closed book.

It was so hard to believe that after it had taken her so long to find the man of her dreams, fate would now deny him to her. When she handed the diary over to Night Fighter, White Shield would soon know, too, that he could not marry Janice.

Nor could she ever bear him sons and daughters!

Her sobs reached all the way down into the parlor, startling Rebecca.

Rebecca tucked her baby into bed, then

slowly climbed the stairs until she came to the top landing, where she could see Janice sitting beside the trunk, sobbing.

"Janice, what's wrong?" Rebecca asked, going over to her. As she knelt down beside Janice, she saw a closed diary on her lap.

Janice shook her head slowly back and forth, for she could not speak the words that would make what she had read truly real.

Chapter Twenty-nine

Seasons, signs,
Ancient times,
Drifting glimpses,
Tease the mind.
—MARY ANN WHITAKER

"Janice, that looks like a diary," Rebecca observed breathlessly. She was panting from the exertion of climbing the stairs so soon after giving birth.

She glanced at the buckskin clothes on the floor, at the open lid of the trunk, then at Janice again. "I don't understand, Janice. I know that must be Hannah's trunk, but why were those Indian clothes in it? And the diary. Let me see it."

She started to go to Janice, her hand already out for the diary, but stopped and looked quickly at the window that faced out to the path leading to the cabin. The sound of an approaching horse and buggy could be heard.

Her eyes lit up. "Seth!" she said.

Forgetting her curiosity about the diary in her eagerness to know if Seth had managed to get their house back from the creditors, she turned and took an unsteady step down the stairs.

Janice saw how Rebecca quickly grabbed for the rail. She sucked in a wild breath when she saw Rebecca's shoulders sway, as though she might be ready to faint. She remembered the steepness of the stairs.

Quickly laying the diary on the floor, she went to Rebecca. "Here, let me help you," she offered, sliding an arm around Rebecca's waist. "Rebecca, you shouldn't have come up these steps so soon after giving birth. You know it's not wise, not only because you are weak, but because it can place a strain on the womb."

"I was worried about you," Rebecca said, sliding her hand down the oak banister as she and Janice slowly descended the stairs. She glanced over at her. "I heard you crying. Why?"

"It's so many things," Janice said, fighting back the urge to cry again when she thought of White Shield and what the diary had revealed.

Reading the diary had changed Janice's future forever. But Janice knew that it was best that she discovered the truth. If she had married White Shield and borne him children, who was to say how they would have turned out?

It was known that if people of blood kin married, the children too often had deformities of some sort or other.

"Yes, I know," Rebecca murmured, interrupting Janice's troubled thoughts. "I do hope that White Shield finds Stumpy Jackson and Lexi."

"He has to," Janice murmured. But this time she did not think at the same time that once her daughter was found she would feel free to marry White Shield.

She *wasn't* free to marry him. Nor was he free to marry her.

Just as they reached the bottom step, Seth was opening the door. As he stepped inside, his eyes filled with pride and joy, both Janice and Rebecca knew that things had worked out for Seth. He *had* managed to get his house back.

Janice wanted to be happy for her brother, yet her heart ached so, it was hard to be happy about anything.

"I did it!" Seth cried, grabbing Rebecca's hands, gazing happily into her eyes. "Darling, it's ours again, lock, stock, and barrel. Come on. Let's get little Seth. We're going home."

He looked past Rebecca and smiled widely at Janice. "Little sis, I did it," he said, breaking away from Rebecca.

He went to Janice and picked her up by the waist and swung her round and round in the middle of the floor. His success at getting his home back seemed to have given strength to his legs, which even this morning were almost too weak to hold him up.

Yes, things were working out for her brother.

But for Janice? Things seemed to get worse by the minute!

"I had just enough money in my pocket to get my house back!" Seth said, his eyes beaming. "It doesn't matter to me that I will have to find other means to open my opera house, even to put food on the table. The important thing is that I have a house to take my family to."

Janice knew that at least for now she had to put herself and her sadness aside so that she could enjoy Seth's happiness.

And she *was* happy for him. When she had first heard that the house was no longer his, it had made her feel almost sick to her stomach. He had drawn the plans for that house. Every inch of it expressed his personality.

"Seth, put me down," Janice said, unable to keep from giggling. "I'm getting dizzy. My head is spinning!"

How could his happiness not be contagious? she thought to herself. And his happiness had always been hers, for she cherished her older brother. It still seemed like a miracle that he was there, alive, well, and oh, yes, so exceedingly happy.

She knew that he was hurting inside over Lexi, but he was the sort who could feel happiness even when a part of his heart was aching.

Seth stopped and put her on the floor. He laughed boisterously. "I'm dizzy as hell, sis, over everything that's happened these past two days," he said, his green eyes bright. "I'm with Rebecca again. I have a newborn son. I have my house again."

Then a veil seemed to fall across his face, his eyes suddenly sad as he remembered what was not good in his life.

His grandmother. He had yet to visit her grave.

And Lexi!

Oh, Lord, he had prayed all night that White Shield would find her.

And then there was his dream . . . the opera house. He would have to invent ways to make money again so that he could open the opera house and give the people of the Northwest something that would take them, at least for a while, away from their troubles.

"Have you heard anything from White Shield yet?" Seth asked, placing gentle hands on Janice's shoulders.

"No, he's not returned yet," Janice said, again fighting back tears. "I'm so afraid that when he does, things will be no different. Something deep inside my heart tells me that I might not see Lexi for a long time, if ever."

Seth swept Janice into his arms and gave her a tight hug. "Never give up hope," he said, his voice breaking. "I survived, didn't I? I came back. Well, so will Lexi."

"Big brother, you always have a way to make things look brighter," Janice murmured, but she was only saying it to make him feel better. She felt guilty for having cast a shadow of doom on his good fortune.

There was no need to make everyone join her suffering when there *was* so much to be thankful for in all their lives.

She eased from his arms. "I'll go and take one last look at my nephew before you take him away," she said softly. "The house will feel empty when you take him with you."

"One day, sis, you'll have your own bundle of joy," Seth said, reaching a gentle hand to her cheek. "If I'm right, it'll be a son for White Shield."

Janice was glad that he had accepted the fact that she was in love with an Indian, had even accepted that she was planning to marry him and give him children. But she could not stand there and talk about something that could never be without bursting into tears.

She placed her hands behind her and tightened them into knots, her fingernails digging into the flesh of her palms as she forced a smile.

"And, big brother, I so appreciate how you

gave your approval of my marrying a Skokomish sub-chief," she murmured. "You've never said much about your feelings for Indians. But I have never heard you speak against them."

"I admire them. They have been forced to endure so much, yet they keep on going, their chins held high, their hearts open to any kindness they may get from white people, the very people who have brought such destruction to their lives," Seth said somberly. "For instance, there is White Shield. He has fallen in love with you, a white woman. And apparently his people approve, or why would so many warriors be with White Shield today, joining him in his search for Lexi?"

"Yes, it's a miracle, isn't it, how they can be so kind to us whites, when they are forced to live on an island, while Tacoma sits on the very land once occupied by the Skokomish people. It's not fair. None of it."

Unable to make any more small talk with her brother while her heart was breaking, Janice went to the bedroom where little Seth was still sleeping soundly after his recent feeding.

Janice bent low over the bed and gently lifted Seth up into her arms, glad that he wasn't hidden by a blanket wrapped around him. The house was so nice and warm from the sunshine bathing it and the fire in the hearth, no blanket was needed.

Janice smiled as she recalled how Rebecca could lie for hours just watching her beautiful son.

Her pride was evident in her eyes.

And her love.

Janice truly believed that Rebecca was not only a good, caring, loving wife, but also a wonderful mother.

"Isn't he adorable?" Rebecca said as she came into the room and stood beside Janice, admiring the baby.

"He's perfect in every way," Janice murmured, then smiled at Seth as he came into the room, all smiles.

"Rebecca, get your things together," he said. "I'm so anxious to go home. I want to see if everything is the way it was left. I hope nothing was disturbed. And it shouldn't have been. No one had laid claim to it yet."

"No, no one has the money for such a grand house," Janice said, nodding. "Thank God you had that amount of cash in our safe at home. If not, you'd never have gotten your Tacoma house back."

"I've got to make plans, though, to find a way to make a living for our family," Seth said, sighing heavily. "And, by God, I *will* have my opera house."

"First things first, Seth," Janice said, laying the baby on the bed and wrapping him in a blanket for the trip home. "We must not get too greedy. Think of all that so many have lost." She gave him a sideways glance. "Be thankful, Seth, that you have what you have. Do not be too eager to get more just yet."

"Yes, I know," Seth said, grabbing up a valise. "Greed is what put Tacoma in the shape it's in."

"I'm ready," Rebecca said, picking up little Seth. She got him settled comfortably in the crook of her left arm, then reached a hand out for Janice. "Things will work out. You'll see."

"Yes, I'm sure they will," Janice said, taking Rebecca's hand and squeezing it affectionately. "And know that I am so very happy for *you*, Rebecca."

She dropped her hand away, went to Seth, and welcomed his arms around her as he gave her one last hug. Then she walked them to the door and waited until they rode away in the horse and buggy.

Feeling so alone, and truly not knowing how she was going to make it through the next several hours, especially the moments when she would have to tell White Shield the truths that would alter both of their plans for the future, Janice halfheartedly closed the door.

She stepped farther into the parlor, then glanced at the staircase that led to the second floor.

The diary.

She must get it and have it ready for when White Shield arrived.

She would show it to him.

He could read, for himself, who her grandmother's lover had been all those years ago.

The fact that her grandmother had been taken captive by the Skokomish did not even seem to matter any longer.

But whom she had fallen in love with *did*, and always would.

"Mema, oh, Mema, what you must have gone through," she whispered, going up the stairs. She stopped when she reached the top and stood staring at the diary.

Something deep inside her told her to place it back in the trunk along with all the other Indian things and force herself to forget what she had read.

But that part of her that always made good sense, and was more rational about things, knew that what she had discovered must not be ignored.

The truth was out.

She must share it now with not only Night Fighter, but also White Shield.

Tears filling her eyes, she swept up the diary and went back downstairs.

But she just couldn't read it again.

The pain was too raw inside her heart.

She opted, instead, to take a hot bath, and while soaking in it she began making plans.

After she disclosed the truth to both White Shield and Night Fighter, she would return to San Francisco.

Thank God she and Seth still owned their large home on Nob Hill.

She would sell off some of the valuable paintings and her mother's jewels to support herself.

Then she would decide what she would do for the rest of her life, for she now knew that she would never marry. She would live in her memories of those few times she had been with the man she loved and hope that she would have her next monthly flow, for a true nightmare would be to have a child not only out of wedlock, but with her own blood kin!

After bathing she prepared herself a meal, but when she sat down at the large oak dining room table, oh, so very alone, she couldn't eat it.

Her whole world was falling apart.

First she'd lost her beloved Lexi.

Now she had to say a final good-bye to the man she loved.

What in life was fair?

How could life keep betraying her?

Was she never to have true, lasting happiness?

She left the untouched plate of food on the table and went back to the parlor.

Just as she started to sit down and go through the diary passages again, she stopped suddenly. She grew pale at the sound of soft footsteps coming up the front steps.

She knew whose they were, for they had the distinct sound made by someone who wore moccasins.

"White Shield," she whispered, grabbing the

diary up next to her heart. "Oh, Lord, it's White Shield."

Then she swallowed back a sob when she realized that she heard only the footsteps of one person. Lexi wasn't with White Shield.

Oh, Lord, how was she to survive these next few moments? She now doubted that White Shield had brought her good news about Lexi, and for certain the news that she had to relay to him was the worst anyone could tell.

Janice's heart skipped a beat and her eyes widened as a thought came to her. "There wouldn't be the sound of a second pair of feet if White Shield was carrying Lexi," she said softly.

Laying the diary aside, her heart thundering inside her chest, Janice went to the door and opened it with a jerk.

Her heart sank and a deep sorrow swept through her when she saw that White Shield was alone. By the downcast look in his eyes, she knew that he had found nothing at all on his search of the heart.

And with so many Skokomish warriors joining the search, surely they had exhausted all possible places to look.

"She . . . was . . . not found," Janice gulped out. Crying, she flung herself into White Shield's arms.

He held her close, his own eyes burning with tears. "She is nowhere to be found," he said, his voice breaking. "Even Blue Rain and his warriors joined the search and did not find her."

Janice leaned away from him. She wiped tears from her eyes as she gazed at him. "You said Blue Rain?" she asked. "He helped? Did you go to him and ask?"

"No, he started the search with his warriors because he wanted to help find her," White Shield said, reaching up and smoothing the last of her tears from her cheek with the flesh of his thumb. "But neither he nor his warriors found any sign of the child ever being in the area."

"But we all know that she was," Janice said, her eyes searching his. "How can someone just . . . vanish?"

"I have more to tell you," White Shield said, taking her hands and holding them.

"What more could there be?" Janice asked thickly. "You didn't find Lexi. You said . . . you . . . didn't find Lexi. So what else do you have to say?"

Then she went pale. She yanked her hands from his. "No, please don't tell me that someone else found her and . . . and . . . they told you she was . . . dead!" she stammered.

"No, that is not what I have to tell you," White Shield said, again grabbing her hands and twining his fingers through hers. "But it is about Stumpy. I, personally, found him. His throat was cut. He is dead."

"Dead?" Janice gulped out. "But . . . how? Who?"

"I knew the man well," White Shield said

somberly. "He had many enemies. He was a gambler. He was the sort of man who cheated while gambling. It is my guess that one of his gambling buddies to whom he owed money caught up with him and finished him off."

Janice frantically shook her head back and forth. "No, lord, no, don't tell me that whoever killed Stumpy has Lexi!" she cried. "If so, my child is in mortal danger!"

Seeing how distraught and out of control Janice was, White Shield slid his hands up to her shoulders and gave her a slight shake.

Janice's knees buckled beneath her as she fainted.

White Shield grabbed and caught her before she hit the floor. He carried her to her bed and sat with her until she slowly awakened.

When she saw him sitting there, and remembered everything all over again, she sat up and moved into his beckoning arms. "I'll never see her again," she quietly sobbed, clinging. "Surely whoever killed Stumpy has taken my Lexi far away."

White Shield was at a loss for words. He just couldn't think of anything to say that he hadn't already said.

"I imagine he had already taken Lexi wherever he intended to take her before he was murdered," White Shield said. "There aren't too many men who would murder a man in cold blood in the presence of a child. She was, I am sure, saved from such a thing as that."

"But where would he have taken her?" Janice cried.

White Shield's eyes widened when he saw Janice suddenly draw away from him, her chin held courageously high, her shoulders squared as she left the bed.

Knowing that she must get all of the pain behind her, knowing that was the only way to find some peace again, Janice gazed at White Shield and held her hand out for him.

She had one more dreaded task ahead of her, and then she was going to have to find a way to accept her losses, for she now doubted that she would ever see Lexi again.

And she knew that as soon as she told White Shield the truth she would also lose him. He would vanish from her life, just as Lexi had.

"Come with me," she said, hating what lay before her. "I have something to show you."

Wondering about the change in Janice's attitude, White Shield went to her and took her hand.

After they were in the parlor, White Shield watched as Janice went to the table and picked up a small book with an old leather binding.

She opened the diary to the latest entries, where her grandmother had written the things that had broken her heart.

Janice could even see tearstains on the pages, where the ink had blurred in some places.

They were a mixture of her tears and her

grandmother's. She imagined that her grand-mother might have felt exactly the way Janice was feeling at this moment: defeated, empty, and so distraught, she might never smile again.

"Start reading here," Janice said, pointing to the entry that would reveal to White Shield a part of his grandfather's past that he had never known.

Raising an eyebrow, White Shield took the diary. He gazed questioningly at Janice for a moment, then began reading, almost noncha-lantly.

When he was finally finished, he closed the diary and looked up at Janice. She was stunned when she saw no look of devastation in White Shield's eyes.

"Well?" she said, her eyes searching his. "Aren't you going to say anything? How . . . do . . . you feel? You don't look at all surprised by what you read."

"I knew of a white woman in my grandfather's life, but I never knew her name, or how it was they came together," White Shield said, laying the book aside. "It took much courage for my grandfather to share such a thing with me . . . that he fell in love with a white woman before he was married to my grandmother."

"But don't you see? Night Fighter's wife *wasn't* your grandmother," Janice said, con-fused to the very core of her being by his strange attitude. "*My* grandmother is *yours*."

She took a shaky step away from him and

gasped with surprise when White Shield smiled. "I have something to tell you that I am sure will change everything you are now thinking," he said, reaching over and sliding his arms around her waist. He drew her closer to him as his eyes smiled into hers. "My sweet Soft Sky, you do not have to fear who my grandmother, mother, or father were. You see I am not related by blood to Night Fighter. Many years ago, before I was even born, a warring tribe from Canada swept down and left death and destruction behind, not only at our Skokomish village, but also in the Haida camp. My father died instantly in the attack, but my mother, who was very pregnant, lived long enough to give birth to a son ... to White Shield. Night Fighter had two sons at the time. One of those sons and his wife took me in to raise me. I lived with them long enough to look at Nighter Fighter as my grandfather. Then my adoptive parents were killed, but this time in a Haida raid. Night Fighter and his wife Winter Dawn took pity on me, especially since I had been orphaned twice. Night Fighter and Winter Dawn thought of me as their true grandson. They took me in. They cared for me and raised me as their own. We, my grandfather and I, have a special bond that even most true grandsons and grandfathers do not have."

Stunned speechless, yet radiantly happy to know the truth, Janice could only stand there, her lips parted, her heart filled with wondrous joy.

White Shield understood. He swept her into his arms and gave her a long, deep kiss. He held her tightly long after the kiss was over.

"I truly thought I had lost you," Janice sobbed, afraid to let him go, afraid that she would discover that he had only made up a story that would comfort her.

"Never will you lose me," White Shield said, breathing in the scent of her hair as he rested his cheek against hers. "And as for who your grandmother's son is, do you wish to know his name?"

"Do you wish to tell me?" Janice asked guardedly. "Or do I already know too much about your grandfather as it is?"

"It is best that you know what I know," White Shield said, taking her by the hand and leading her over to the sofa. "Sees Far, my shaman uncle, is the son born of your grandmother's and my grandfather's love. It seems that when your grandmother did her sleuthing to discover which son of Night Fighter was hers, she chose the wrong one of the two. In truth, her son was still alive. She could have known him before she died, had he known that she was there, wanting to meet him. He was told long ago that his mother was white. He longed to know her."

"Then Sees Far is my true uncle," Janice said, marveling over the discovery. She hugged White Shield again. "I do wish Mema could have known him. He is such a special, dear man."

"I am sorry about Lexi," White Shield said thickly as he stroked his long, lean fingers through Janice's lustrously soft red hair. "But you must go on. I believe the best way to do that is to get married. Soft Sky, will you marry me? Will you marry me soon?"

Having almost lost him once, Janice would not allow anything to threaten their happiness. She held her head away from him and gazed deeply into his eyes. "*Ah-hah*, yes, please, White Shield? Let's get married—even *tomorrow*."

He laughed throatily. "You do not want a large celebration?" he asked, his eyes beaming into hers.

"Despite our love for one another, I don't feel much like a big celebration," Janice said, swallowing hard. "Do you understand?"

"*Ah-hah*, the celebration will come later," he said, then framed her face between his hands and kissed her softly and tenderly.

Chapter Thirty

Midnight groves,
Darker, darker,
No moonbeams
On the water.
—MARY ANN WHITAKER

Janice's knees were shaky and weak as she stood just outside Night Fighter's large longhouse.

She glanced down at the diary she held in one hand, and then at the feather in the other.

She knew that it was necessary for Night Fighter to read the diary, to finally know the truth about the woman he'd loved so long ago . . . where she had been all these years, with whom, and what she had done with her life.

Janice hoped the eagle feather would bring good memories into his heart about the moment he had swept the feather out of the water and given it to the woman he loved.

Unfortunately, it had not been a good omen, as he had said it might be. When Hannah had been forced to leave him after she had given birth to a son, it had surely torn a piece of Night Fighter's heart away, yet he had done as the council had ruled. If he had refused, he would have lost his right to call himself Skokomish ever again, for the council would have banished him forever from the tribe.

But he *had* kept a piece of his white woman: the child. Sees Far looked nothing like his white mother, yet surely somewhere inside him were parts of her, in his fiery spirit and his goodness.

Janice gazed heavenward. The sky was filled with fluffy white clouds today. She believed that her grandmother was there somewhere, looking down upon her today, smiling at what she was doing.

Yes, by giving Night Fighter the diary, Janice was, in a sense, reuniting two people who had loved with tragic intensity.

"Are you ready?" White Shield asked, having stood quietly beside her, watching her, knowing that she was torn over what she was about to do. He was not sure he understood her hesitation, yet he was patient and would help her if she faltered after entering his grandfather's lodge.

He looked over at Sees Far's lodge. Soon, he,

too, would know the identity of his true mother. He only hoped that Sees Far would not feel cheated that he had never met her even though she'd lived so near.

Being the sort of man Sees Far was, White Shield expected him to take the news gently. As a shaman, he knew how to work through all sorts of emotions with a warm heart.

This news today would be no different, especially since he had adored the woman who had raised him as her own.

"Yes, I am ready," Janice said, swallowing hard. She gave him a soft, pleading look. "Will you do the talking for me? Surely you will know the best way to tell Night Fighter about everything."

"I only hope that his heart is strong enough to bear these revelations," White Shield said somberly.

"Maybe we shouldn't even tell him," Janice said, turning quickly and starting to walk away.

When she felt a hand on her arm, stopping her, she turned slowly and smiled weakly up at White Shield.

"We must do this now, no matter the outcome," he said thickly. "My grandfather has the right to know." He took the diary from Janice. He gave it a lingering look, then sighed and turned back toward the longhouse. "Come on inside with me. I sent word moments ago that we would soon be with him for a private council."

Janice hesitated, then went to the door and

after White Shield opened it, walked inside ahead of him.

She stopped and her heart skipped a beat when she found Night Fighter sitting on a pallet of furs beside his fireplace. She knew that he had been waiting for her and White Shield, for he sat facing the door.

As her eyes met and held his, she tried to look past his age and see why her grandmother had fallen in love with a man who had taken her captive. And although she knew that Night Fighter and White Shield were not true blood kin, she could still see many resemblances between them.

It was said that often, when two people lived together for a long time, they began not only to act, but to look, the same.

And now, imagining Night Fighter as a young man, she could picture him being as handsome and as intriguing as White Shield.

She could see how her grandmother had forgiven the man for taking her captive when she had fallen head over heels in love with him.

Janice could even understand why her grandmother had kept on loving Night Fighter even after he had sent her away.

"You have come for council?" Night Fighter said, reaching a hand out toward White Shield and Janice. "Come and sit beside me. Tell me the reason for this private council."

He waited until Janice and White Shield sat

down before him, then he placed a gentle hand on Janice's shoulder. "I want to apologize for having behaved strangely in your presence," he said, his voice deep and steady. "You remind me of someone from my past. I have had to work through much in my heart since I first saw you."

"Grandfather, have you succeeded in working it out in your heart?" White Shield asked, drawing his grandfather's old eyes to him.

Night Fighter lowered his hand away from Janice. His gaze fell on the small leather-bound book in White Shield's hand; then he smiled at White Shield. "*Ah-hah*, as best I can," he said thickly. Again he gazed at the diary. "And what is this you bring into my lodge today? What is the need for this strange-looking book?" He gazed with narrowed eyes at the white eagle feather. He looked slowly up at Janice, then gave her a questioning look.

Janice and White Shield exchanged quick looks, then White Shield held the diary out toward his grandfather as Janice took the feather and laid it down beside the elderly man.

"This book has a name. It is called a diary," White Shield softly explained. "Grandfather, white people use such a book to record their daily thoughts. This is a book of thoughts of someone you once knew. I thought you would like to read it."

Night Fighter's thick gray eyebrows rose.

"Who is this someone you speak of?" he asked, his hands trembling slightly as he took the diary from White Shield.

"Her name was . . ."

"Day Star," Janice quickly interjected, drawing the old man's eyes quickly to her as he gave a low, surprised gasp.

"How would you know that name?" he asked, his voice wary.

"Because I found it written in this diary," Janice said, now courageous enough to speak her mind.

"But only one person besides myself knew the name," Night Fighter said, his eyes widening as he held the diary out before him and stared at it. "She would be the only one who would write it."

"*Ah-hah*, and it was she who did write it in her diary, as she wrote of a love so true and special," Janice said, almost choking on a sob of emotion when she saw the old man's eyes fill with sudden tears. "It is my grandmother's diary, Night Fighter. In it she explains how you met, how you fell in love, and how she . . . how . . . she gave her son up to you before she was made to leave the Skokomish village."

"This . . . book . . . is my Day Star's book?" Night Fighter said, suddenly placing the book over his heart. He clutched it there as though it might be his beloved. "She wrote about me and Sees Far in the book?"

"She wrote about you and your son, but the name she called your son was Aaron," Janice murmured. "She never knew what Indian name you gave him."

"Sees Far is his name," Night Fighter said, slowly nodding. "And this is Sees Far's mother's book."

"And I believe Sees Far should have the opportunity to read it, also," White Shield said softly.

"And the feather?" Night Fighter said, gazing at it. "I know of such a feather. And if it came with the book, I know the very day it was swept from the water, and why."

Night Fighter looked slowly from Janice to White Shield. "Will you leave me alone now with my memories, and your grandmother's?" he asked, his voice breaking. His eyes lingered on White Shield. "And, grandson, will you inform Sees Far that I would like to see him?"

"*Ah-hah*, I will do that for you," White Shield said, rising. He took Janice's hand. She rose up beside him. "But how long should I wait before I tell him? You want time to read the diary in private and absorb everything in it inside your heart, do you not?"

"As usual, you are astute about your grandfather," Night Fighter said, smiling. "*Ah-hah*, wait awhile. Wait until the sun sets on the horizon. Then inform Sees Far that I wish to have private council with him."

"I will do that," White Shield said, turning to leave. But when his grandfather spoke his name, he stopped and turned to see what else he had to say.

"Did you tell this woman that I am not your blood kin?" he asked softly.

"*Ah-hah*, I did, and now we plan to marry, and *soon*," White Shield said, smiling when he saw that comment did not surprise his grandfather.

"*Ah-hah*, grandson, marry her *soon*," Night Fighter said, still clutching the diary to his heart. "Do not be foolish like your grandfather and let the true love of your life get away from you." He swallowed hard. "Now, do not misunderstand. I did love Winter Dawn. But it was in a different way than I loved my Day Star."

"I understand what you mean," White Shield said, sliding an arm around Janice's waist. "I could never love another woman in the same way I love Janice."

"Give her an Indian name soon," Night Fighter said. "It will be something no one can ever take away from her. Even when my love was away from me, she always had the name I gave her."

"I have named her Soft Sky," White Shield said, smiling down at Janice. "Is not that a beautiful name for a beautiful woman?"

"She *is* soft in voice and behavior like the sky in spring and early summer," Night Fighter said. He smiled at Janice. "*Ah-hah*, it is a name that fits you well."

He lowered the diary to his lap. "There is so much about you, Soft Sky, that brings Day Star alive inside my heart again. Thank you for that. I will forever be grateful." He gazed down at the diary and placed a hand on it. "And also for this. With this, I have a piece of my Day Star back with me again."

He waved a hand toward the door. "Go now," he said softly. "I must have privacy to read my woman's words."

Janice brushed a tear from her eyes, then hand in hand with White Shield, left the longhouse.

Suddenly a tiny voice cried Janice's name. She turned on her heel and found little Pretty Fawn running toward her.

Janice knelt down and held her arms out for the child.

Pretty Fawn hugged Janice. "I was told you did not find your daughter," she said. She stepped away from Janice and placed a tiny hand on her cheek. "If you wish, I will be your daughter when you need a child to hug and talk to."

Taken heart and soul by the child and her sweetness, Janice swept her into her arms again and hugged her. "Thank you, Pretty Fawn," she murmured. "I shall be glad to have you to talk to and to hug when I need tiny hugs."

"I will be there for you, always," Pretty Fawn said, then broke away when she heard her friends calling her name from a circle of children.

Janice watched the child scamper away, then looked up at White Shield. "That child has so much love to give," she said, her voice breaking. "I wish that Lexi could be here to be a recipient of it."

"We will continue searching for Lexi," White Shield said, taking her hand and leading her toward his lodge.

"There comes a time when one must give up," Janice said, her voice quivering.

"My grandfather never gave up hope of having his first love with him again," White Shield said, opening the door of his lodge for Janice. He turned to her. "Today he finally was reunited with her."

"Only by way of a diary," Janice said, sighing.

"Did you not see?" White Shield said. "That seemed enough."

"It just can't happen that way for me," Janice said, then stepped into the lodge.

Janice watched as he added wood to the fire in his fireplace. She was filled with many emotions, but she was learning how to concentrate on the here and now.

She took joy in the love White Shield felt for her, and that which she felt for him.

And they were going to be married tomorrow in a quiet, private ceremony.

She could hardly believe that she had found such a man as White Shield.

She felt so *blessed*.

When he went down on bended knees and

held his arms out for her, she sank to her knees and fell into a big, deep, wonderful hug. "I need you so much," she murmured. "Take me away, White Shield. Take me far away from my heartache."

"There is only one way that I know to do that," he said huskily, his hands already at the hem of her buckskin dress, slowly raising it.

"That is exactly how I wish to be transported, my love," Janice said, lifting her arms as he drew the dress over her head and tossed it aside.

She placed her hands at the waistband of his breechclout and slowly lowered it past his hips. She sucked in a wild breath of ecstasy when the part of him that brought her such pleasure came into view, thick, long, and ready.

After they both were fully undressed, their moccasins sitting side by side before the fireplace, White Shield lifted her into his arms and carried her to his bed.

"Soon this bed will be *ours*," he said as he laid her atop it. "What is mine is yours."

"And what is mine is *yours*," Janice said, then gave him a downcast look. "But I do not have all that much to bring into our marriage. I recently lost so much."

"You are all that I want," White Shield said, brushing her hair back from her face, spreading it out across the blanket beneath her in a pillow of red.

"Am I truly enough?" Janice asked, her eyes searching his.

"For always and always," White Shield replied, his mouth bearing down upon hers, exploding in raw passion as they exchanged a frenzy of kisses.

His mouth seemed more sensuous, hotter, more demanding than ever before, Janice thought to herself, her body yearning for his as he moved over her, his one knee softly spreading her legs.

A wild, sensuous pleasure swept through Janice when he thrust himself into her softly yielding folds.

She lifted herself toward him, the flesh of her thighs soft against his as she strained against him.

Their bodies sucked at each other, flesh against flesh, as she moved sinuously against him.

Her breathing was ragged as the kiss deepened and his hands went to her breasts, kneading and caressing.

Overwhelmed with desire, filled with such a sweet, painful longing, Janice ran her hands up and down his muscled back, then splayed her fingers out across his hard buttocks and pressed him closer and closer to her building heat.

"My woman, my Soft Sky," White Shield whispered against her lips, then bent low and flicked his tongue across one of her nipples, and then the other.

Then he leaned away from her and moved so that he was kneeling between her outstretched legs. That part of her that had been awakened to joyful bliss throbbed in anticipation.

When he bent low and ran his tongue across her, where all her senses seemed to be centered, warm pleasure blossomed deliciously sweet throughout her, making Janice close her eyes and slowly toss her head back and forth, moaning.

As he sucked that tight nub of hers between his teeth and then ran his tongue back and forth over it, Janice was almost mindless with pleasure.

She was glad when he came back up over her and filled her again with his thick, wonderful shaft, for she was not sure just how much of that deep, dark pleasure she could stand.

She now moved her body with his.

She twined her arms around his neck and clung to him.

He kissed her with passion-hot lips, then moved his mouth to the hollow of her throat and groaned out his pleasure against her flesh as his thrusts pounded wildly into her.

She quaked against him as her own pleasure peaked.

And then they both lay quietly clinging, their breath coming in short, raspy gasps.

"Did I carry you far enough away?" White Shield asked, as he looked slowly into her eyes. "Or do you need to be transported again to another plateau of passion?"

"Take me where you wish, for as long as you wish," Janice said, her eyes dancing. "But only as long as you promise me . . . *assure* me . . . the same pleasure you just gave me."

"The same as you gave me?" he teased back.

"Well, I hope you felt the same passion that I just felt," she said, laughing seductively.

She closed her eyes and let her head fall back when he bent low and swept his tongue over one breast, and then the other. He kissed his way down her body until again he was sending her to clouds of wondrous bliss with his tongue and fingers.

"Yes," she whispered, tangling her fingers through his thick, brown hair. "It is so wonderful, White Shield." She swallowed hard and shivered sensually. "Oh, so very, very wonderful. Please . . . don't . . . stop!"

Chapter Thirty-one

Dance moonbeams on the water,
Dance moonbeams, chase evil spirits away.
                    —MARY ANN WHITAKER

Ten years later

It was an exciting evening for Janice's family, especially Seth. Seth had gone to and returned from the Yukon, where he'd regained his wealth in the goldfields.

Although it had taken him longer than he had hoped, tonight his longtime—almost his life-time—dream was coming true, yet in a different way than he had originally planned.

Instead of owning an opera house, he now owned one of the first cinemas in the Northwest.

Tonight was the grand opening. A young actress who was making her first appearance in the exciting new world of movies was coming to Tacoma for a personal appearance. All of the arrangements had been made by her movie producer, Frederick Hopper, leaving the actress yet to meet the theater's owner.

The sidewalks outside Seth's cinema were crowded with people who had come to take a quick look at the beautiful star.

Inside were those who had paid well for a closer look, and who would even be sharing pink champagne and Beluga caviar with the young woman.

Later, the most elite of the group would sit down to a gourmet dinner of duck consommé with ginger, a mouthwatering roasted lobster, tournedos of salmon, sautéed breast of duck, and roasted pigeon.

Janice was standing back from the crowd inside the cinema, watching this exciting moment.

White Shield stood beside her. For her alone he had made the sacrifice of coming to a place where, except for his son, he was the only one with red skin.

He glanced down at Janice now, proud that she had chosen to wear a doeskin dress to this event, instead of trying to fit in with the other women who wore silks, satins, and sparkling jewels at their throats and wrists.

She was clad in a soft doeskin garment of

simple shift design that could not hide her lithe figure nor conceal the fullness of her breasts. She also wore ankle-high, unadorned buckskin moccasins on her tiny feet.

Her glossy red hair was twisted into a single braid that fell down the middle of her back. Tiny red rosebuds were pinned into her hair just above her ears.

White Shield had seen her pride in who she was, and to whom she was married. It showed in Janice's every smile and how she ignored the snide remarks from tiny clusters of prissy women.

But White Shield knew that Janice was thinking what White Shield was thinking— that these women, whose riches were flaunted in the way they were dressed, and by their expensive jewels, had been among those who only a few years ago had done anything to get a meal of clams set before them on their dinner table.

For a while they had lost everything, but as Tacoma had jumped back from its lost days and was now as rich and boisterous as before, so had the people who had suffered for a while because of their lost riches.

Like Seth, many of the men went to Alaska and returned with much money in their pockets, which they tripled in no time on their stock market gambles.

As for the Skokomish people, they were still happy on their island, the salmon runs and whaling ventures keeping them comfortably fed and healthy.

And miracle of miracles, White Shield's wife and Blue Rain's were the closest of friends. Even the children had become as one. There was no room for enmity in their sweet and caring hearts.

White Shield's gaze moved elsewhere. His chest swelled with pride when he found his twins standing back with other children, giggling, those dressed in the fancy clothes of rich whites seemingly ignoring the fact that Lexi and Jacob wore the clothing of the Skokomish people.

Lexi, named after her half-sister, wore a doeskin dress that matched her mother's in beaded design, while Jacob Half Moon wore buckskins that matched his father's attire.

The twins, five winters of age, could talk of nothing else this morning at breakfast but the pretty star who would come for an appearance at their Uncle Seth's cinema house.

They had heard little Seth, who was not all that little now at the age of ten, talk endlessly about his father's dream finally coming to fruition.

The excitement had become contagious, and for the past several weeks Lexi and Jacob Half Moon could talk of nothing else.

White Shield looked slowly around the room, his gaze stopping when he found little Seth standing in his fine tuxedo beside his beautiful mother, his eyes never leaving his father, who was chatting with the mayor of Tacoma.

The two—father and son—had been almost inseparable since Seth's return from Alaska.

White Shield's gaze shifted to Rebecca, who looked no more than twenty winters, the age of the arriving actress. Today she was radiant in an elegant evening gown of peach satin trimmed with lace and velvet ribbons. A mink stole drew much attention her way, as did her diamonds.

Her black, lustrous hair was worn in a top-knot of flowers and ribbons, with only a few ringlets of curls falling across her pale brow.

White Shield glanced down at his wife and caught Janice looking at Rebecca. He recognized a worried look in his wife's eyes and knew why. She had voiced a concern about Rebecca, whose excitement about this special day seemed different than her husband's.

White Shield had also sensed that Rebecca seemed more jealous than happy about the arriving actress, since it had never been a secret that Rebecca herself, had aspired to star on the stage in one way or another.

But even though everyone seemed to believe she longed for stardom, she never voiced this desire aloud.

Janice edged closer to White Shield. She stood on tiptoe and whispered into his ear. "I

Cassie Edwards

see you looking at Rebecca," she said. "She has not smiled once since we arrived. And see how anxiously she watches the door? Do you believe it's because she is anxious to meet the cinema producer? Do you think she still has fantasies of being a star, herself, and will try to impress this upon the producer today?"

"You are reading too much into her behavior," White Shield whispered back. "Relax, sweet wife. This is a day to enjoy, not to be uneasy."

"*Ah-hah*, you are right," Janice said, sighing heavily. She smiled as she looked over at their children. "Don't the twins look adorable standing there with the other children all circled around them, as though Lexi and Jacob are as important as the movie star? It's because their uncle owns the cinema. It makes them very special in the eyes of the other children."

"They *are* special," White Shield said softly. "Look at Lexi. She is the very image of you, her mother. What young man could not enjoy being with her?"

"And look at Jacob," Janice said, her eyes warming as she took in her son, who looked so much like his father. "What girl his age could not be totally captivated by him?"

"Look at us," White Shield said, chuckling as he brought Janice's eyes to him. "Are we not the proudest parents in the world?"

Janice laughed softly, and melted inside when he slid an arm around her waist and brought her closer to his side.

As he went quiet, so did she, but her eyes continued to take in everything. She was so happy for Seth. He had done everything right. His cinema was the talk of not only the Northwest, but also San Francisco, and even as far away as Chicago!

He had selected a lovely headland overlooking the bay on which to build his cinema house. Outside, its broad terraces and gardens rose tier upon tier from almost the water's edge to its vast, grand entrance.

The front windows of the cinema were made of etched glass with a bird's-nest pattern in the middle and marginal lines of blue and yellow along the sides.

Inside, one stepped in on marble flooring, with elegant European carpet reaching away from the entry in all directions. Red velvet drapes hung at the ceiling-high windows. Murals of cherubs holding garlands of flowers had been painted on the walls.

More than one handblown crystal chandelier, resembling large concoctions of delicate spun sugar, hung from the tall ceiling. A graceful winding staircase on each side of the lobby swept up to the second floor, where lush red velvet box seats were prominent on each side of the theater.

It did seem such a perfect day for the family, except for one missing ingredient—long-lost Lexi. Although the passing years should have helped ease the pain inside Janice's heart, it was still there every day when she awakened, and at night, just prior to going to bed.

She would gaze at the rising sun each morning, wondering if Lexi was seeing it.

Each night she would gaze at the stars and wonder if Lexi might also be sighing over such a wondrous sight.

Janice had accepted that she would never see Lexi again, but she would never allow herself to think that her daughter had come to a bad end. She had convinced herself long ago that Lexi was alive and happy, but had somehow lost her memory of who her family was, and where they resided. She had heard of such things, how amnesia robbed a person of the past.

That optimistic belief was the only way Janice could survive the tragedy of having lost her daughter.

Yes, her older daughter was still alive, she kept telling herself. But where?

Janice was resigned to never knowing.

Loud squeals and shouts from outside the cinema house made Janice's heart skip a beat. "It must be her! The movie star!" she said, looking quickly up at White Shield. "She's arrived! Darling, do you care if I go and take a quick look? You said earlier that you didn't want to get so involved, only to stand back and observe."

He leaned over and brushed a kiss across her brow. "You go and enjoy every moment of your brother's big day, and, *ah-hah*, I will stand here and watch from afar," he said, laughing to himself when he looked past her and saw their twins running and squealing toward the double doors with the other children.

Janice elbowed her way through the crowd until she reached Seth.

Breathing hard, she stepped outside with him and Rebecca. The elderly mayor, in his stiff tuxedo, stood beside them, his old eyes anxious.

Janice stood on tiptoe and got a glimpse now as a carriage came into view. She saw a tiny gloved hand waving from a window.

Janice clasped her hands together before her, beaming as she glanced at her brother and saw the excitement in his eyes as he enjoyed this moment of glory so long dreamed about.

She looked slowly around her and knew that it was not only Seth who was caught up in the moment. The whole city of Tacoma was crazy to see this Chinese actress whose face was said to be as beautiful as a porcelain doll's. When Janice had heard that the actress was Chinese, she thought that maybe she shouldn't come to the event today, for fear that seeing the lovely girl would renew her hopeless longing for Lexi.

But for Seth, she had made herself brush such thoughts from her mind. It was his day. She would not spoil it.

But now, as she waited to see the pretty actress for the first time, Janice could not help thinking of her own porcelain doll . . . her Lexi who would now surely be a raging beauty.

Again she fought back the agony of memories and focused on the wonders of the moment.

And as the carriage stopped and the crowd was held back by muscled men, Janice gasped when she caught her first glimpse of the hauntingly beautiful star as she was helped from the carriage. She wore a stylish gown of brocaded silk in a delicate floral pattern, her ankles surrounded by billowing lace petticoats. Three-quarter-length white gloves protected her delicate hands.

The star's long, thick black hair was parted and brought back in curls that fell to her shoulders. Her large, slanted, liquid dark eyes were radiant as she smiled at everyone who openly gaped at her.

Janice stared at Madeline Hopper disbelievingly. She grabbed at thin air, finally latching onto Seth's arm. Although the actress was older than the child she'd known, Janice knew that she couldn't be anyone but Lexi! *Her* Lexi!

As a child, hadn't Lexi dreamed about being on the stage . . . being a star?

When Janice heard Seth gasp Lexi's name out loud, she knew that he, too, saw the resemblance.

"Seth, is it?" Janice asked, bringing his eyes to her. "Can it be?"

Seth's lips parted to say something, but he was

stopped when Frederick Hopper swept Madeline, his daughter-in-law, over toward them. He was a tall, lean, well-dressed man. He wore a cutaway, opened in front to disclose a white waistcoat; trousers of a peachy hue creased gracefully over patent-leather shoes; and a baby-blue tie fastened with a diamond pin.

In his free hand he carried a Malacca stick, over the head of which was folded a pair of immaculate kidskin gloves. His hair was cropped short just above his collar line and it was snow white.

"Can we go on somewhere private before meeting the crowd inside formally?" Frederick asked, protectively sliding an arm around Madeline's waist.

"Certainly," Seth said, brought out of his stunned state. He grabbed both Rebecca and Janice by a hand and turned toward a side door, where there was more privacy.

"Come, children," Janice said as she looked over her shoulder at little Lexi and Jacob Half Moon. "Come with us."

Wide-eyed, and totally in awe of the lovely Chinese lady, they followed and stood aside after the adults went into a smaller lobby where a lone chandelier hung low overhead, its lights bright.

"This is more like it," Frederick said, laughing softly as he glanced from Seth to Janice, and then gave Rebecca an obviously appreciative look that made her smile. "It was once my dream to be a star," Rebecca murmured, her eyes twinkling as Frederick took her hand.

"You don't say," he replied, politely kissing her hand as his eyes held hers.

"Dearest, you *are* a star," Seth was clever enough to say. *"Mine."*

"Yes, so I am," Rebecca said, easing her hand from Frederick's and gazing adoringly up at Seth as she linked an arm through his. "Thank you, darling. You do say the sweetest things. You know that I am exceedingly happy."

Seth gave her a pleased look, then turned slow eyes to Madeline as Frederick slid an arm around her waist and led her closer. "This is Madeline," he said, pride obvious in his words. "Not only is she going to be my top box-office draw, she's my daughter-in-law. Only yesterday she married my son Thomas. He is not the sort who enjoys the limelight, so he has stayed behind at the hotel."

"I am so very pleased to meet you," Madeline said, her eyes warm and bright. She offered her hand first to Janice. "And you are . . . ?"

Spellbound by the young lady, and certain that she was Lexi, Janice realized that she did not recognize her mother or Seth. Janice's fingers trembled as she took Madeline's tiny hand. "My name is Janice," she murmured. Although she was married to White Shield, she dared to mention the name that Lexi would have remembered. "Janice Edwards, Madeline. My name is Janice Edwards."

"Such a lovely name," Madeline murmured. Then before she had the chance to meet Seth formally, Janice's daughter Lexi and son Jacob Half Moon rushed up, squealing that they wanted to meet the movie star.

"Jacob, *Lexi,* where are your manners!" Janice gasped, reaching for her children as she tried to quell their excitement.

Then she saw Madeline's eyes waver strangely as she stared at Lexi. Janice's heart skipped a beat when saw the actress rub her brow.

"Lexi?" Madeline said, her voice faint. She stared down at little Lexi, and then looked questioningly at Janice. "You . . . called . . . her Lexi?"

"Yes, that's her name," Janice said gently.

Oh, Lord, Janice thought to herself. Could this be happening? Could this young woman only now be remembering . . . ?

"Suddenly I am so dizzy," Madeline said, her shoulders swaying. She looked desperately at Frederick. "I . . . I . . . don't feel well. I think I'm going to faint."

Frederick grabbed her into his arms. "What's the matter, child?" he asked, searching her eyes as she gazed up at him. "What's caused you to feel like this?"

"Lexi?" Seth said, his voice gentle but quite audible.

Cassie Edwards

Little Lexi, his niece, went to his side. "Yes?" she murmured. "Uncle Seth, do you want me?"

Seth placed a gentle hand on her head. "No, child, I was not addressing you," he said, his voice revealing his nervous excitement. "I . . . I . . . was speaking to your *sister.*"

Madeline visibly stiffened. She jerked away from Frederick and gazed, wide-eyed, at Seth. "Uncle Seth . . . ?" she murmured.

She turned tear-filled eyes toward Janice who was in a state of shock at the realization that her daughter had just been returned to her.

"Mother?" Lexi cried. She went to Janice and flung herself into her arms. "Oh, Mother, I forgot everything . . . until . . . now. When you spoke the name *Lexi*, something just seemed to snap in my mind. Mother, oh, Mother, I didn't mean to be gone for so long. I just didn't remember!"

Sobbing, clinging, Janice looked across her shoulder at White Shield as he came into the room. "White Shield, this is Lexi," she said, her voice breaking with emotion. "White Shield, she's come home to me."

White Shield gazed in wonder at the young woman, his own eyes misting with tears, for he knew that his wife had never forgotten the child whom she had given up to the raging waters of the Sound so many years ago.

And now, finally, as though by magic, here she was! Lexi was here for his wife!

He was touched deeply as he watched the emotional reunion.

Seth couldn't hold himself back any longer. He went and grabbed Lexi from Janice's arms and held her as though he would never let her go again, for he had always felt responsible for her disappearance. If he had only held on to her more tightly in the Sound, she never would have been separated from him.

"I don't understand any of this," Frederick said, nervously kneading his brow. "Are you saying she is your child?"

Seth swallowed hard, then eased Lexi from his arms. She went and snuggled into Janice's arms again, her cheek resting against her chest.

"How long has she been with you?" Seth asked, his eyes narrowing angrily at the thought of this man having possibly gotten Lexi in some sort of underhanded way.

"Many years ago, my wife and I came to Tacoma to help a relative who had survived the terrible shipwreck in the Sound. As we were traveling through the forest in a rented horse and buggy to get to the home where my cousin was recovering, my wife and I happened upon a scene in the forest that was most deplorable," Frederick explained. "There was a filthy man slapping a young girl as she tried to reach our buggy. She finally managed to get free. The man drew a knife and came after her. I jumped from the buggy and wrestled the knife away from him. In the scuffle, the knife . . . sank . . . into his chest. He died instantly. Not wanting to be arrested for something that was accidental, my wife and I fled with the child."

Tears came to Frederick's eyes as he gazed lovingly at Lexi. He took a handkerchief from his front pocket and dabbed his eyes dry, then continued with his tale of how Lexi had come to stay with him and his wife. "My wife and I fell instantly in love with the child. And since she was obviously a victim of something terrible that may have happened even before knowing this man, her memory totally erased from the tragedy, we took her in. We adopted her. She and my son became instantly close. They were inseparable. I have never seen my son so protective of anyone or anything as he became of Madeline. It turned to love. Like I said earlier, they were married only yesterday."

"Thank you so much for caring for my child," Janice said, stroking her fingers lovingly through Lexi's black hair. "I am sure she has blocked much from her mind that is painful. At the same time she lost all that was good, which was us, her family.

"Thank heavens you rescued Lexi so soon after Stumpy Jackson took her from the Haida village," Janice said, sighing heavily.

Lexi stepped away and gazed questioningly at Janice. "Who are the Haida? Who is Stumpy Jackson?" she asked softly.

"Stumpy Jackson is the ugly part of your past," Janice murmured. "The Haida are a good part. They took care of you after the shipwreck that separated our family. Stumpy Jackson came for you, saying that his name was Seth, pretending to be your uncle."

"I don't remember any of that," Lexi said, frowning. "But, of course, except for you and Uncle Seth, I don't remember anything before I met Frederick and his family."

"My wife passed away last year," Frederick said, coming to take Lexi's hand in his. "She would have been proud to see this day . . . the day our child was reunited with her mother."

Then his eyebrows lifted. "But you aren't Chinese," he said softly.

Janice smiled. "No, I'm not Chinese." Then she told the whole story about how she had found Lexi and taken her in as her own child. She told him everything else as Lexi listened and became acquainted all over again with her past.

When people began applauding and cheering, they were all reminded of why this movie star was there in the first place. Janice reached her hands to Lexi's face and smoothed tears from her beautiful cheeks.

"Are you ready to meet your adoring fans?" she asked softly, thrilled to the very core that she was there, as Lexi's mother, to enjoy this moment with her. For a child who began with nothing when Janice found her on the streets of San Francisco, she now had so much!

"Yes, and I'm so thankful and excited about everything," Lexi said, her eyes gleaming.

"First, you have more family that I want you to meet," Janice said, reaching out for little Lexi and Jacob Half Moon. "This is your brother and sister."

She could see an instant love enter Lexi's eyes as she knelt down and swept both children into her arms at once.

She introduced Rebecca and Seth Eugene, and then she smiled over at White Shield. "And this? This is my wonderful husband White Shield," she said.

White Shield reached out and drew her into his arms. "I have heard so much about you," he said softly. "It is as though I have known you forever."

Janice stood back, her whole world now back together again, as though a magic wand had been waved over her.

Seth looked at her and smiled broadly. "Sis, isn't today the best?" he said, glad when Rebecca snuggled close, her tear-streaked face proof that she had also been touched deeply by Lexi's reappearance in their lives.

"Madeline! Madeline! We want Madeline!" The chant rang out from the waiting crowd.

Smiling, she turned toward the door.

"Go on," Janice said softly. "Enjoy!"

Madeline, who was in truth Lexi, nodded and left the room.

Everyone quietly followed and watched a star being born as people stood around her, asking questions and requesting autographs.

Janice sighed with pride and happiness. The waiting had been long and grueling, but, oh, so very worth it!

Chapter Thirty-two

Sunset's charm,
Slithers on,
Darkest nights,
Captive Dawn.
—MARY ANN WHITAKER

A loon called to its mate across the water somewhere in the distance. Stars glittered overhead—pulsating. The full moon cast a silver
sheen across the land. Janice stepped out onto
the porch of her cabin and stood in the muted
shadows. She gazed with a wondrously happy
heart at her grown-up Lexi holding hands with
her golden-haired husband beneath the moonlight and stars.

When they turned to one another and slid into each other's arms to kiss, Janice sighed and clasped her hands before her.

Her Lexi, gone from home so long, was with her again!

It was nothing less than a miracle that Seth's dream of having his cinema had also made Janice's come true.

Janice had never been more glad that she and Seth had kept their grandmother's cabin in the family instead of selling it when Janice married White Shield and moved into his longhouse.

Since then, the cabin had been used as a family retreat, where anyone could get away from the real world and enjoy the serenity of the forest for a night or two.

Before Night Fighter's death three years earlier, he had come often, alone, to be with his memories of the woman he'd loved and lost.

At times, Sees Far had joined him, to also capture something of his true mother inside his heart.

Sees Far had regretted the fact that he'd never had the opportunity to meet his mother, but he had never voiced his feelings aloud to his ailing father. Night Fighter had lived with his own regrets ever since the day he had sent Sees Far's mother away.

"*Here* is my wife," White Shield said as he slipped up behind Janice and slid his arms around her waist. He turned her slowly to face him, then eased her out into the moonlight.

"You are radiant beneath the moonlight tonight, my Soft Sky," he said. "It does not have anything to do with Lexi, or should I say, Madeline, does it?" He glanced past Janice's shoulder and gazed at the newlyweds, who were now walking hand in hand farther into the shadows of the forest.

"She is a part of my happiness," Janice said, gazing proudly up at her chieftain husband. He had acquired that title and its responsibilities the very day Night Fighter had taken his last breath of life. "It's everything, darling. Grown-up Lexi, little Lexi, Jacob Half Moon, Seth . . ."

Chuckling, White Shield slid a gentle hand over Janice's lips. "No more," he said. "It is easier to say that your life . . . *ours* . . . is complete . . . *whole*."

"Well, there *is* just one more thing left to make that statement true," Janice murmured, touched that White Shield had agreed to stay at the cabin tonight with the rest of her family. Seth and Rebecca and their children, Sees Far and his wife and children, even Frederick were there for the night.

The house was filled with warmth and love.

All the bedrooms were filled to capacity, even overflowing, for cots were set up before the fireplace in the living room.

"Oh?" White Shield said, arching an eyebrow. "What is that?"

"Not *what*, but *who*," Janice said, her eyes twinkling.

"Who could you mean?" White Shield said, even more intrigued by his wife's mysterious behavior.

"Darling chieftain husband, give me one of your hands," Janice said, so happy she felt as though she might burst. She had such marvelous news to add to a day that had already been heaven on earth for her.

White Shield held his right hand out toward Janice.

She took it, and as their eyes met and held, she placed his hand on her belly.

"White Shield, when our baby is born and can be held in our arms, our world will be truly whole," Janice said, smiling sweetly as she watched his eyes light up with surprise, and then an intense joy. "Darling, where your hand rests? Just beneath it lies a child. White Shield, as though today's miracles weren't enough, another miracle will be born to us in eight months."

"I did not think you could have any more children," White Shield said, his eyes wavering, his happiness now tinged with concern. "When Sees Far was unable to help your condition when you were having problems carrying the twins, we went to Doc Rose for medical attention. After you gave birth to our twins, Doc Rose said that you could not get pregnant again . . . that it had something to do with the way you carried the twins."

"Seems he's wrong," Janice said, lifting her

chin proudly, her eyes dancing. She was almost giddy from happiness. She giggled. "I am pregnant, White Shield. I have missed my monthly flow by one whole month now. I can *feel* the pregnancy deep inside my soul. We *will* have more children, White Shield. As many as your heart desires."

He swept her into his arms. He gazed at her a moment longer, then kissed her with a gentleness and sweetness that made Janice know all over again why she loved this man. Although he was a powerful chief, revered by so many, and again had white lumber barons seeking his advice daily about the forest trees, he never forgot that other side of his life—his family.

Never could children have had such an adoring father as White Shield.

Never could a wife have such a caring, gentle, devoted husband!

White Shield!

He was everything to their family.

Janice felt so blessed that he ... was ... hers!

Yes, he was a leader ... a father ... a husband ... an adviser ... a man of savage devotion.

CASSIE EDWARDS
SAVAGE HERO

To the Crow people the land is a gift from the First Maker, a place of snowy mountains and sunny plains, where elk and antelope graze by brightly tumbling streams. But Chief Brave Wolf knows that proud heritage is threatened by the pony soldiers under Yellow Hair's command, for they spread death and destruction wherever they ride.

To Mary Beth Wilson, Custer's Last Stand means the end of her marriage and a lonely trek back east with her young son David. When renegades attack her wagon train, rescue comes in the form of a powerful Crow warrior. This beautiful man is both her savior and her enemy, her savage hero.

Savage Honor
Cassie Edwards

Shawndee Sibley longs for satin ribbons, fancy dresses, and a man who will take her away from her miserable life in Silver Creek. But the only men she ever encounters are the drunks who frequent her mother's tavern. And even then, Shawndee's mother makes her disguise herself as a boy for her own protection.

Shadow Hawk bitterly resents the Sibleys for corrupting his warriors with their whiskey. Capturing their "son" is a surefire way to force them to listen to him. But he quickly becomes the captive—of Shawndee's shy smile, iron will, and her shimmering golden hair.

___4889-2 $5.99 US/$6.99 CAN

SAVAGE LOVE

CASSIE EDWARDS

Monster bones are the stuff of Indian legend, which warns that they must not be disturbed. But Dayanara and her father are on a mission to uncover the bones. Not even her father's untimely death or a disapproving Indian chief can prevent Dayanara from proving her worth as an archaeologist.

Any relationship between a Cree chief and a white woman is prohibited by both their peoples, but the golden woman of Quick Fox's dreams is more glorious than the setting sun. Not even her interest in the sacred burial grounds of his people can prevent him from discovering the delights they will know together and proving his savage love.

SAVAGE LONGINGS

CASSIE EDWARDS

"Cassie Edwards is a shining talent!"
—Romantic Times

Having been kidnapped by vicious trappers, Snow Deer despairs of ever seeing her people again. Then, from out of the Kansas wilderness comes Charles Cline to rescue the Indian maiden. Strong yet gentle, brave yet tenderhearted, the virile blacksmith is everything Snow Deer desires in a man. And beneath the fierce sun, she burns to succumb to the sweet temptation of his kiss. But the strong-willed Cheyenne princess is torn between the duty that demands she stay with her tribesmen and the passion that promises her unending happiness among white settlers. Only the love in her heart and the courage in her soul can convince Snow Deer that her destiny lies with Charles—and the blissful fulfillment of their savage longings.

_4176-6 $5.99 US/$6.99 CAN

Cassie Edwards Savage Moon

Night after night she sees a warrior in her dreams, his body golden bronze, his hair raven black. And she knows he is the one destined to make her a woman. As a child, Misshi Bradley watched as one by one her family died on the trail west, until she herself was stolen by renegade Indians. But now she is ready to start a family of her own, and Soaring Hawk is searching for a wife. In his eyes, she reads promises of a passion that will never end, but can she trust him when his own father is the renegade who destroyed her life once before? As Soaring Hawk holds her to his heart, Misshi vows the tragedies of the past will not come between them, or keep her from finding fulfillment beneath the savage moon.

SAVAGE TEARS

CASSIE EDWARDS

Bestselling author of *Savage Longings*

Long has Marjorie Zimmerman been fascinated by the Dakota Indians of the Minnesota Territory—especially their hot-blooded chieftain. With the merest glance from his smoldering eyes, Spotted Horse can spark a firestorm of desire in the spirited settler's heart. Then he steals like a shadow in the night to rescue Marjorie from her hated stepfather, and she aches to surrender to the proud warrior body and soul. But even as they ride to safety, enemies—both Indian and white—prepare to make their passion as fleeting as the moonlight shining down from the heavens. Soon Marjorie and Spotted Horse realize that they will have to fight with all their cunning, strength, and valor, or they will end up with nothing more than savage tears.

___4281-9 $5.99 US/$6.99 CAN

SAVAGE WONDER
CASSIE EDWARDS

Hunted by the fiend who killed his illustrious cousin Crazy Horse, Black Wolf fears for the lives of his people, even as a flash flood forces him to accept the aid of gentle, golden-haired Madeline Penrod. Pursued by the madman who murdered her father to gain her hand in marriage, Maddy has no choice but to take refuge from the storm in an isolated hillside cave. But the breathtakingly virile Sioux warrior who shares her hideaway makes the nights far from lonely.

___4414-5 $5.99 US/$6.99 CAN

Dorchester Publishing Co., Inc.
P.O. Box 6640
Wayne, PA 19087-8640

SAVAGE SHADOWS

CASSIE EDWARDS

All her life, Jae lived in the mysterious region of Texas known as the Big Thicket. And even though the wild land is full of ferocious animals and deadly outlaws, the ebon-haired beauty never fears for her safety. After all, she can outshoot, outhunt, and outwit most any man in the territory. Then a rugged rancher comes to take Jae to a home and a father she never knew, and she is alarmed by the dangerous desires he rouses in her innocent heart. Half Comanche, half white, and all man, the hard-bodied stranger threatens Jae's peace of mind even when she holds him at gunpoint. Soon, she has to choose between escaping deeper into the dark recesses of the untamed forest—or surrendering to the secrets of passionate ecstasy in the savage shadows.

___52355-8 $5.99 US/$6.99 CAN

SAVAGE FIRES

CASSIE EDWARDS

Josephine Taylor Stanton has given up on love after losing both her mother, and her desire to walk, in a train wreck. But when the tall, handsome Indian chief, Wolf, walks into her office, she is drawn to the proud Ottawa leader and longs to feel his strong arms surround her. Wolf has come to Jo to help fight for the rights of his people, but from the moment he sees her sweet smile, his heart is lost to her forever. Lying together in front of the crackling fire, he sees only the sparkling blue eyes and tender heart of a woman of courage and strength, a woman the Ottawa would be proud to claim as their own. And when he tastes her sweet kisses, her love speaks to his soul and unites them as one for all eternity.

___4551-6 $5.99 US/$6.99 CAN

Dorchester Publishing Co., Inc.
P.O. Box 6640
Wayne, PA 19087-8640